Praise for *The Goblets Immortal* Series

'A promising series opener with a rich supporting cast of characters. Packed full of adventure and ending with a cliffhanger that leaves readers anxiously awaiting a sequel.'
Booklist

'Fast-paced and can be read in a day – perfect for a long airplane ride.'
SciFiMoviePage

'*The Goblets Immortal* is a very interesting and unique fantasy story. It is fun and chaotic, and I really enjoyed the read.'
FanFiAddict

'I had a blast reading this compelling fantasy with a wonderful, character-driven plot led by a kick-ass main character! I highly recommend this book!'
The Haunted Fae

BETH OVERMYER

TEMPERED GLASS

Blade and Bone Book Two

This is a **FLAME TREE PRESS** book

FLAME TREE PRESS
6 Melbray Mews, London, SW6 3NS, UK
flametreepress.com

US sales, distribution and warehouse:
Simon & Schuster
simonandschuster.biz

UK distribution and warehouse:
Hachette UK Distribution
hukdcustomerservice@hachette.co.uk

Thanks to the Flame Tree Press team.
The cover is made by Flame Tree Studio, working with the fine and wonderful artist Broci who created the illustration especially for this book. The art is © Broci 2024.
The font families used are Avenir and Bembo.

Flame Tree Press is an imprint of Flame Tree Publishing Ltd
flametreepublishing.com

A copy of the CIP data for this book is available from the British Library and the Library of Congress.

PB ISBN: 978-1-78758-875-2
ebook ISBN: 978-1-78758-877-6

Printed and bound in Great Britain by Clays Ltd, Elcograf S.p.A.

BETH OVERMYER

TEMPERED GLASS

Blade and Bone Book Two

FLAME TREE PRESS
London & New York

'Nearly all men can stand adversity, but if you want
to test a man's character, give him power.'
Abraham Lincoln

PART ONE

CHAPTER ONE

One week passed and then another since Verve had promised to return to Letorheas, the land of Faerie. The longer she remained with her family, the more convinced she became that she was safe and not a danger to those around her.

There was little time to worry about what was not, she told herself. The bills needed paying, and she was the most fit to work and earn them a living since Father had been murdered. Not that anyone – well, anyone *human* – besides her younger sister Helena believed him to be dead. Mother and Davinia still held on to the hope that Father would return and things would go back to normal.

They wouldn't. Father had been killed by Dacre, a fae lord who wanted the Cunning Blade, the only weapon capable of killing high fae. Fortunately, the blade had been destroyed and could no longer benefit anyone evil. Unfortunately, Verve had absorbed all of its powers, which made day-to-day living a challenge, but nothing she couldn't handle. Not for the first time that day did she touch her face, making certain her mortal appearance was holding. Without it, her ears would be pointed, her face would be pale and glowing, and others would see that her eyes were not quite human. Her hand brushed a sticky barrier, and she was reassured she would appear normal to anyone who might intrude upon her solitude.

Verve sat in the attic in the stifling heat of late summer, sixteen months since she had promised her fae husband, Fenn, she would summon him and they would leave Etterhea – the mortal realm – together. The story she was writing would not co-operate, as her mind was pulled in a million different directions: Fenn, home, her strange powers, and pretending to be normal were chief among them.

"Where is Verve?" asked Dav. Verve could hear her youngest sister all the way down in the kitchen. She imagined Davinia's fair brow puckering and a golden lock falling across her face. "She said she would walk with me to town."

Anna, the Springers' housekeeper, stirred a pot of jam on the stove as she waited for their bread to bake. Verve's hearing picked up the monotonous clanking of the wooden spoon against the metal sides of the pan. "Leave her be. She's working on her latest story."

Dav snorted, and Verve accidentally snapped her pen in two.

"Blast," she said, for she was now covered in ink. After a quick look around, she put both ends against each other and they joined together with a satisfying *click*. As a result, the air smelled of hot spun sugar, the smell produced after she had used magic, an odor also known as a residual burst. A quick wave of her hand took care of the ink, though it made her hands tingle with the need to use more of her power.

"She's always writing these days," Dav complained. "She might as well run off and be a governess again."

Mother sighed, and Verve set her pen down before she could do any more damage to it. "I would not complain so loudly, Davinia. She's helping us out from under all those bills, after all."

There was a pause and Verve moved away from her desk. This was one reason it was so hard to write: she could hear every blasted noise in the house and the surrounding area. Sometimes, she heard conversations in her neighbors' respective homes and even as far away as town. Those instances tended to come upon her when she was tired and her guard was down, making sleep nearly impossible. Not that she needed sleep much these days.

"I think there's a man," said Dav.

"Oh, do you, now?" said Anna. "You've seen one around, I reckon? Perhaps tucked between her books?"

"You can tease all you like, but she's moody and more unpredictable than ever. Someone's on her mind." *If only she knew.*

On the floor below the attic, Helena stirred. The poor girl had caught another cold and wouldn't let Verve help make it better. Hel was the only one of the family whose memory couldn't be tampered with, and thus she knew what Verve was. Being a middling – a middle child – gave her the ability to resist certain magic, such as memory spells. It wasn't true of every middling, however; Verve herself had had her memories tampered with when she was still mortal. Verve wished she or Fenn could cast that particular spell on Hel, as the girl remembered her short yet horrible captivity in Letorheas. Midras, the fae king, had held Verve's family hostage, hoping to exchange them for Verve's power. It had not ended well for him.

Verve shuddered and ran a hand over the gooseflesh on her arms. She'd better go down and check on Helena and then stop her family from gossiping; they might alight upon the truth, and she didn't trust herself to tamper with their memories without Fenn's help.

She was on the bottom stair when she thought she scented limes. Her heart's beating quickened. *He can't be around. I haven't heard from him in months.* Though curious to see what she might find belowstairs, she stopped and rapped on Helena's door. "I'm going down to the kitchen. Do you need anything?"

Silence.

"Water? Some fresh juice? I think Anna's cooking with limes again."

There was a sigh on the other side of the door. "I'm fine, but you need to tone it down. They'll suspect you're different."

Verve pulled a face and checked her reflection in the hallway mirror. Her magic was still muted, as she had felt earlier. Fenn had reluctantly taught her how to disguise herself. "You mean my voice?"

"I can...*feel* you. Even through the door."

That made Verve scowl. "I can hardly help how I make people feel." She paused, knowing she oughtn't be cross with her favorite sister. "I'll try to rein it in." With that said, Verve turned and went downstairs. *She's still getting used to the new you. Be patient with her.*

Pasting on a smile, Verve entered the kitchen, where Anna was removing bread from the oven. The old cook looked up from her work and grunted. "Oh, good. You're done writing. Now you can take Davinia to town and stop her from pestering me."

Verve sniffed again, having caught another whiff of limes. "It smells wonderful in here. What all did you make?" Without having to look, she saw, in her mind, Dav roll her eyes and set aside her charcoal drawing.

"Blackcurrant preserves, which you can easily see bubbling here on the stovetop," said Anna, giving the pot a stir. "And brown bread."

"Did you make anything with limes?"

Anna frowned. "Limes? Dear, there are no limes to be had here, save for what your sister bought pickled from the shop."

Could that be what I smell?

Dav apparently could wait no longer to be attended to. "Verve, you said you would walk to town with me. You know I ought not go by myself and sully my reputation." She rubbed her nose, leaving a black smudge where her fingers had been.

"All right." Verve dipped a finger into the jam and licked it.

"Don't burn yourself," warned Anna, eyeing Verve warily. "Are you all right? You...you seem strange today."

Verve checked a grimace. If Anna noticed as well, Verve hadn't expended enough of her power. Fenn had warned her if she left too much unused, it would seek other ways to escape. *But I used so much last week.* "The duke is about to propose, but someone's beat him to it."

"Not your stories again."

"Enough, Davinia," said Mother, not looking up from her crocheting. "You shouldn't speak to your sister like that, especially since she's agreed to do something nice for you."

Cheeks crimson, Dav rose from the table and would not quite look at Verve. "I thought there might be a *real* man. And don't say you'll never marry, because I know there's someone you fancy."

Oh, the things Verve would like to say in response. Instead, she found herself counting backward from twenty, trying to regain control over her temper, which always led to magical mayhem, usually in the form of fire. "I truly don't aim to marry." ...*Because I already* am *married*. They were not to know, however. "Now, do you want to go to town or continue arguing about my lack of a romantic entanglement?" She quirked an eyebrow at her youngest sister and headed for the door, remembering then that she had neglected to put on her gloves. *I'll just be extra careful not to touch anyone.*

Before Verve had triumphed over Dacre, the fae lord had managed to curse Verve, making it perilous for anyone to touch her skin if they didn't share a blood bond with her. Since Verve had already been remade into a fae, her familial blood bonds had been broken, and her kin were in danger of harm should their skin make contact with hers.

"Wait." Dav hurried after Verve, smoothing out her golden hair as she ran. She caught up with her elder sister and attempted to thread an arm through hers, but Verve managed to sidestep her at the last minute. "All right, Miss Touch-Me-Not."

Verve cringed and magicked a pair of long gloves onto her hands while Dav wasn't paying attention. "We're looking at dresses and not buying anything." As convenient as it would be to make money out of feathers as she had seen done, Verve didn't trust herself with the details. That and it was a morally questionable thing to do.

"Yes, I know. But just because we're too poor to afford the latest fashions, it doesn't mean I can't enjoy looking at them." She stepped around horse droppings and picked up her pace to match Verve's. "What are you *really* writing about?" It wasn't like Dav to be so perceptive...or so interested in Verve's fiction writing.

"What makes you say I'm not writing about the duke and his conquests?" In truth, she had given up writing romance and mysteries and was trying her hand at fables. Her family knew about her quitting mysteries; she had sworn off the genre when no one believed her about Father. But romance? She should not even think about it.

Dav shrugged. "What you write tends to reflect what mood you're in, and lately, you've been nothing like your old self."

At the words, Verve's pace slowed. "Helena said as much."

"You're not leaving again so suddenly, are you?" Dav pursed her lips and looked up at Verve. "I know we don't get along as well as sisters ought, but it wasn't the same without you around."

A lump formed in Verve's throat and she swallowed around it. "That's not part of the plan. You know I love—"

"Oh, I forgot my hat," said Dav suddenly, turning on her heels and running. "Go on without me. I'll see you later."

Frowning, Verve watched her sister run back home. *What's gotten into her?* Verve turned and began the short trek after her, but she caught a whiff of citrus borne on a breeze and froze. "Using magic on my sister isn't fair," she said below her breath, loud enough for the fae she sensed behind her to hear. She felt his gaze boring into her back, but she didn't turn, didn't want to see the disappointment and anger in those dark eyes that haunted her dreams.

"How else was I to get you alone?" asked Fenn.

Verve rolled her eyes. She sensed him moving nearer and knew she should leave. There was nothing to be said, nothing he could do to convince her to abandon her family, no matter how much he insisted it was for the greater good. But her feet didn't seem to want to co-operate.

Before she could blink, his arm ensnared her waist and he pulled her off the road and into the woods surrounding. "You're doing a poor job of hiding," he said, gently pushing her up against a rather wide oak.

Now she did dare to meet his gaze and was surprised by the lack of judgement she found. There was a hint of anger, though she could be mistaking it. "What brings you here?" Verve meant to keep her tone light, casual, but Fenn seemed to have different plans for their reunion.

His eyes darkened to the edges, and his skin began to glow golden. "You know what brings me here, Verve."

"No."

Fenn licked his lips. "Come with me."

"I don't want to." She dropped her gaze.

He leaned in and rested his forehead against hers, bending over quite a-ways in order to do so. She'd forgotten how impossibly tall he was. "I could make you want to."

A pleasant chill went down her spine, and she stopped a shiver just in time. "My family needs me." Verve jutted out her chin, hoping to end the discussion.

Fenn sighed but didn't pull back. "*I* need you, wife." He twirled a strand of her reddish blonde hair around one of his fingers and kissed her eyes closed. "*Letorheas* needs you."

That made Verve snort. She opened her eyes and glared at Fenn, whose hands had found their way to her waist. "What could that realm possibly need from me?"

"You killed its king."

Verve squirmed, not wishing to think about Midras, but Fenn held her fast. "I had no choice," she said.

"There is a balance to things, Verve." He kissed her cheek. "You left us leaderless and lacking in power. First the blade—"

"Stop."

"Then the king. Then Dacre."

Her stomach churned at the mention of the fae who had imprisoned her the previous year after killing Father. The horrible man had fallen in love with her, in some twisted sense of the word, and had attempted a painful ritual to turn her into something he could use as a weapon. He'd succeeded in part, changing her into a half-fae. But most of her abilities now came from the Cunning Blade.

Fenn was relentless in his lecturing. "You can't take so much power out of Letorheas and expect it to run like it ought. It needs you, Verve." His grip on her waist tightened. "Come home."

But Verve was already shaking her head. "I can't. Don't ask me to."

"Middlings are going missing."

That made Verve pause. "Why middlings? And what has that got to do with me?"

Fenn gave her a searching look. "They're going missing from Etterhea." Fenn pulled his face away from hers. "Everywhere I go, I hear murmurings of strangers, talk of young men and women gone missing. When I look into the matter, it's always a middle child who's been taken."

"Fenn—"

"They're connected, Verve. And they're a fae's doing." His brow furrowed, and it took all of Verve's self-control not to reach up and smooth out the lines of worry. "You could be next. Or your sister."

Verve flinched at the mention of Helena. "I can protect her." Her hands moved to Fenn's and she attempted to remove them from her waist, but didn't know how to do so without breaking his fingers.

"You're practically a beacon, you know," he said. "My wards can only keep out so much. One of these days, someone is going to find or create a hole, and I can only hope I'm there before...."

She wanted to tell him to stop worrying, to keep to a topic and stop hopping from one subject to the next; it was making her dizzy. There was no opportunity to say anything else as he pressed his lips against hers.

This kiss was needy, desperate, not the tender one she last remembered receiving. Verve responded with the same urgency, having not touched another living soul since the last time their paths had crossed.

His hands slid up her front, over her neck, and moved into her hair, tangling in her locks and loosening them from the knot at the base of her skull.

It would be prudent to stop him, she knew. Already she could feel the damper she put on her powers lifting. Magic pulsed in her veins, begging to be released. But she couldn't allow herself to let it free, not here, so close to civilization. Frightened of herself now, Verve pushed Fenn back, and he went flying away from her, righting himself at the last minute ere he could hit the ground.

His eyes were fire. "You need to let it out."

She chewed on her lower lip, drawing a bead of silver blood, which she at once licked away. "How exactly do you propose I do that?"

He approached her cautiously, as one might a feral cat. "Do you trust me?"

Her stomach flipped. "I'm not going back to Letorheas."

"Just for an hour." He must have known she was on the edge of declining, because he quickly added, "If you don't, your power will find a way to escape. You could hurt someone."

"Promise you won't try to stop me from returning."

Fenn cocked his head to the side and frowned. "I won't promise that." Before she could protest, he added, "Perhaps I wouldn't be able to keep you there, but who knows? Maybe you're too weak-willed to resist." It had obviously been meant as a taunt, and Verve bristled, the reaction she knew he wanted.

Her temper enflamed, Verve knew at once she had better leave Etterhea for the suggested hour, and quickly; she didn't want to accidentally set the wood ablaze. The thought of returning to Letorheas was not one she relished, and on instinct she looked back toward the road her home sat on. Would they be safe while she was away?

Taking advantage of her distraction, Fenn grabbed her hand and tugged her at a dizzying speed toward the nearest hawthorn tree. It didn't take long to create a gateway. Fenn had only just pressed his hand against the silver bark when the trunk split into two parts, forming an entry to the world of fae. He nudged Verve ahead of him and ran in after.

Verve had hardly a chance to take in her surroundings – it was early evening and stifling hot – when Fenn pulled her against him. She gasped and he captured the sound with his mouth. He hadn't brought her back to Letorheas to release pent-up magic, after all.

Fenn tumbled to the ground with her, but Verve stayed him with a touch of her hand on his chest. He froze.

She ran a hand through his dark hair. He'd let it grow down past his shoulders, and it was rather unkempt. Her eyes roved over him, and she was startled to notice he had lost weight. Dark circles ran under his eyes, and he smelled of dirt and sweat. "Oh, Fenn."

The words seemed to break him, and he recoiled, crawling off her prone form. "I don't want your pity. I want *you*." He scowled. "But if you're going to keep looking at me like that, we might as well fight."

Before he could rise, Verve threw out a hand, knocking him onto his back. It felt good to use her magic, even though it was at Fenn's expense. In a blink of an eye, she straddled him and pinned his hands at his sides, and tugged on his lower lip with her teeth.

Fenn stilled and seemed perfectly happy to lie there and let her win. His eyes were on hers, expectant, hopeful.

"You can have me…if you can catch me first." She grinned at him and took off running, the ghost of his touch nipping at her waist.

His approach would have been inaudible, even to a fae, but Verve was different and Fenn might as well have announced his presence with a trumpet. He had run around her, probably meaning to take her by surprise and cut her off.

Without trying, Verve's gaze bored right through the tree he was hiding behind, seeing him as clearly as though he stood in front of her. With a thought, she sent a great wind his way, bending the trunk.

There was much cursing and laughter as the wind uprooted the tree and knocked it over, forcing Fenn from his hiding spot. He gave her a lopsided grin and dodged a bolt of golden light she had released from her fingertips. Had it struck him, he would have obeyed her every whim. "You really should have left the tree out of this," he said from behind her, yards away. "It had no quarrel with you."

She didn't need to look to know he was holding a rope made out of light. It shot out and would have ensnared her, had she not batted it away at the last possible second.

The rope dissolved and reformed in its creator's hands. "You could at least have the decency to face me when we're fighting."

Verve turned, and he took advantage of the moment to knock her off-balance with a gust of his own. Annoyed, she allowed him to lasso her, only to seize the rope and rip it out of his hands. She smirked at him and attempted a lasso herself. But the rope had other plans. It crawled up her arm and squeezed, cutting off blood circulation and thus distracting her enough to let Fenn get closer.

He almost caught her, but she tossed him away with a mere thought, breaking his connection to the rope, which shattered in a flash of light and was no more. Again Fenn came at her, this time with a net of blue light, one that Verve tried and failed to bat away. It covered her and dragged her to the ground, tightening as it fell.

The rope the net was made of had more magical substance to it, and for a worrisome moment, Verve thought she might have lost their play fight. But one look at Fenn, who still stood a few yards away, told her he was expending a lot of energy on his magic, far more than Verve was. She didn't need to escape the net yet. All she had to do was to keep him at bay or exhaust him enough so the net broke on its own.

"Would you like to surrender now?" Fenn stalked toward her, his eyes bright and alert.

Verve snorted as the net ceased tightening, allowing her enough room to sit hunched forward. "You would like that, wouldn't you?"

He grinned. "Is that a yes?"

With a blink of her eyes, the ground beneath Fenn moved, earth and grass twining around his legs and dragging him away from where Verve sat. Now a stretch of grassless muck lay between them and a rolled-up carpet of green sat at his feet. For a moment, the netting around Verve flickered but at once solidified again. Verve caused the ground on which Fenn stood to swallow him up to the knees like quicksand, and then harden like concrete.

Fenn shook his head. "You've been practicing?" His concentration broke, freeing Verve from the netting.

She gulped and reluctantly admitted, "Well, Dav might have annoyed me more than she ought, and my control might have slipped while we were walking on the neighbor's property." A few vines from above snatched her by the wrists as Fenn freed himself from his prison.

"That's why you need to be trained," Fenn said, tightening the vines holding her.

Verve threw up an invisible barrier between them, effectively stalling her husband's approach. "I didn't ask for power."

"And yet you have it." He placed his hands almost reverently on the wall she had created. His eyes narrowed as he no doubt looked for weaknesses. "You're dangerous, Verve."

"I haven't hurt anyone," she countered as the tip of a vine leaf stroked her face.

"*Yet.*" He tapped his fingers against the barrier. It made a soft ringing sound, much like a handbell Verve had played as a child during Winter Festival. "It's only a matter of time before you lose your temper and slip. God help the fool who's in your way then."

That stung, but Verve didn't let him see how much his words had hurt her. They couldn't be true. She wouldn't *let* them be true. Verve's temper seeped into the vines holding her, and they recoiled, releasing her and twisting in a furor as they attempted to put distance between themselves and her.

Fenn grinned and stepped through the barrier, emerging on the other side soaking wet. He shook himself like a dog, and Verve jumped back to avoid getting drenched. "You know, if you really had wanted to keep me out, you should have tried something more substantial."

"Oh, really?" Verve raised her hands and deflected a bolt of yellow light, which bounced back at Fenn.

He leaned to the right, avoiding his rebounded attack. "Well, if you had been properly trained, you wouldn't be focusing so hard on not hurting me."

Verve winced.

Fenn raised his hands, his expression contrite. "I don't think you *can* hurt me, Verve. I'm sorry to distress you." For the entirety of their mock fight, Fenn had avoided using any gestures to enhance his magic. But now he surprised Verve by breaking his own personal rule. He threw his hands out, and the air filled with the scent of citrus as his magic gathered behind Verve and pushed her toward him. He snatched her around the waist and pulled her to his chest.

"You cheated," she said into his shirt.

His whole body vibrated with silent laughter. "We never set any rules that said I couldn't take an advantage." He rested his cheek on the crown of her head. "Do you feel any better?"

Despite herself, a slow smile spread across her face. "Maybe." She did feel somewhat better, as though she were not wound so tightly, ready to explode with magic at the merest touch. Verve hadn't realized how dire things had gotten; she would have to exercise her magic more often, with or without Fenn to help her.

They stood there in each other's arms for some time, until her breaths grew slow and even and the sky began to darken. Fenn's fingers dug into her bodice, staying her when she stirred.

"Don't return. Please," said Fenn.

Verve pressed her right hand over his heart, which leapt beneath her touch. "Can you give me more time?" She tipped her head to look up at him. Perhaps it was only wishful thinking, but it seemed to Verve that Fenn perhaps looked less haggard than when they started.

He didn't answer at first, his expression tightening. Then, leaning down, he pressed his lips to her forehead before whispering, "Why would I agree to that without asking for something in return?"

If Verve was in any doubt what Fenn meant at first, she was no longer when he tasted the sensitive skin of her throat. Breathing heavily, she allowed him to guide her onto the ground, and they lay there entwined until the stars came out.

★ ★ ★

When she returned to Etterhea, the first hints of morning were creeping over the horizon. Fenn had refused to accompany her back and wouldn't make a gateway for her, something Verve had trouble with now that the trees were so afraid of her – ever since she had been transformed into the fae's Fire Queen, a powerful being that had been prophesied ages ago. When she had once asked Fenn why, he reasoned it was because she could destroy them with a mere touch. The trees' terror was an annoyance, but she shrugged it off as she felt her face, making certain her magic wasn't showing.

Maplehurst's lights shone brightly upon her arrival. Verve heard five human heartbeats within the walls and frowned. She slowed her steps and listened more closely, and was startled to hear a masculine voice she did not recognize. Not waiting to discern if it was friend or foe, Verve took off at an unnatural speed and arrived at the side door within the blinking of an eye. "Hello?" she called out.

There was an exclamation from the kitchen, and four sets of feet came rushing at her. "Oh, Verve," said Mother, before breaking down with sobs.

Verve took a step back as Anna helped support the matron of the family and led her to the sitting room. "What's wrong?"

"What's wrong?" snapped Anna. "Been gone for three days and she asks what's wrong. What happened to you, child?"

"It's really been three days?" she asked, looking at Helena for confirmation. Verve had forgotten time moved differently in Letorheas.

Her favorite sister nodded and attempted a smile, which trembled on her lips and then faded entirely. "I thought you'd been taken again," she confided in a whisper as all the Springer women staggered after Mother. Following closely from the kitchen was the town constable, his expression turning from relieved to wary upon taking a better look at Verve.

"You gave us quite a fright, Miss Springer," he said. "Would you care to tell us where exactly you've been?"

Verve sighed inwardly. How was she going to explain this away? "No harm has come to me. Why worry about where I've been?"

Dav moaned in the corner. "I shouldn't have left you on the road the other day. I don't know what made me do it." She rested her head in her hands, her shoulders shaking. It wasn't like her to become this distraught over anything to do with Verve. Something else must have occurred.

Verve knew she should come up with a lie, and quickly. "I stayed with some friends in town. I thought I had told you," she said.

"Then where is your overnight bag?" Anna demanded.

Looking to her mother, Verve frowned. "What has truly happened?" She waited expectantly, her eyes moving from Mother, who was still near hysterics, to Dav, and then to the constable, the only one in the room who didn't seem ready to start sobbing.

The lawman cleared his throat. "A few women from the area went missing the same day you did. They haven't returned."

The hairs on Verve's arms stood on end. "Who?"

"Carrie and Violet and some girl from town," said Helena. Carrie and Violet were the only two offspring of Daniel and Martha Woodhouse, their next-door neighbors.

"Middlings are going missing." But Carrie and Violet weren't middle children...that she knew of. Had Mrs. Woodhouse lost children? The girls' disappearance had to be unrelated to Fenn's warning.

"Have you seen the missing girls?" asked the constable.

Verve shook her head. "No. Their poor families." Her stomach twisted, and she felt the color drain from her face. Something was very wrong about this.

"And you say you were in town with friends?" When Verve nodded, the constable frowned. "And is there anyone who can verify your story?"

Those words roused Mother from her stupor. "What exactly are you insinuating, Officer? If Verve says she was with friends, she was with friends." Her voice broke as she looked at her second-eldest daughter, who wanted to sink into the floor just then.

I should have never left Etterhea. Aloud Verve said, "I'll supply you with their names and place of residence, if that will help." She looked into the officer's eyes and, remembering Fenn's second lesson in magic he'd taught her, Verve pushed a false memory into the man's mind.

The officer blinked, his expression slackened, and the air filled with the aromas of toffee and other sweets. "Thank you, Miss Springer. I should be on my way now." He pulled his black cap from under his arm and smoothed it out in his hands. "If you see anything strange, please report it immediately."

"I'll show you out," said Anna, giving Verve a peculiar glance, one that was both suspicious and fearful.

Verve's eyes sought Helena's, but the girl immediately looked away. Hel didn't like it when Verve used magic, especially on other people. Thankfully, from what Verve could tell, the damper she kept on her power still held. But the way Anna had looked at her made Verve wonder if the old maid was perhaps a middling herself.

Mother held out her arms for Verve, and it took all of Verve's strength to smile and not embrace her. At length, the woman's expression faltered and she dropped her arms. "Are you sure you're all right, Verve? The day you went missing, Helena and Dav mentioned you seemed strange." Even as she studied her, Mother flinched. Innately she must have known her daughter was dangerous.

"I'm fine. Honestly."

Dav, who was still sniffling, looked up at Verve, a frown on her face. "What friends do you have in town? I didn't think you liked anyone there."

A headache was forming behind Verve's right eye. Now she wanted to be alone and think over what she should do about Fenn, who she knew wouldn't leave her alone for long. The thought of him made her face warm, and she had to look away from Dav and the others and stare instead at the floor. "They are more acquaintances than friends, but the girls said they liked my writing and wanted to hear more of my stories."

At her words, Helena left the room, her expression sour. The others didn't seem to notice her departure.

"You might have at least sent a note," said Mother. "We were so worried."

"And besides," said Dav, "you missed the news."

Verve looked at her sister sharply. "What news?"

Dav tittered and Anna, who had returned with a steaming mug of tea, rolled her eyes and handed the beverage to Mother. "Old Mr. Franz is getting married. La! Can you imagine?" Dav shook her head.

"If you ask me, he's getting a mite up in years to be wanting a wife." Anna fussed over Mother, smoothing invisible wrinkles out of her shawl.

"I wonder whatever happened to his nephew," said Dav. "He was such an agreeable man."

Verve cringed at the mention of Dacre, who had only posed as the old man's nephew to ingratiate himself with the Springer family and get close to Verve. She thought Fenn had wiped the memory of the fae from everyone's minds, but apparently she had been wrong. "I'm sure he's moved on to bigger and better things." Before anyone could bombard her with more news and speculations, Verve turned and made for the staircase in the hallway.

Mother called after her, "Where do you think you're going?"

"I'm tired. I thought I might get ready for bed. Why?" She slowed her steps and looked around at her family.

It was Anna who spoke next. "Is gone without word for three days and doesn't have time for her mother and sisters." She glared openly at Verve, sparking the latter's temper.

"Anna, what's gotten into you?" Mother snapped.

Dav started sniffling again, further trying Verve's patience.

She knew she needed to get away from them and quickly, before she accidentally incinerated the room. "I'm sorry. I-I'm not myself tonight, I guess. I'll see you in the late morning." Fingertips pulsing hot, Verve turned again and fled at a speed that must have further raised Anna's suspicions. And she was just in time. No sooner had she entered her bedroom than her hands burst forth orange flames, which she aimed toward the log in her fireplace. The wood was immediately engulfed, and Verve held her hands over the grate until the heat went out of her temper and the fire in her hands diminished and was no more.

CHAPTER TWO

Anna was still cold toward Verve for the next fortnight, so Verve spent most of her time in the attic, the one place the old maid didn't venture due to arthritic knees. There she struggled to write the story she had been attempting to put down on paper, and instead wound up losing control of her magic and accidentally burning the page in front of her more often than not. The whole house had begun to stink of sweets, the smell Verve's residual bursts had taken on since her transformation. No one but Anna complained, for only Anna – along with a much quieter Helena – could smell it.

Ripping at her hair one colder morning, Verve stepped away from the scribbled notes on her desk and took to pacing the attic floor. Bills were coming in, and Verve knew she needed to produce something quickly if the Springer women didn't want to see themselves further impoverished or, worse, imprisoned in a workhouse. So she crept down to her room and locked the door behind her.

There she went to her pillow, tore it open, and plucked a handful of feathers from its insides. These she carried to the fireplace, where she sat cross-legged, and set them next to her on the floor. Currently there was a shortage of metal, thanks to the building of a new railroad. The territories still hadn't recovered from the war, which had eaten up metal and caused many haberdashers and seamstresses to lament the scarcity of pins.

Verve tried to clear her mind of worries and doubts, things that would inhibit her transformative magic, but the house below her was in a tizzy. Mr. Franz's upcoming nuptials to a widowed heiress had turned the household upside down, as the Springers had been asked to help with the festivities following the outdoor ceremony.

"Davinia, child, what are you doing with all these ribbons?" Anna demanded belowstairs, just as Verve had begun to transform a feather into a sewing pin. The feather wilted in her hands and fell to the hearth with a loud *plunk*.

"Mrs. Biddle dropped them off," said Dav. "She says I'm so artistic that she wants me to sew them together into a bouquet."

Verve clenched her jaw and relaxed it again. There would never be a truly silent moment for her ever again, thanks to her enhanced hearing, which exceeded that of even a fae. *I'd better find a way to cope.* She reached for another feather and tried again, this time succeeding almost as soon as she touched the plume. Encouraged, Verve set the sewing pin aside and was about to transform another feather, when the side door slammed, interrupting her concentration.

"They're getting married tomorrow, child. Do you think you have enough time?" Anna was saying.

"I'm certain," said Dav.

"Has anyone seen Verve?" Mother asked. "It looks like rain, and the washing is still out on the line."

With a sigh, Verve abandoned her attempts at magic and went downstairs so she wouldn't accidentally set the house on fire. "Here I am," she said, tramping down the stairs. She was met with silence. Verve entered the sitting room, and was confused to find it empty. In fact, the whole house sounded free of breaths and beating hearts. She could hear her family, but they were next door, not downstairs as she had first perceived.

The side door opened and slammed, admitting Dav, who glowered at Verve. "I hung up the washing like you were supposed to."

"B-but Mother just said to bring it in. That it looked like rain."

Dav blinked at her. "But Anna just washed it." Her eyes narrowed. "You're not going mad again, are you?" Indeed, everyone had thought Verve to be crazy after Father was murdered. No one had been able to find the body, after all, and the scene of the crime had been thoroughly tidied up and wiped of any evidence after Verve had left it to get help. There had not even been any tracks left in the snow.

Verve's pulse quickened. She couldn't have been hearing things… could she?

Laughter outside interrupted their conversation, which Dav mercifully lost interest in. "Mrs. Biddle is going to drop ribbons off later. She says I'm artistic and wants me to make them into a sort of floral bouquet."

The side door opened and slammed closed again, jarring Verve, who resisted putting her hands over her ears. She didn't have time to think about what might be going on with her sanity, because Anna entered the room laughing and talking to Mother, only to stop and flinch at the sight of Verve.

"Looks to be a fair-weather day," said Mother, oblivious apparently to Anna's suddenly sour expression. "Thanks for hanging up the washing for Anna, Verve."

"Dav—"

"Could you see to the chickens? No one's gathered eggs yet today."

In a daze, Verve nodded and stumbled out of the room, her eyes unfocused. She snatched a basket from the kitchen and left the house, only half paying attention to where she was going and what she was doing.

The hens clucked at her as she traipsed past them and ducked into their enclosure, which smelled strongly of waste and straw. She picked up one egg, accidentally crushing it in what she had thought to have been a gentle grip. Touching her skin, the whites and yolk bubbled and sizzled and cooked fully until she shook them off. She dropped the basket and retreated from the henhouse. The birds scattered at the sight of her, and Verve's hands began glowing with blue light. "No." Verve shook her hands, and sparks went flying, which she quickly stomped out in the grass.

With a nervous glance first at the house to make certain no one was watching, Verve turned and ran through the back gate and sped toward the Woodhouse property abutting their own, knowing she would be truly alone there to sort out whatever was happening to her.

Verve's hands continued to glow and spark as she ran, until she came to a stop in the middle of a puddle. There things seemed to calm for a moment, but soon waves of pure white light exploded from Verve's body with a deafening boom, knocking over the trees immediately surrounding her and scorching them as well. With a strangled sob, Verve lowered herself to the ground and sat in the puddle, which began to bubble and evaporate until it was nothing. She paid it little mind, hugging her knees to her chest as tears stung her eyes. "What's happening to me?"

At her voice, the trees began to stir, righting themselves, their trunks mending where they had snapped, until they stood proud and tall once more with no signs they had even been burned. The air smelled strongly of toffee and sugar, and Verve choked on a cough. She'd been in control for most of her time back in Etterhea. What had changed? Fenn couldn't be right about her being a danger... could he? Verve attempted to dry her eyes, but new tears spilled forth.

"What's the matter?"

Verve's head snapped up at the sound of Fenn's voice, and then crumpled again to her chest. "What're you doing here?" She didn't look up but could hear his soft tread approach her, feel the wind stir around her as he stopped a few feet away.

"I thought you might need me."

She shrugged. "Are you here to say 'I told you so'?"

Fenn lowered himself next to her, their arms brushing as he settled. Comfortable silence sat between them for a moment while Verve attempted to bring her tears under control. When they would not subside, Fenn wrapped an arm around her shoulder and pulled her closer. "The change has been hard on you."

A snort escaped Verve's lips. "That's an understatement."

She waited for him to beg her to return to Letorheas with him, to submit to his training and instruction, but instead he gave her shoulder a gentle squeeze and simply said, "Tell me your woes."

Verve launched into a short explanation of how she had started hallucinating and glowing and involuntarily knocking over trees.

When she'd finished, she looked up at Fenn, only to find him watching her lips. "What?" she asked.

He blinked and looked into her eyes. "It doesn't sound like you were hallucinating. It sounds like you were seeing ahead." Here he brought a hand to her face and cupped her jaw in his palm. "It's nothing to be afraid of, love. In fact, it might come in useful." He kissed her softly, taking her lower lip between his teeth and gently tugging on it. She could feel a shudder ripple through his body, and he smiled as he pulled back, his eyes twinkling. "As for the energy bursts, it might be a good idea to leave for a while. Just to keep everyone safe."

Verve groaned and got to her feet. "I told you I'm not ready to return to Letorheas." She sounded like a sulky child and she knew it.

But Fenn was kind and did not push her. Instead, he got to his feet as well and took her hand and kissed it. "I didn't necessarily mean Letorheas. There are other places, Verve."

She scowled as he tapped her nose playfully with his finger. "My family needs me. We've been over this."

Gently he led her farther into the woods, leaves crackling lustily beneath their boots. "I'm sorry. I don't wish to lecture. Come, let's walk until you forget what's troubling you."

The air held a nip to it, though the cold no longer affected Verve in quite the same way. In a sense, she almost missed a runny nose and chapped lips. "I need to get back soon," she said, stopping Fenn, who seemed intent on leading her away. "The wedding's tomorrow and I'm supposed to be helping."

"Wedding?" Fenn tilted his head to the side.

Verve rolled her eyes. "Our neighbor, the eternal bachelor, is settling down." She sighed and pulled her hand from Fenn's. "The ceremony and reception will both be outside at his house, unless the weather is foul."

"I'd love to see a mortal wedding," Fenn said, a distant look in his eye that Verve didn't understand.

She laughed, suddenly feeling shy. "Well, you're welcome to come, if you want to play witness."

His eyes flashed to hers. "You're inviting me?"

"Why not?" She threw up her hands. "The more the merrier."

"And it's on your neighbor's property?" A slow grin spread across his face. "I'm welcome on your property as well, I imagine?"

A jolt went through her body. It was good to see him happy. He'd been so downtrodden yesterday – or had it been three days ago? Whatever the case, he seemed more alert, hopeful. "Of course you're welcome anytime at Maplehurst. Maybe you can even help me put a better damper on my magic." When he leaned down to kiss her again, she sighed, relieved to no longer feel so out of control as she had been moments prior.

He took her face in his hands, pulling out of the kiss with apparent reluctance. "How I've missed you, Verve." His thumb stroked her chin once and then he released her and began to walk away backward. "I'll see you tomorrow?"

Cheeks heating, she nodded.

"Good. I look forward to it and perhaps seeing your family." Smiling softly, he turned and began a slow retreat, only to turn once more and ask, "Are you certain you won't walk a little farther with me today?"

Verve scoffed. "No. I have work to do."

He shrugged, his eyes flashing. "You can't fault a man for trying. Tomorrow, then."

She watched him leave, noticed the buoyancy in his step, and smirked in puzzled contentment. Well, as long as he was happy to leave her be for now, there was no use attempting to figure out why. Her own steps lighter, Verve reached a hand to her face, making certain her power was muted and not apparent in her appearance, and then trekked home.

Apparently Verve had been gone for more than two hours, leaving the others to fulfill her household duties and make speculations as to her whereabouts. Even before she slipped in through the back gate, Verve could hear perfectly well what everyone in the house was saying.

"If'n you ask me, something's not right with Verity," said Anna, causing Verve to slow and listen. "You know the stories where I'm from, of children being snatched and changelings being left in their places."

Verve nearly choked on her own saliva at the words. How far and yet how close to the truth! She was still Verve, and yet...she had been changed. The housekeeper was too observant, and Verve resolved then and there to be more careful and avoid the woman as much as possible. She'd already taken to hiding and washing her own laundry, as certain changes to her body would be evident on some private articles of clothing. Mercifully, no one had commented on this strange behavior...yet. Verve worried her lower lip and closed the gate behind her.

"Anna, you are overly superstitious," said Mother.

Dav was quick to chime in as well, however. "I don't know. Even Helena doesn't seem to want to go near her, and don't tell me Verve wasn't once her favorite."

The words brought Verve's spirits crashing to the ground once more, though she no longer felt as though she were about to lose control of her magic. Head down, Verve pushed through the side door and went straight upstairs to her room, ignoring the others' calls to her, asking where she had been and what she was doing now. After shutting and locking the door behind her, Verve sat in front of the fire, drew in a steadying breath, and proceeded to produce seventy pins from the feathers she had left behind earlier. The magic felt natural, and each pin was perfectly straight and sharp. Hopefully, she would be able to sell them to the local seamstress in town and put more food on the Springer table.

★ ★ ★

The preparations for the wedding went smoothly, and Verve managed to stay out of the way up in her room and in the attic until the next morning, skipping meals. She fell asleep at her desk, and when she awoke, the sun had already made its appearance. With a yawn, she rubbed ink from her hands and went downstairs.

All was a bustle of activity, and Verve was surprised she had slept through all the noise. Anna was in the kitchen, tending to bread in the oven, by the sound and smell of things, and Dav was placing cutlery on the dining room table.

"Good morning, Verve," said Mother, her hands full of boxes. "Would you mind taking these linens next door? I was up late last night, ironing them."

Careful not to touch Mother's skin, Verve took the boxes in her arms and moved toward the side door. "Will our neighbor be up and about, you think?" She looked over her shoulder, but Mother had disappeared into the kitchen.

"You slept in, Verity," said Mother, her voice raised to an unnecessary volume that made her daughter cringe. "It's nearly ten."

Swearing below her breath, Verve balanced the three boxes and managed to carry them through the door, which she shut behind her with the tips of her toes. The air was cool but tolerable, and the skies were clear of signs of rain, a mercy. Though Mr. Franz's house was large, Verve doubted it could comfortably fit the one hundred people who had been invited to attend the nuptials and the ensuing festivities, should they need to be moved indoors.

She left the linens with a servant, again careful not to touch the woman, who gave her a wary look, stole the tablecloths inside, and shut the door in Verve's face. With a frown, Verve caught her reflection in a window and noticed her eyes were glowing softly. "No wonder she was so rude. I terrified the poor woman," she said with a groan and attempted to regain control of her magic before returning home. Closing her eyes and breathing slowly seemed to work as she wrestled with herself, and when she opened her lids again, her eyes had ceased to shine. Just to be certain she didn't cause any further suspicion, Verve made herself scarce for as long as possible, wandering in the woods where she had seen Fenn the day previous.

When she returned home, she only had enough time to slip into a high-necked blue dress and a yellow shawl. Downstairs she could hear the others getting ready as well, all but Anna, who had offered to take a last-minute look over the seating and the tables set up in the yard behind.

"Verve, dear, there's someone down here who wants to see you," Mother called up the stairs.

Had Fenn arrived early? Who or what had he introduced himself as? As far as Verve knew, he'd entirely wiped himself from Mother's and Dav's memories. "Coming," she shouted back, taking the steps at a gallop. But the person waiting for her was only her elder sister, Ainsley, whom she hadn't seen for over a month now.

Ainsley laughed at the sight of Verve's face. "You look like you were expecting someone else." She leaned in to embrace Verve, who backed away, nearly bumping into Dav, who was rushing past. "*Were* you expecting someone?" Ainsley sounded more interested in the notion than Verve liked.

"I was hoping you'd bring my brother-in-law," Verve said, putting a careful smile in place. Markus had taken a disliking to Verve since she had returned from Letorheas, and Verve was secretly pleased to see him nowhere around.

The smile on her elder sister's face faded slightly. She shook her head and sighed. "You know Markus. He's always working on our little home."

Verve grunted. "Well, as long as he still treats you well, I have no reason to complain."

"Have you seen my gloves?" Dav asked.

"No. I thought you said you were going to lay them somewhere where you wouldn't easily forget them," Verve reminded her.

Dav shook her head. "I think.... Oh, yes, on my bookshelf. Hello, Ainsley." She pecked her eldest sister on the cheek and ran off, pushing around her hooped skirt in the process.

After breakfast, the Springer women made their way next door, where a string quartet had situated itself on the back lawn, welcoming guests with familiar tunes as they arrived. Rows of white chairs tied with champagne-colored bows were lined up on either side of the aisle with a white satin runner placed smartly down the middle. Verve trailed behind her mother and sisters, opting to sit behind them in an aisle seat in case she lost control of herself and needed to leave quickly.

Thankfully, that did not end up being the case. The guests arrived and sat, and the quartet played as the soon-to-be Mrs. Franz walked down the aisle to meet Mr. Franz. It was sweet, watching the couple holding each other's wrinkled hands, gazing into each other's eyes with such joy that envy tugged at the pit of Verve's stomach. To grow old with someone and love them without complications, or fears of hurting them: the thought made Verve ache. But she kept hold of her magic and saw the couple pronounced husband and wife, which was met with generous cheers and applause.

Fenn had not made an appearance. At least, not that she had noticed. There were too many mortal heartbeats and other noises surrounding Verve for her to be able to separate any immortal ones.

As the aisles were dismissed, Verve sneaked away so the bride wouldn't attempt to embrace her. It wouldn't do to have the woman collapsing in a fit of agony. She headed for the far back, where tables sat between trees, all decked in white or champagne-colored bows. It was beautiful and festive, and Verve ought to be happy, but the longer she watched everyone, the more she began to feel as though she no longer quite fit into their world.

"There you are," said Anna, snapping Verve's attention. But the housekeeper wasn't talking to her; she addressed Dav, who also must have left the ceremony early. "You can man the punch bowl."

Dav sighed. "Wasn't the ceremony romantic?" She practically floated over to the table where the crystal punch bowl and ladle lay. "Verve, why are you just standing there looking so sad?"

Verve shrugged but made no other answer. Instead she moved toward a round table next to the one bearing the punch, upon which gifts of varying shapes and sizes sat. As busy as she'd been trying to keep herself, she had forgotten to get the newlyweds anything. But what could the rich couple possibly need?

Wishing to avoid the crowd heading her way, Verve turned and walked back toward her home. Surely no one would miss her. But she didn't make it very far. Someone took her elbow and she tensed, fearing for that person's safety. When she turned, her heart tripped all over itself.

Fenn stood there in mortal attire, his hair trimmed and neater than it had been during their last meeting in the woods. He gave her an amused smile before turning her and guiding her back toward the party. "Thought you would escape the festivities so easily, did you?"

Verve groaned as their hands entwined. "If you've seen one wedding here, you've seen them all."

"Yes, but I haven't had the same privileges as you in that respect. I'd like to see more." He steered her around guests, who tried their best to avoid them anyway, no doubt sensing his otherness, and led her to the punch table, though Verve protested.

"My family will see you," she warned.

"Let them," Fenn said with a laugh.

Dav was busily filling punch glasses and didn't look up at first. "Twenty-nine, thirty, and...." She sloshed some of the red punch onto her white gloves. "Blast."

After snatching a glass, Verve attempted to tug Fenn away, but he reached for a glass as well and seemed in no rush to leave. "A lovely wedding."

"Yes," said Dav, removing her sodden gloves and paying attention only to those. "It was lovely. I—" She looked up from her work and caught Verve's eye. Then her gaze moved to Fenn and their joined hands. Her jaw dropped.

Uncomfortable, Verve freed her hand from Fenn's, but it was too late. "Dav, this is Fenn. He's someone I met at the boarding house." She tried to say it with nonchalance, but her youngest sister wasn't so easily fooled.

"Why didn't you tell me you'd found someone?"

Verve rolled her eyes and tried changing the subject. "Where is Helena? Wasn't she supposed to be helping you?"

Dav blinked rapidly as though she didn't quite follow the sudden turn in the conversation. "Oh, she complained of a headache and had to go lie down."

"A shame," said Fenn. "I would have liked to meet her." It was a bold-faced lie. Fenn had met Helena already, and Dav, for that matter, all those months ago when they had been prisoners of the fae king, Midras. None of them but Helena would remember that, however. "I hope she recovers quickly."

With a blush, Dav looked down at what she was doing. "Verve, might I speak to you alone for a moment?"

"Can it wait?" Verve asked, knowing her sister was going to interrogate her about Fenn.

Fenn sipped his punch and looked back and forth between the two, clearly amused. "I'll be right over there by the shrubbery." To Verve's surprise, he kissed her on the cheek and retreated.

Dav at once squealed, causing more than one old woman to clutch her pearls and stare at the young blonde spectacle. "I knew there was a man. But he was rather forward, kissing you so in public. It isn't proper, Verve. You should have a word with your beau." She narrowed her eyes at her elder sister. "He is your beau, isn't he?"

It was suddenly much too hot in the early autumn air. Verve removed her shawl from around her shoulders and folded it up in her arms. "Well, I suppose he is." *If only you knew.* Verve cleared her throat and looked around for signs that someone else had witnessed the kiss. *I shouldn't care. He is my husband, after all.* But the problem was no one else knew that, save for Helena. "Perhaps I had better check on Hel. The poor thing has been sick more and more often."

She turned to leave, but Dav caught her with the words, "He was staring at you during the whole wedding, so I knew he had to be a love interest." Dav sighed happily. "Is he rich?"

"Wait a moment," said Verve, shaking her head. "He was here during the ceremony?"

Dav passed a few more glasses of punch to the guests. "Why, yes. You must not have seen him." A giggle escaped her lips. "He is very handsome, Verve. Do you think he'll ask for your hand?"

"It's not…I mean, I don't…." Why was she suddenly so flustered? And why hadn't Fenn admitted to having witnessed the wedding? It wasn't like him to tease her so much.

Now Dav let out a heartier laugh, her eyes crinkling. "You love him, don't you? Why else would you suddenly start acting so bashful about things? It isn't like you."

Aware Fenn would be able to hear every word they were saying, Verve knew she had to be careful not to hurt him or say anything to encourage her youngest sister's teasing. "Never mind all this talk. I'm going to take a slice of cake to Hel. Perhaps that will lift her spirits."

"You can run for now, Verity Springer. But sooner or later, you are going to have to tell me all about your adventures at the boarding house. Does he have a brother?"

Verve rolled her eyes and left Dav to the line that had been forming in front of her table. By the appearance of things, the youngest Springer woman would be kept busy for some time. With a quick look around, Verve spied Fenn standing where he had promised to be waiting, a smug look on his face. "What?"

He motioned for her to follow him toward the back of the property, his eyes sparkling with mischief. When she reached him, he took her hand once more and led her away from all the wedding guests who were milling about. "There are a lot of people here." He squeezed her hand. "Is it making you anxious?"

"Well, it is, now that you mention it," she said, shoving him playfully. It was nice being around someone she could actually touch, who knew what she was and loved her anyway. "I don't know if it was wise of me to attend. I might've accidentally touched someone, and then where would we be?" She tried to keep her tone light, but the worry was real and it gnawed at her.

Fenn must have sensed her changing mood, but he didn't comment on it or scold her, thankfully. He opened his mouth to say something only to stiffen and turn Verve around. "Let's go this way," he whispered.

Verve frowned. "Why? Did you see something?" Already her muscles were tensing, her magic pulsing in her veins, ready to flow. Several passersby gawped at her and quickly moved on.

"Careful, Verve," he warned as the smell of toffee filled the air. "There's no danger. I just saw someone looking at you oddly and wanted to get you away from them."

"Oh." That ought to be comforting, but Verve's senses had been awakened and her magic needed releasing. Despite her best efforts to shove it all down, her hands began to glow. "What do I do?"

Hastily and with little care, he pulled her past staring party guests and toward the front of the house, where more people still had congregated. It would be difficult not touching anyone here.

"Fenn," she groaned.

"Verve!" said a familiar voice from a-ways behind her, a man's voice.

At her side, Fenn stiffened. Of all things, he released her hand and seemed ready to run off. "You'll be all right. Imagine the light dissolving in your veins. And keep your hands tucked inside your skirts." He leaned in, kissed her on the cheek, and attempted to disappear inside the crowd, which took to suddenly blocking him.

The air smelled of citrus and a hand came to rest on the small of her back. "Are you all right?"

Confused, Verve looked up at the man next to her and was startled to see Fenn standing there. But he was also in front of her, smirking.

"Twins!" someone from the crowd cried.

The Fenn at Verve's side was ashen, his eyes widening apparently at the sight of himself and then narrowing once more. His hold on Verve tightened, and he made to move her behind his back, but she was having none of that.

She wrenched her arm from his grasp. Her heart was fit to beat right out of her breast, and her breaths came in small gasps as she looked from one to the other, not knowing who was her husband and who was the shape-changer. As it was, she sidled away from the

Fenn at her side, and he let her. Up to that moment, her magic had barely been under control, and now she knew it was ready to burst forth from her body. Mindful not to touch anyone in the crowd, Verve hastened around and through them, moving at a speed more than one person would certainly think odd. Verve sensed rather than heard both men following her.

"Verve," called out one of the Fenns. He caught her by the elbow.

"Let her go," said the other, the one with slightly longer hair.

This didn't make any sense. How were both men able to touch her without getting hurt? One was an imposter who certainly didn't share a blood bond with her. Shouldn't that man have been writhing on the ground in agony?

The one with shorter hair shook his head. "Stay back, fiend. Verve, are you all right?"

Verve shook that Fenn's grip off as well. Her hands were glowing golden. Hastily she tucked them into her skirts, but she was aware her face was beginning to shine as well. Turning her back on the two, though it went against every instinct, she hastened onto the Maplehurst property. Only one of the men followed her.

This one kept his distance, watching her like a hawk ready to swoop in as she thrust her hands into the earth, which shook with the force of the magic escaping her body. Next door, a few guests cried out and plates rattled, but the tremors ceased, and Verve sat on the grass, panting. "Who are you?" she demanded.

"The real question is who the shape-changer was and how he was able to touch you." This Fenn shook his head and took to pacing. "I should never have let you return to Etterhea alone. I am so sorry, Verve."

"Prove that it's you," Verve said, her voice rising in hysteria. "T-tell me something only you would know." She swallowed a sob, cringing when he began to approach her.

Thankfully, he stayed where he was and answered, "Your magic used to smell like coffee and chocolate. But it changed after you touched the Cunning Blade and absorbed its power." He looked her directly in the eyes. "It smells like toffee and sugar and other sweet things now." He stopped pacing and sat on the grass several feet away from her. "Your greatest fear is being trapped, but you would risk anything to be there for your family, even if it trapped you even more."

Verve sniffed.

"And, if you will let me perform some magic, it should prove it really is I." He gave her a small, reassuring smile. "May I?"

She hesitated a moment and then nodded. "All right. Just don't – don't hurt anyone."

His smile softened further still. "I won't." Without moving or gesturing, this Fenn conjured an empty jar labeled *blackcurrant jam*, which settled on the ground between them. Accompanying this magic was the aroma of oranges and limes, causing Verve to relax somewhat.

A crease formed on Fenn's brow. "I don't understand how an enemy fae was able to enter that property. The wards I put up were powerful ones and should have covered all of that and most of your other neighbors' lands." He paused. "Did you see anything unusual in the last few days?"

Verve shook her head. "No."

"Then—"

"I mean, yes. Just what you saw."

Fenn's frown deepened and he got to his feet. "What I saw?"

"Yesterday, I mean, with the trees and my magic."

That did not seem to enlighten the fae. He approached Verve slowly, until she instinctively bared her teeth at him and sprang to her own feet. "Verve, there's a difference between the passage of time in Etterhea and in Letorheas. Perhaps you ought to clarify." The look he gave her was expectant, but he did not attempt to approach her again.

"Yesterday. In the woods next…door." A chill ran up Verve's spine as Fenn's eyebrows rose. "It wasn't you in the woods yesterday, was it?" She swore. "I invited the shape-changer to the wedding… and onto my property. But…are you sure it wasn't you?"

He shook his head. "It's been at least four days in Etterhean time since I've set foot in this realm. When I took you back to Letorheas, I had no intention of returning so soon."

"Then why did you?"

The tips of Fenn's pointed ears turned pink and he seemed suddenly ill at ease. "Because I was going to attempt again to talk you into returning to Letorheas...for good this time." Before Verve could get one word out against the idea, Fenn raised his hands in a truce. "The wards are no good against him – or her – now, whoever they are. A direct invitation from you was the only way for them to break in." Now he did approach Verve, slowly and deliberately, even though she showed him with her posture what she thought of him taking such liberties. "Verve, this isn't safe. Please, stop pushing me away."

Verve laughed bitterly. "I'm not. Can't we live here in Etterhea?"

He scrubbed a hand over his face and his shoulders sagged. "You need to come with me." His voice held an edge to it Verve didn't like, and he stalked slowly toward her, his movements suggesting he was contemplating aggression.

A feral hiss escaped Verve's lips, but Fenn continued his approach. "I'm sorry, Verve, but I'll never forgive myself if I don't try. And I expect you'll never forgive me either if I let you hurt your loved ones by my inaction."

"What do you—" The words had barely left her mouth when Fenn was upon her, pulling her into his chest.

"It's all right, my love. I'm not going to hurt you."

Verve squirmed, knowing full well she could break Fenn's hold on her...but not without physically hurting him. He must know and be depending on her fear of harming him, curse the man. She laughed without humor, and he tightened his grip. It would have been painful, had she still been a fragile mortal. "You said you would give me more time."

He made it two small steps ere she dug in her heels and forced him to stop. "That was before you were almost abducted."

"You think that was the shape-changer's plan?" Verve leaned back against him, meaning to push him, and he swiftly released her and moved away, causing her to lose her footing.

At once Fenn took advantage of her misstep and lifted her into his arms. "I'm convinced it is."

"And how is that different than what you are trying to do now?"

Fenn paused, and that was all the hesitation Verve needed. She placed her hand near his heart, her fingers contorting into strange positions as she fed golden light into his chest.

Under her control, he set her down and stepped back, hurt and betrayal written across his fair features. "Verve."

"Just go," she snapped. When he seemed ready to fight her hold on him, tears formed in Verve's eyes. "You promised." Magic was building beneath her skin once more, threatening to escape her in a wave of pure devastation. Verve tried to fight it and to hold Fenn back at the same time, but her control quickly slipped, just as the side door swung open.

CHAPTER THREE

The noise startled Verve and broke her concentration.

"Verve? What's happening?" Helena's voice rose and was immediately swallowed by the roar of Verve's power exploding outward. A wall of energy hit the fragile mortal in the chest, knocking her backward in a perfect arc, arms flying out.

That the house had been destroyed with a series of deafening bangs was only given a moment's consideration. Fenn was already by Verve's side, working his own magic to contain hers, which he gathered into his arms in a ball of blinding light and thrust sky-high. They looked like many fireworks bursting, all colors of the rainbow, but Verve was too frozen in horror to react to them.

Helena lay on the ground with her limbs sticking out at odd angles. Dark red blood trickled from her nose and mouth and from her eyes, which were open and glassy.

"Hel?" Verve asked.

Fenn created an opaque wall of light between them and the crowd of onlookers from next door. "Don't touch her."

Her hand flew up to her mouth as she tapped Helena with the tip of her shoe. "I hurt her." All around Verve, a wind swirled and lifted her skirts, threatening to pull her into the sky.

"Control it, Verve." Fenn was on his knees, feeling for a pulse in Helena's neck.

Before he even looked her in the eye and shook his head, Verve knew her sister was gone. A silent scream formed on her lips, and Fenn took her into his arms and held her as she shook.

"Shh. You need to calm yourself."

What was the point of controlling anything? Helena – sweet, innocent, *good* Helena – was dead. And it was Verve's doing. Power pulsed behind her eyes, and another wave of explosions threatened to burst forth from her.

The intense smell of citrus mingled with sweets told Verve her husband was fighting against her magic, taking it and throwing it heavenward, where it exploded. Day turned to night as ash rained from the skies. Her feet nearly left the ground, though Fenn held her fast by the waist, anchoring her to the earth. At length, exhausted from grief and numb from shock, Verve collapsed with a strangled sob and sat there trembling while Fenn returned the house to its foundations and attempted to repair it.

He worked silently, using gestures to aid his magic, though he kept them to a minimum. A crowd formed behind the wall of magic Fenn had put up: Verve could sense them, heard their cries of dismay and terror.

I'm a powder keg, thought Verve. *If allowed to go on, I will destroy everything I touch.* She had been blind and foolish, and now everyone was paying the price.

Fenn worked quickly and quietly, sweat beading on his neck. When he finished, the house had been put back together and was resting on its foundations as though nothing had happened. He crouched over Helena and closed her eyes and then approached Verve, slowly and warily. "I'll alter their memories, but then we need to leave here immediately."

A blow across the face would have been preferable to the kind look he gave her now. Mutely she nodded and remained where she was as Fenn stepped through the barrier he had erected.

There were cries and sobs one minute, and the next everything went silent. The air smelled of oranges and the wall of magic dropped, revealing that the revelers had returned to what they had been doing before the explosions. No one could see Helena's body over the now-repaired hedges, it would seem.

"Can you walk?" Fenn asked, holding out his hand for Verve. When Verve took it, he pulled her up and led her at a ridiculous speed onto the Woodhouse property. There were several hawthorn trees there, and Fenn selected the first one they came across, making a portal while Verve stared on in silence. "I removed your presence at the wedding from as many memories as I could, including your mother's and sisters'. They think you received an urgent summons to the boarding house and will resume work as a governess there."

I will never see them again. She didn't even get to say goodbye. *It's your own fault…murderess.* She hadn't said any of it out loud, but Fenn looked at her sharply.

"It was an accident, Verve."

She stared through him to the gateway. *An accident that could have been prevented.*

Again Fenn held out his hand for her. "Please, dearest, don't torment yourself."

Meekly she took his hand once more and followed him into Letorheas. There in the land of fae, the skies were a dull gray and dim. A mist hung in the air, which was cold enough to freeze. Verve thought nothing of its strangeness and followed Fenn like one in a dream, not bothering to mind her steps. She saw nothing as they walked hand in hand, only pictures of the devastation she had caused flickering in her mind's eye. At length the image of Helena lying dead could no longer be avoided. It was now seared into her brain as though it had been branded, and she knew it would haunt her until the day she died. *Fae don't die, they're killed…and only by* you, said a mocking part of her mind.

Fenn led her onward through shadow and fog, clearly with a destination in mind. Never once did he release her hand or show signs of slowing. Soon they emerged from the haze and into a clearing surrounded by magical wards and a tall iron fence with spikes mounted atop. "This was my father's home growing up."

Verve startled at the sound of his voice, which dragged her out of her thoughts. Half-interested, she followed him to the wide gate.

"It doesn't open. One has to share a blood bond with the master to walk through." His tone was conversational, his words spilling out as though he were making up for their silent trek. It was more likely, Verve thought, he was trying to distract her. When she made no response, he continued in the same calm staccato. "I only rediscovered this place recently, or else I would have taken refuge here ages ago. It's perfectly safe from intrusion." His calloused thumb smoothed over the skin of her right hand as he pulled her to the iron bars. "Would you very much mind introducing yourself?"

She blinked at him, not understanding what he meant her to do. "Do I say something?" Her voice was dull, dead to her own ears.

The look on Fenn's face told her it sounded the same to him. "You just need to present your hand. It will tickle," he warned and kissed her on the cheek. He lifted their entwined hands and set her palm against one of the cold bars, which wriggled beneath her touch.

He had been right: it did tickle, but not for long. The metal, which had been solid moments earlier, softened under her hand and vanished in a black fog.

"After you," said Fenn, gesturing for her to step through the gate. His back was now to the wall, his eyes fixed on the mist beyond.

Verve frowned. Was something out there that had him nervous? Her senses, which were stronger than his, picked up light footfalls. But her hearing was good – *too* good. She might be listening to sounds from miles away without realizing it.

As if reading her thoughts, Fenn urged her to make haste. "Someone is out there. I don't know if it's your would-be kidnapper, but whoever they are, they don't feel friendly."

That piqued her curiosity, despite herself. She wanted to ask him about his ability to discern friend from foe through feeling, but it took all her energy to control her fear as she stepped through the gate. The house loomed ahead. It was an elegant mansion that boasted five stories, all built of tan stone and inlaid with tall, opaque-glass windows. On either side of the grand staircase sat a turret with a tattered green flag whipping in the breeze.

This feels wrong, her magic seemed to whisper. *You are a wild thing he wishes to trap*. Verve pushed the thoughts aside as Fenn followed her through the iron bars and once again claimed her hand.

The inside of the house proved as imposing as the outside. The floors were cold stone with dark blue runners leading from end to end and room to room. From the walls hung ornate tapestries depicting battles and men on steeds, all of which seemed to come to life before Verve's eyes until she blinked. Here and there, between tapestries, stood tall suits of tarnished armor, some holding swords and others, lances. To this point they had encountered no sources of light, relying on fae sight and intuition to guide them. But as they left the antechamber and emerged into a round ballroom, a fire roared to life in a grate at the far back.

Verve jumped, calling magic to her free hand instinctively.

Gently squeezing her other hand, Fenn led her to the right end of the room, down a narrow, cold hall, up a short flight of stone stairs, and into the first room on the left. "You don't have to worry. No one can get to you here." Her hand still pulsed with magic flame until she calmed.

When she spoke, her voice was raw and hoarse as though from disuse. "Could I have brought her back? I mean, the Cunning Blade had a lot of power and I think I absorbed most of it. Maybe if I had touched Helena, something might've happened…."

The look of pity Fenn gave her was more than her heart could bear. She cried out and ripped her hand from his.

"No fae, no matter how powerful, has ever raised the dead."

She felt him move closer. "You're certain?"

"It is beyond what is natural."

The intonation of his words gave Verve pause. There was something there, something he was not telling her – there had to be. Fighting back tears, Verve rubbed a hand under her nose and attempted to press the issue. "But has anyone tried?"

Fenn tugged her hair out of its coif and ran his fingers through the reddish strands. "It's not something you want to look into, Verve. Madness and grief lie that way." He planted a kiss on the crown of her head. "Are you hungry?"

Verve let out an impatient huff. "No." Her stomach growled in disagreement.

"Wait here. I'll find something for us to eat." He squeezed her shoulders and turned to leave. "My magic works differently in this house and doesn't allow me to transport things more than a couple feet." Still he lingered. "I won't be long."

She nodded and moved forward to explore the room, her pulse ticking behind her right eye. When she heard Fenn shut the door behind him, pause, and then pad away, Verve walked toward the drapes on the far end of the bedroom. She pulled them back and was frustrated to find they opened into an enclosed courtyard. *You're not trapped, you're just…upset about Helena.* If it were safe for her to return home, perhaps they hadn't taken away Hel's body yet, and she could…. The thought did not bear finishing. Verve closed the blue drapes and smoothed a hand across the stone walls.

Firstblood.

Verve frowned and paused. "Hello?" She spun around, her back to the right-hand wall. A chill shot down her spine and her skin broke out in gooseflesh. "Is anyone there? Fenn?"

Someone's cold breath blew at the hair hanging down her back, and Verve had to choke down a scream. Magic lighting up her palms, Verve spun around, ready to attack. But no one was there.

Abomination.

The voice sounded as though it was right in front of her, but all she could see was the wall and the fireplace set within it.

You'll kill him.

A fire roared to life in the grate, and Verve's hairs stood on end when an image flickered within the blaze. A man made of flame danced with a woman made of blue light. They twirled and the embers swirled beneath their feet. Little by little, the male figure seemed to lose strength, but the blue woman continued at a frantic pace, dragging him on and on until he shriveled into ash.

You were meant for another, murmured a woman's voice. *Leave ere you kill this one.*

With a *poof*, the fire vanished along with the images within. The air smelled heavily of chocolate.

The door flew open, and Fenn was there, a tray in one hand and a ball of magic light in the other. "What's happened?"

Verve pointed at the fireplace. "There was something there. A specter or – I don't know what."

Fenn set the tray on the table inside the door and hastened forward, never once letting his magic drop. He sniffed the air, his eyes narrowing as he bent over to better look at the fireplace. With a sigh, he released the magic in his hand and let it join the blaze within the grate. "No one could have gotten in here unless they were blood bound to me." Fenn shook his head. "But that doesn't mean powerful magic couldn't have found its way in after us." He held out his hands for Verve. "What did it do? Are you hurt?"

"There were some creatures dancing in the flames and then the air smelled of magic. Dacre's magic."

A shadow passed across Fenn's face, and when he spoke, it was with care. "Other fae have the same residual burst as he did, Verve. It couldn't possibly have been him."

Verve shivered. "You buried him."

"I buried him."

Verve nodded and smoothed her hands down her dress, trying to control the fear that threatened to take hold of her. She didn't resist as Fenn led her toward a chair by the fireplace and bade her to sit.

"I'll put up extra wards to keep others' magic out." He brought over the food tray and handed her a plate. "It's nothing to worry about, Verve. Whoever sent the images wants to frighten you into doing something rash." Fenn handed her a chalice full of what smelled like honey and alcohol.

Without hesitation, she downed the liquid in several large gulps before coming up for air, coughing. Her family did not drink alcohol. Mother always had preached against the vile sort of people who would imbibe and indulge their baser desires. Thinking of Mother, Verve stared at her cup, wishing it would refill itself.

Fenn raised an eyebrow when she hiccoughed, but said nothing of it. "There's a library on the premises. I've been looking for books that might help us in the days to come, and found a few that show promise. It's a large collection, so it will take both of us to go through its contents."

"Could you put up the wards now?" Verve snatched Fenn's chalice out of his hand and downed its contents as well. Her chest warmed pleasantly, and her cheeks grew hot.

After giving Verve a concerned look, Fenn got to his feet and walked about the room. "*Frisonem atta aflar. Choel nees bettem manique.*" At his words – which Verve understood to roughly mean 'Safe may you keep us. Bid no magic enter' – the house shook on its foundations and the air filled with the scent of bergamot and limes. When Fenn looked at her again, his eyes were glowing like those of a cat. "You should really eat something. It's not good to have so much alcohol on an empty stomach." He returned to his chair and handed Verve a slice of soft, fragrant bread that had been smothered with butter and blackberry jam.

Not wishing to start an argument or arouse concern, Verve ate what he had given her, along with a sausage and some strange pink fruit, without complaining.

★ ★ ★

Late that night, as they lay in bed, Verve tried to rest. Fenn had dozed off hours prior, but sleep would not claim her. Every time she shut her eyes, Helena was there, cold and lifeless. Verve tried distracting herself by reciting poems she had learned as a child, but each one made her think of her family and caused grief enough to nearly suffocate.

Fenn rolled her way in his sleep, threw an arm over her, sighed, and settled down again. His presence was soothing, reassuring. But Verve knew she didn't deserve it.

Had the strange voice really meant to frighten her? Was she actually a danger to Fenn? Perhaps it had meant to warn her, to save her from herself. She had killed Helena without any effort, after all. Would it be much more difficult to accidentally kill her husband? Verve shuddered at the thought, and Fenn's hold on her tightened.

His lips pressed against the nape of her neck, which he then nuzzled into, his hands roaming over her. "I love you, Verve."

Tears prickled her eyes even as desire flooded her being. "Are you trying to distract me?"

He chuckled into her hair and rolled her onto her back. His lips skimmed hers as he crawled astride her, his touch feather-light. He kissed away her tears and laid his cheek against hers, whispering sweet things into her ear.

It felt good to be treated so, and Verve let herself relax beneath him.

Fenn did nothing more than kiss and touch, his fingertips gently teasing her, telling her what he wanted but would not take. He remained so until first light broke through the slit in the curtains, and Verve fell asleep.

When she woke perhaps three hours later, the sun had made no further progress other than to weakly shine from behind dark, brooding clouds. Violet lightning streaked across the skies, and rain began to pelt against the glass over the enclosed courtyard. Verve rubbed her eyes and sat up. It was quiet, besides the rain, which suited her mood fine. She noted the fire within the grate had been tended and a tray of food and drink sat on the table by it, along with a piece of parchment with a note.

Tearing into toasted bread and cheese, Verve read what Fenn had to say:

Verve,

I'm in the library. Please follow the blue ribbon to find me at your convenience.

Yours,

Fenn.

A frown tugged at Verve's lips. He had mentioned the library the night previous, about searching through books there to aid them in the days to come. At the time, she hadn't had the wits or the heart to ask him what he meant.

She downed the remainder of her toast and cheese and gulped a mug of hot tea, which did not scald her as it would have had she still been mortal. Still her stomach rumbled, so she ate the sausage that had been left for her as well. Then, licking her fingers, she left the room and, as promised, found a long, blue ribbon stretching down the hall, hanging from sconce to sconce.

The ribbon led her farther down the hall she had entered last night – south, if her bearings were correct – turning left and then right, up a flight of stairs, which led to the end of a hallway where sat a set of heavy-looking oak doors. As if sensing her presence and desire to enter, the doors creaked open, letting out the smells of parchment, ink, woodsmoke, limes, oranges, and dust. Yellow light flooded the entryway and spilled into the hall, causing Verve to squint and hold up her hand to shade her eyes.

A peal of thunder made Verve jump. "That one was close," she murmured, her hand to her chest.

"The Royal Weather-Makers are a disorganized lot these days," said Fenn, his voice muffled slightly. Verve inched into the room, whose doors closed behind her. "They have no one in charge and they cannot agree on who should be in control. So the more powerful ones make it storm nearly every day."

"Why?" Her jaw dropped at the height, breadth, and depth of the room, its walls entirely covered in bookshelves.

Soon, Fenn emerged from a closet in the corner, dust on his shoulders. "Because they can." Two orbs of yellow light circled around him, making Verve think of a mythological sun god she had once read about in a foreign novel. As if noticing her staring, the two orbs shot away from Fenn and into a far corner, where they hovered and bobbed with several others like them. He crossed the room and stooped to kiss her on the cheek. "Are you rested?"

She shrugged. "I don't need much rest these days."

That made Fenn cock his head to the side, but he did not pursue the answers to the unspoken questions in his eyes. Instead, he took her hand and led her to the enormous fireplace in the room, the one spot of wall where there were no books. Two chairs sat in front of the blaze, along with a table that came up to Verve's knees. Fenn gestured to the three large tomes resting on the tabletop. "These two are all I've found so far on curses," he said, pointing to the red book and the blue book. He jabbed a finger at the third, a thin tome covered in black leather. "And that is all I have come across about mastership magic."

Verve nodded as though the latter made any sense to her. She approached the black book and reached out to take it, but Fenn took her hand and guided her away from the table. "What?"

"That is a conveyable text."

She frowned. "Which means…?"

"Conveyable texts are much like conveyable weapons." He handed her the red book and led her to the chair on the right in front of the fireplace. "The Cunning Blade was one: when you touched it, you claimed each other and the magic that had been woven into the metal was absorbed into your being. These texts carry magic, which, unlike the Blade, can be absorbed by up to ten people. However, the magic weakens with each fae who takes it. And most fae can only absorb so much power before they start to lose some of their older abilities." He nudged her into the seat and pointed at the book in her hands. "This text is more like a regular book."

Verve cracked open the spine, and the book groaned in her hands. She scanned the page, thinking she'd see some familiar words or letters, but the pages were covered in golden nonsensical scribbles. "And I'm to read this?" Irritation flaring, Verve slammed the book shut.

Fenn took the book from her and replaced it on the table, lifting instead the blue book. "Interesting." He handed the blue tome to her. "Try this one instead."

"What's interesting?" She opened this book and was surprised to find the pages completely empty.

"Your curse seems to extend to at least some magical texts as well." His voice held a note of concern, but when he caught Verve chewing on her lower lip, he gave her a reassuring smile. "Don't worry. I should be able to read them again eventually. They just need time to recover from your touch." He took the blue book from her as well and replaced it on the table. "One thing we haven't done is to test the limits of your magic." Her expression must have soured, because he raised his palms in a truce. "When you're ready, of course. But it will have to happen sometime." Fenn held out his hand for Verve and pulled her to her feet.

"How are you finding what you need in all this?" Verve gestured at the shelves upon shelves of books, her fingers itching to pull each one from its place so she could breathe in its scent.

Fenn swung their hands between them as he led her over to the shelf next to the fireplace, where sat a tall wooden ladder on wheels. "It's been a matter of reading each spine and sending magic out to each book to make certain they're not conveyable. Nothing is organized, sadly. Texts on magical flora and fauna are where I would normally expect to find books on curses. There are biographies among the cookery books, and fiction is tucked here and there, while poetry keeps cropping up among the weather-making texts." He blew out his cheeks and squeezed her hand. "It would be nice to take a rest from all this."

"How far have you gotten?" Verve asked after he reeled her toward him.

With her back pressed into his chest and his hands resting against her stomach, Fenn rocked with her to and fro as though he were preparing to twirl her around in a dance. "Well, I started in the other room." He blew on a strand of her wild hair; his breath tickled her scalp.

"You mean the closet?" She pulled away and moved toward the place he had emerged from.

Fenn sighed and followed her. "No, I mean the other room. I'm about done with the second bookcase on the right."

Verve peeked through the doorway and groaned. This room was half the size of the main library but it still was huge, and the walls were covered in shelves of books, with stacks more of them on the floor. "Are we going to search through all this?" She began to enter the room, but paused when Fenn laid a hand on her shoulder.

"Are you able?"

She knew what he alluded to and shuddered. "I need to keep busy. Please."

Concern marred his handsome face but he didn't question her. He removed his hand and allowed her to lead the way into the second room of the library. In here, the air smelled of musk and vanilla with hints of citrus, which told Verve Fenn had recently used magic.

"Where did you say you left off?" She found the nearest ladder and climbed three rungs before Fenn's voice stopped her.

"Be careful to read the title first. And if it feels like it's conveyable, please call me over and don't touch."

Verve nodded and looked around for anything she thought might be useful. She would do anything to escape her thoughts.

They worked silently near each other. Fenn allowed her to use the ladder while he searched through the texts on the lower shelves. Every now and again, Verve couldn't read a title, either because the spine was too cracked, the text had faded with time, or the words simply vanished when she tried to take a better look at them. It was slow, frustrating work, but it did take her mind off things.

Fenn seemed to be faring better. He'd already removed two books from the shelves and set them aside by the time Verve had finished the second row of her unit.

They went on like this as the storm raged without. During one particularly loud peal of thunder, Verve lost control of her magic and the room seemed to disappear around them. She could see the woods beyond and the heavens above, but she didn't dare look down, knowing full well she wouldn't be able to see the floor below.

This disorienting experience had happened to her once already by accident. Fenn called it through-sight – something so easy, she knew she could do it on purpose if she tried. He had told her to close her eyes and wait. So she closed her eyes now. When she opened them again, though, dizziness overtook her and she swayed on the ladder.

"Verve!" Fenn shouted as she lost her footing and tumbled toward the floor.

Time seemed to slow as she fell. She could see every detail around her, from Fenn ready to catch her, to the ruby-red housefly buzzing about. She felt weightless, buoyed by power somehow, and unwittingly soared to the uppermost step of the ladder, where she clung to the shelf in surprise.

Breathing unsteadily, Fenn held the bottom of the ladder, his eyes wide with wonder. "Well, that is very interesting. Please come down from there."

Verve found her footing and climbed down the ladder, her whole body shaking, not with fear but with exhilaration. "What was that?"

Fenn's face, which had paled, split into a pleased grin. "We don't need to test you for flight. You have that ability, apparently." He shook his head, amused, it would seem. "The crueler among fae parents will test their young for flight by pushing them off great heights."

"What?" The thought made Verve feel sick.

"Fae bones don't break as easily as a human's," he reminded her. "But for now, perhaps you ought to stay on the ground."

But Verve had had a taste of flight, and it had only whetted her appetite. She wanted to climb the ladder again, to pitch herself from the top rung and defy gravity once more. The feeling of falling and then flying had effectively distracted her, more than reading book titles had. Even now, standing there doing nothing, the weight of the previous day settled back on her shoulders.

Shaking her head to rid herself of her darker thoughts, Verve took Fenn's place at the shelves below with a sigh. "What subjects are we looking for again?"

Fenn climbed the ladder with ease and scanned the shelves where she had left off. "Anything to do with curses, the Fire Queen, prophecy of the First and Second Ages, the Cunning Blade, and mastership magic."

Verve reached out to touch the book in front of her, but drew back her hand when she sensed it was a conveyable text. "What is mastership magic, exactly?" She squinted at the book's title, which declared the book to be about counter-magic.

"Mastership magic has to do with controlling a less experienced fae's abilities." He looked down at her. "Did you find something?"

"A book on counter-magic."

His face lightened up. "Ah, perfect. I knew there had to be one around here somewhere. Is it safe to touch or conveyable?" Fenn was already climbing down the rungs.

"Conveyable." She pointed at the green binding with golden letters. "Mastership – you mean like what Dacre might've been able to do with my magic?" That had been the reason Verve and Fenn had wed. Dacre had attempted to transform Verve into a fae, which would have given him ownership of Verve's magic. But with the marriage rites, the ownership would have passed over to Fenn. It did…until Verve absorbed the Cunning Blade's magic, which, as far as Verve knew, was under no one's control but her own.

The air smelled of Fenn's magic as he produced a handkerchief out of thin air and used it to grab the book Verve had found. "Yes and no. Fae property rights give a fae natural access to their creation's magic. Mastership magic is usually agreed upon between a teacher and pupil. It puts a temporary damper on the latter's powers for the safety of everyone involved." He turned the book over in his hands, not touching the cover or even the edges of the paper with his bare flesh. "This one's a good find, Verve. It might have what I've been looking for."

But Verve wasn't distracted from the topic of mastership magic, all thoughts of flight pushed aside. "Why do you need a book on that sort of magic?"

"That sort of magic hasn't been seen in centuries, fae being the suspicious beings we are. I'll have to see if any of the power still lingers in the text."

Verve grimaced and followed him to the other room, where he placed the newly found books near the other three. "Are you avoiding my question?"

Fenn shook his head. "No, I'm trying to think of the best way to answer it." He folded his arms across his chest and paused. "What I hope to do is to put a temporary leash on your powers."

It felt as though a cold hand had clenched her heart. "What exactly would that look like?"

"Well, it would allow me to decide when and how your magic would be used." The words hung between them, and Verve's stomach soured. "Just for a time, 'til you've learned better control."

Verve flinched. "It was an accident." Power began to swell inside her as her temper rose, pushing against her skin, which suddenly felt like it was too tight an encasement. But she tamped it down, forced it aside, and brought herself under control ere it could erupt.

All the while, Fenn watched her with apparent interest, his muscles tensed, as though he were ready to come to her rescue if needed. Only when Verve had mastered herself did he relax, and even then the tension did not quite leave his eyes. "I know it was an accident." His voice was soothing, careful. It made Verve want to smash something. "But that doesn't mean we shouldn't be proactive."

"No."

Fenn held up his hands. "I know it sounds unnatural. But it would only be temporary. Please, think about it."

The thought was more than unnatural. It sounded very much like being controlled by someone else – trapped. Unbidden thoughts and images of her captivity months and months ago entered Verve's mind, causing her to shudder and move away from Fenn, fear bubbling inside her.

"Verve?" He took a cautious step toward her.

She shook her head and fled from the room. Verve ran without direction, going as far and as fast as her legs would carry her. At first she was aware of Fenn's pursuit, but soon she left him so far behind, she could have sworn she had left the grounds, how faint his pulse and breathing had become to her ears. She turned this way and that, going up one staircase and then another, then down again. At length she ran out of house and found herself in what appeared to be an attic, dusty and full of the ghosts of old furniture shrouded in white cloth. Magic made her fingertips burn. She tried to control her power, but it was fed by fear and anger and insisted on release.

The nearest window, one that led onto a balcony overlooking the front grounds, flew open at a mere thought, and she directed her energy toward the open sky. Silver bolts of lightning shot from her fingers and lit up the dreary sky, pounding Verve's sensitive ears with every resulting *boom*. The air smelled of toffee, and she knew fae would be able to scent it for miles, perhaps drawing them to her. That thought, of being discovered and having to explain where she got such power from, caused Verve's fear to rise once more. The winds picked up outside, and a funnel cloud formed beyond the front gate.

Imagine the winds dying down, she told herself. She tried. It did little good, as her magic was intrinsically linked with her emotions. What had Father always told her to do when her feelings were out of control or she was having an attack? It was something to do with counting.... *In for a count of ten, out for a count of fifteen?* Verve attempted to focus on her breathing, and was mostly successful: the funnel cloud disappeared, the winds died down to small gusts, and the lightning ceased. But as things stilled, Verve became aware of a second presence in the room, one that was not Fenn.

CHAPTER FOUR

Not wanting to hurt the person in case she was wrong about them not being Fenn, Verve held herself steady and allowed a ball of fire to form in her right palm, ready to throw at any intruder. Spinning around, she was at once struck with a mighty gust of wind, and the air smelled of ginger. The force of the blow knocked her off her feet and sent her sailing against the wall, where she hit her head against the large balcony window, shattering several panes and rattling the rest. A metallic taste filled her mouth and her ears rang, but she knew herself to be otherwise unscathed. She wasn't going to give away that information to her attacker, however, and instead feigned unconsciousness.

Fenn was shouting in the distance, his footsteps racing through the house as he tried to find Verve.

For whatever reason, her attacker didn't strike again. "I know you're not knocked out," said a familiar feminine voice that took Verve a moment to place. "You need to stay down, halfling."

With a scowl, Verve gave up the pretense and opened her eyes. The woman was as Verve remembered from her vision over a year ago now: tall and muscular, the warrior-like she-fae had half of her blonde hair shaved on one side, and intricate braids ran throughout what was left. *Fenn's ally in the flesh.* They had never met, but Verve wasted no time in addressing her. "How did you get in here, Tilda?" Verve asked conversationally, taking pleasure when the other's eyes lit up with surprise.

She looked over Verve slowly, raising her hands as though expecting a fight. "Not a halfling, then. Interesting. Who and what are you? And how did *you* get onto this property?"

Verve sprang to her feet, and Fenn's friend struck out with a fireball, but Verve was ready this time and threw up a wall of defense. Tilda made a move to strike again, but Fenn was there, taking her by the throat and hauling her up against a wall.

"Are you all right?" he demanded, not taking his eyes from the woman kicking at him and attempting to free her neck from his grasp.

"I'm fine." Verve's tone was brittle, but Fenn seemed to take no note of what she had said.

Fenn growled at the woman he had pinned. "If you so much as scratched my wife…."

Tilda stopped struggling; her eyes rolled back in her head and she went limp.

"Fenn," said Verve. She had never seen him so truly angry. "She didn't hurt me. Put her down."

After a moment's hesitation, Fenn sighed and let the woman's feet touch the ground but did not remove his hand from her throat, though he loosened his hold. "Stop being so dramatic," he warned Tilda.

With a snort, Tilda opened her eyes and attempted to shake Fenn off. "*This* is your wife? I thought you had married a halfling."

Verve didn't need to see Fenn's face to know his left eye had twitched in response. "What are you doing here?"

"Is that any way to greet me?" She sounded bored, but Verve could sense her fear. Tilda's eyes darted to Verve and then back to Fenn. "Besides, you may be head of the Larknott family now, but that doesn't mean you can decide who comes and goes."

"It most certainly does," he said, his voice calm and cold. "Why did you attack my wife without provocation?"

Tilda scoffed, and Verve hastily shook the glass shards out of her hair. "What makes you think it was unprovoked? You weren't even in the room." There was a tense silence in which Verve heard Tilda's heart take off at a gallop. "She was ready to incinerate me." Even as she said the lie, the she-fae continued to stare Fenn in the eye. "It was self-defense."

Fenn didn't look Verve's way either but sniffed the air and swore. "Are you bleeding?"

"Of course not. I can handle myself."

"That's good to know, but I wasn't talking to you." After dropping Tilda, Fenn turned his back on her with apparent reluctance and was at once examining Verve, combing more of the glass shards from her hair and looking her over for goodness knows what he thought he'd find.

"From the power I feel coming off her and the storm she created moments ago, I'd say your wife can take care of herself as well."

Verve batted him away, mindful to be gentle. "She's right. I'm fine."

There was a glint in his eye she did not like. It promised they would have words later. "You've healed already. That's good," Fenn said lightly. He gestured to Tilda. "This is my cousin and the last remaining woman of the family. Or rather, she was until recently." There was a note of gloating in his voice that made Verve roll her eyes.

The she-fae eyed her suspiciously and did not extend a hand for Verve to shake. Neither did Verve. "Last I saw our Fenn, he asked for my help saving your family and then said the Cunning Blade had been destroyed."

Verve shrugged. "I know he did." Indeed, she had witnessed the whole meeting in a vision.

"Let's discuss that another time," said Fenn. With pronounced care, he moved Verve behind his back, shielding her from his cousin and perhaps her scrutiny. "You have one chance, Tilda. You may remain here for a week, but stay away from my wife and out of the west wing."

Tilda picked at her nails, feigning boredom, apparently, though her annoyance and barely suppressed rage screamed at Verve almost loudly enough to be heard. "Anything else?"

Fenn nodded at her boots. "Leave the knives outside."

"Really, cousin, you trust me so little?"

The grin Fenn gave Tilda was positively deadly. "With you, your *stolen* blades, and my wife under the same roof? Why need you ask?"

Tired of being talked about and hidden away as though she wasn't there, Verve stepped out from behind Fenn and strode toward the door, feeling two sets of eyes on her back. She didn't stop, even as she sensed Fenn following her. The halls were long and branched off into others, and Verve could only guess at where the outside door might be. *Out. I need to get out, even if just for a moment.*

Fenn continued to follow but kept his distance until the hall ended in a set of double doors. For something to do, she tried them, but they did not budge. It took all her self-control not to kick the doorframe. Afraid Fenn would press the issue of managing her powers, Verve turned and said, "I didn't know you had any family around."

His eyes were weary, and at once an ache blossomed in her chest. "When I was born," he said, "my family was terrified." He leaned against the wall on his right and regarded her. "My parents weren't powerful fae. We have elfin blood in our line, so to conceive something like me was not expected. Tilda's family raised me when things went wrong. She's the only blood relative I have left now."

Verve frowned, and when she spoke, her voice was very small. "You speak of your family as though they're no longer living."

"Most are not," said Fenn, his expression grim. "All of my family is either dead or moved on to another realm."

That made no sense. Fae were immortal.

Perhaps reading the confusion on Verve's face, Fenn straightened and said, "It's true high fae live forever, but my parents were not high fae and their lack of magic made them vulnerable. They were perhaps seven hundred years old when I killed them."

Verve stilled. "What do you mean?"

Fenn looked her in the eyes. "Mother died birthing me, a bad omen. Then I lost my temper with my father when I was three and he didn't survive it. My grandparents and uncle fled the realm when I was sixteen, I am told. Tilda's parents were tortured by Midras when I was...younger, and they never recovered their sanity." He shrugged.

"Anyone else is either hiding because they're afraid of my power or dead because of it."

The way he said it all was so casual, so lacking in emotion, it must have happened a very long time ago. *Just how old* are *you?* Verve wrapped her arms around herself. "I'm sorry for your loss." When he said nothing but continued to gaze at her, Verve cleared her throat and attempted to walk around him, but Fenn's hand shot out and caught her gently by the arm.

"Sooner or later, we're having a conversation about managing your magic. The display you put on earlier with the wind and the lightning – that was only a shadow of what I sense is to come if you don't learn more control."

She started to argue, but he cupped her face in one hand, effectively distracting her and staying her words.

"As long as Tilda's here, please stay away from her. I don't want her guessing where your powers originate." He leaned in and pressed his lips against hers.

His mouth was demanding, driving all objections out of Verve's mind. Long fingers wove themselves into her hair as he backed her into the wall and pressed his body into hers. Gasping, he dragged his lips down her throat and up again.

There were footsteps in the near distance, and Fenn pulled back with a sigh. "Later," he promised, stroking her cheek. "Let's find something to eat, shall we?"

Though her legs now seemed to be made of jelly, Verve walked arm in arm with Fenn down the hall whence they had come.

★ ★ ★

It soon became apparent Tilda didn't mean to abide by Fenn's rules. She didn't encroach on their side of the mansion – not exactly. But Verve sensed her presence flirting near the divide, heard the she-fae's heart beating around corners almost everywhere she went. And of course wherever Verve went, Fenn followed.

They ate at separate times in the house's one kitchen, though Verve knew the she-fae wasn't far. What exactly she wanted, it wasn't clear, and any time Verve thought to ask Fenn, she decided against it in fear it would remind him about their postponed conversation. In fact, she didn't speak to him much at all.

He asked her once if she was all right. She lied and told him she was fine, effectively stopping the questions burning in his eyes. After that, he watched her even more closely.

On the third day of Tilda's stay, Verve had had enough of being followed by the two of them and she stayed in bed late that morning, waiting for her husband to leave for the library so she could sneak off. Unfortunately, this seemed to make Fenn suspicious, and he took longer than usual getting up and ready for the day.

"Aren't you interested in the books I found last night?" he asked Verve as he finished dressing. They were books on curse-breaking, both conveyable texts. Fenn had been excited upon finding them, wondering aloud if they would give instructions for breaking a curse bestowed by a now-deceased fae. "Since Dacre is dead, it makes little sense to me why we shouldn't be able to at least weaken the curse's potency," he had said. Now, his eyes roved over Verve, searching for something and then narrowing. "You are all right, aren't you?"

Verve sighed. "I'm just tired."

That seemed to do nothing to ease Fenn's worry. "You've been aloof since Tilda's arrival." He made up his side of the bed, which he then leaned across. "Has she offended you?" He stilled. "Have – have *I* done something to offend you?"

She didn't want to fight, not now. If he only *suspected* she was angry at him, maybe he would leave her alone. But if he *knew for certain* how she felt, Fenn would become even more vigilant, and Verve would never have a moment to herself. So she maintained careful control of her expression and voice as she answered. "I really just want to be alone for a while." There, that was true enough.

Worry creased his face as he leaned down and kissed her on the cheek. "All right. I'll put up some extra wards to keep her at bay. But if you feel threatened, please, come find me." He seemed to want to say something more and stood at the door, his eyes alert.

"Let me know what you find today," Verve said, rolling over onto her side facing away from him.

Fenn remained a moment longer and then closed the door behind him. His presence lingered outside the door, and Verve could hear his reluctant steps pattering away, even as the smell of limes filled the air, signaling he had put up more defensive spells against Tilda.

Using through-sight, Verve saw him reach the library and begin to look through the many rows of books. It was perhaps wrong to keep things from him, but she didn't know what else to do. Would he lock her away if he found out what she was planning? There was no way to be certain.

After relaxing and closing her eyes, Verve opened them and her normal sight returned. She went to the wardrobe in the corner and pulled out a pair of tan trousers and a deep green tunic, both of which Fenn had helped her make out of feathers the night previous. The transfiguration process was getting easier for Verve, much to her relief, and the clothes fit her nearly to perfection.

She devoured a piece of toasted bread and cheese, washed it down with a large gulp of water, and then made her way toward the central part of the house. It was obvious where Fenn had set the magical boundaries. There was a visible line of green light on the floor, and the smell of citrus was intense. *Will he sense if I cross over?* That was a concern. Biting her lower lip, Verve nudged her toe through the boundary and paused when she heard Tilda approaching from the south-east end of the house.

The she-fae would have been too quiet for Verve to hear, had Verve been a normal fae. Tilda's steps were measured, quiet, and she had silenced her heart's beatings.

Verve waited for the creature to reveal herself, could feel her watching from a short distance. She looked over and smirked when she spied Tilda looking at her through a small hole in the wall opposite. "You can come out," said Verve, keeping her voice low so that Fenn might not hear from the other end of the house.

The eye in the hole disappeared and its mistress materialized moments later from the room across the hall. Both women stared at each other in silence. It was obvious from Tilda's expression she didn't know what to make of Verve and she was still striving to hide the terror she felt. She looked down at the floor between them and whistled. "That is an impressive spell. He really doesn't want me anywhere near you." The air smelled of ginger as Tilda reached out with her magic toward the line Fenn had made, stopping shy of the boundary.

Verve could see the she-fae's magic. It was white and it sparkled as it moved gracefully upward, exploring the boundaries of whatever spell Fenn had set up. The closer the white got to the green, the deeper in color the line grew, until Tilda pulled it back suddenly. Her eyes narrowed when Verve looked back up at her.

"You can see my magic, can't you?" Tilda asked. "Don't deny it. I saw your eyes following its progress. Something as weak as a testing spell shouldn't be detectable."

Instead of answering, Verve shrugged and changed the subject. "What do you want?"

The she-fae leaned against the wall to her left, mirroring Verve. "You know I've been trying to find a way to get to you, then?"

The non-answer grated at Verve, made her wonder if trying to speak with the woman was a good idea after all. For a moment she took her eyes off Tilda, using through-sight to make certain Fenn was where she had left him. She didn't have to look to know Tilda had thrown something at her, but reached out and caught it, her hand passing through Fenn's invisible barrier. She turned to look at what was in her hand. It was a wadded-up piece of paper. Verve straightened it out and read, *The Gate of the Dead is open again. Run, little Firstblood. Run.* Frowning, she looked up to demand an explanation, but the creature had gone.

It was obvious now that the paper's passage through the barrier had triggered an alarm, because Fenn was there moments later, a knife in his hand and a wild look in his eyes. "What happened?" His gaze traveled to the piece of paper in her hand, and as it did, the letter dissolved into ash and fell through her fingers, leaving the reek of ginger behind.

"It said, 'The Gate of the Dead is open again'," Verve murmured.

Fenn cursed and replaced his knife in its sheath with apparent reluctance. "Did she write anything else?"

With a sigh, Verve told him the rest of the text. "What is the Gate of the Dead and why should I run?"

Gently, Fenn took her by the hand and led her away from the barrier, his pulse pounding so hard in his veins, Verve could easily feel it. He waited until they were back in the bedroom, the door bolted, and more protective spells put up. The air smelled strongly of grapefruit and lemons, and Verve knew there was no way they would be overheard or intruded upon. "What she wrote is a reference to a poem about the Fire Queen, one that paints her as a saint – a *martyred* saint." His expression and voice were both calm, but Verve could feel anger radiating off him in waves.

"Oh?" asked Verve, leaning against the far wall.

Fenn scrubbed a hand over his face and recited,

"The Gate of the Dead is locked—
But two shall hold the key.
Fire flows in her veins,
Through his dread certainty.
He tied what is hers to his own,
That cunning thief to the throne."

Here Fenn paused and leaned against the door. "We're now certain of the first person mentioned in the poem, the woman, the Fire Queen – you." He nodded at her, and she scoffed. "It's you, Verve. You're fitting more and more the prophetic description with each passing day.

"The second person in the poem, the man, has been a point of some debate among scholars. Most schools of thought believe him to be the Fire Queen's spouse or mate. Others believe it is someone who learns to manipulate her. But," said he, shaking his head, "I think there's a better explanation." He watched her carefully, his eyes asking if he could continue or if he should stop. When she nodded, Fenn went on. "'He tied what is hers to his own'. Who fits that description in your life, Verve?"

She thought for a moment, and her blood seemed to freeze in her veins. Adamantly, she shook her head. "I thought you said he was dead. That you buried him after I – after it happened."

Fenn nodded. "Yes, and I still believe Dacre is dead. But that doesn't mean someone isn't acting on his behalf."

Verve groaned.

"It is possible to pass on one's legacy to another fae. What if Dacre knew you might destroy him? He would seek out a progeny of sorts, pass on some or most of his abilities to her or him, and charge them with fulfilling his purpose."

"And that purpose is what?"

Now Fenn took to pacing, his left eye twitching. "That is the question. I'm not as well versed in Second Age prophecy as I ought to be. I thought the Fire Queen wouldn't be found for another ten generations at least...if she were to exist at all."

Verve thought back to the note Tilda had given her. "But what about what was on that scrap of paper? 'The Gate of the Dead is open again. Run, little Firstblood. Run'? Did Dacre's progeny or what-have-you open the gate?"

"Tilda seems to believe so. The last part is a taunt that might be entirely of her own making. Which means I need to find a way to banish her." Fenn ceased pacing and moved to the door, but Verve used magic to lock it from across the room, filling the air with the smell of toffee. He looked back at her.

"You can't throw her out on the streets."

"Verve—"

"She's your family." Weariness settled on Verve's shoulders and she sat near the window.

With a sigh, Fenn moved across the room toward Verve and sat on the edge of the bed facing her. "*You* are my family now. Tilda and I have a long, complicated past. Sometimes we've been the best of friends, other times, each other's greatest enemy. That she would threaten and taunt you in that note, making it destroy itself before I could see it.... She must have believed you wouldn't tell me." Fenn shook his head.

Dread tightened Verve's chest. She had lost Helena, and now she was making Fenn lose his only remaining family. *What sort of monster am I?* "She hasn't harmed me."

His eyes met hers. "Tilda is no longer welcome here. She knew what she was doing, and now there have to be consequences." As one decided in their course, Fenn rose and moved to the door, pausing to say, "What troubles me is how she guessed so quickly you're the Fire Queen. Did you say anything to her upon her arrival? Anything about the Cunning Blade?"

"No. Nothing that would have made her suspect I had anything to do with it."

Fenn nodded, his eyes distant, calculating. "Then she must have been drawn to your power. And with some prophecy yet to be fulfilled – some I have only recently learned of – it's not your time to ascend. It would throw Letorheas and possibly Etterhea into chaos."

"Ascend?" Verve asked, the small hairs on the back of her neck rising. "Ascend what?"

The look he gave her was confused and then incredulous. "The fae throne."

Verve felt the color drain from her face. "What? I thought that was metaphorical."

"She's called the Fire *Queen* for a reason, Verve. She's meant to reign and restore balance between the realms...or, at least, that is what half the prophecies claim. We need to make sure you're not discovered before your time. Or the other prophecies...." He closed his mouth and his pupils dilated slightly, alerting Verve that he was afraid.

"What do the other prophecies say?"

Fenn hesitated a long moment and finally said, "It doesn't matter. Besides, they're heavily debated."

"Fenn," Verve said. "What do those other prophecies say?" A sudden wind swirled around her, whipping her hair out of its braid and nearly lifting her from the ground as angry sparks flew out of her fingertips.

"They say," said Fenn, his tone measured, "either you destroy the 'cunning thief to the throne' or death devours you whole."

The words hung between them heavily. Around Verve, the wind died down to a gentle breeze as she mulled over what Fenn had just told her. She didn't want to die, feared it, but did she deserve to live? That was a matter for another time. Her thoughts strayed to the fateful day of the wedding. Whoever had attempted to kidnap her must know what she was...and could possibly be the so-called thief to the throne – or, at least, could be working *for* them. Perhaps it was time to stop hiding. Whether or not she was the Fire Queen might be irrelevant if others believed she was. She'd be hunted all her days for merely holding as much power as she did. "I want to know more of these prophecies."

Tension seemed to tighten Fenn's shoulders. He nodded and folded his arms across his chest. "As I said, I don't know them all. Not even close to a fourth. And I'm not having much luck finding books on the subject."

"First and Second Age prophecies?" The breeze ceased, leaving Verve's hair a tangled mess she had to brush out of her face. She had seen two books on the subjects; she only had to remember where and when.

"First Age prophecies speak of the creation of the Cunning Blade and hinted at the possibilities of a power to come. They also foretold many things that have already come to pass. Second Age prophecies deal with the Fire Queen, the thief, and the futures of Letorheas and Etterhea." He sounded distracted, turned inward. "I'll interrogate Tilda before I send her on her way. And then we're going to look more closely at mastership magic." He turned and strode out the door, shutting it with a little extra force than was necessary.

Verve tugged at her hair. Even if giving control of her magic to Fenn meant fewer people would be able to find her, it was no way to live, someone else pulling her strings. How did this make Fenn any better than Dacre, who had sought to control her through transformation? *Trapped.*

The walls seemed to close in on Verve. Her head pounded and her hands were slick with sweat. "Get a hold of yourself." She needed to clear her thoughts, to formulate a plan. If she had a full-blown attack, which she hadn't done for over a year now, that would leave her vulnerable and Fenn might be able to....

No, she couldn't think like this. *In for a count of six, hold for a count of ten, out for a count of seven.* Controlling her breathing helped a little. She also tried tensing and then relaxing each muscle.

They were loud, the two cousins. There was a great deal of shouting, many accusations, and then the fight began.

Effectively distracted, Verve left the relative safety of the bedroom and then wound through hallways until she arrived at the house's antechamber and entry. Both Tilda and Fenn held shields of glowing magic in front of them, and the air reeked of lemons and ginger.

"It was just a harmless warning," Tilda was saying as Fenn lobbed a fistful of angry red magic at her, dissolving her shield.

"How did you figure out she was even here?" He plucked the dagger she threw at him out of the air and then threw it back, pinning Tilda by the neck of her tunic to the wall.

She snarled and growled at him as he approached. Each threw more magic at each other as he gained ground. "Her magic is so strong, I could smell and sense it for miles." Tilda lashed out and struck Fenn across the face before tearing her tunic in her effort to free herself. This bought her enough time to make a leap for the door, but Fenn was faster.

He caught Tilda by her upper arms and hauled her against the wall, where she writhed and kicked at him, all to no effect. "Why did you seek her out?"

"Curiosity. Who wouldn't want to know where that amount of power came from?"

"You know I can discern lies," said Fenn. "Why do you even try? I wonder...."

Verve cringed. That was new information to her; she thought fae lies were indiscernible. She would have to watch her words around Fenn more closely.

Tilda howled in rage or pain as Fenn wove a spell between his fingers and shoved it into her forehead. With a scream, she fell to her knees and clutched her head. Fenn stood over her, barring her escape.

Though she didn't wish to be seen, Verve didn't know how much more of this violence she could take, especially when it was dealt on her behalf. She was about to intervene when Tilda convulsed and Fenn lifted her from the ground. Whether or not he was surprised to turn and find Verve standing there staring at him, she couldn't be certain.

"She's been bewitched," said Fenn, carrying her past Verve. "I should have known she was acting strangely."

Verve followed him down the hall until he reached a door that flew open for him. He carried Tilda inside and lowered her onto the lone bed in the room, even as she continued to thrash and shake. "Tilda!" he said sharply. "Can you hear me?"

The she-fae's eyes fluttered open and she looked about her in confusion. When her eyes landed on Verve, she cringed. Then, of all things, she began to sob. "I'm sorry. I'm so sorry." Again and again she repeated her apologies as Fenn checked her pulse and covered her with a blanket.

"Who bewitched you?" Fenn asked.

Tilda sniffled and shuddered mightily. "I didn't see who did it."

"Where were you when it happened?"

She was silent for a moment, besides the odd whimper, and then whispered, "I don't remember."

Fenn produced a glass of water out of thin air and poured some of it down his cousin's throat. "Do you remember what you were compelled to do?" His tone was compassionate enough, but Verve sensed his impatience and dread.

Tilda hiccoughed. "I was supposed to come between you and her, make you two fight." She snatched the glass from Fenn and downed the rest of the water, clearly wishing it was something stronger. "If that failed, I was to find a way for the house's wards to be penetrated. Oh, cousin, I am so sorry. I should have kept my guard up." She passed the glass back to Fenn, who made it vanish.

"And this mystery party didn't compel you to do anything else? They didn't give you any motivation? Stay where you are, dearest."

Verve, who had been ready to move closer, stopped. "What? Why? You lifted the bewitchment."

Fenn grimaced. "The bewitching is perhaps removed, but that doesn't mean there won't be any residual effects." He turned his attention back to Tilda, who looked truly wretched. "Are you compelled to harm her?"

Tilda shook her head.

"Answer, out loud, please."

"No, I wasn't supposed to harm her." Again she shuddered and drew the blanket more tightly under her neck. "You must believe—"

Fenn held up a hand, effectively staying her words. "If you weren't to harm her, why did you attack my wife when you first arrived?" His expression was calm enough, but his eyes.... Verve knew he was struggling with himself.

"I was allowed to attack to defend myself, should I feel threatened. But the spell – it told me I couldn't truly harm her. That's how I guessed she was the Fire Queen."

"And the note? Were you compelled to write it or were you attempting to circumvent the bewitching?" A vein pulsed in his forehead, and he shook his head at Verve as if to say, *"This isn't looking good."*

Tilda closed her eyes. "I'm sorry. I can't say."

"You can't or you won't?"

She swore and sat up in bed, her expression incredulous. "I was *bewitched*, Fenn. I'm the *victim*, not the enemy."

He rested his head in one of his hands. "Nonetheless, you shall leave here as soon as you've recovered from the counter-bewitching."

Tilda opened her mouth at the same time as Verve to argue, but Fenn put up his hand. "My mind is made up." He looked pointedly at Tilda. "You know why."

Tears prickled Verve's eyes, and when Fenn moved toward her and the door, she turned her back on him and stormed to the room they were staying in. How could he be so cold-hearted to his own flesh and blood? She slammed the door in Fenn's face, as he was fast on her heels, and she had half a mind to lock him out with magic.

There was a tentative knock on the wood and the door creaked open. "Verve?" He stepped toward her, but paused when she turned her back to him. "So you *are* angry with me."

"Of course I am," she spat over her shoulder. "How can you treat your own family this way?"

"You take an eager interest in someone who does not like you one bit."

Verve went rigid as he moved closer. "That doesn't excuse your behavior."

"She will harm you if given the chance, Verve. Tilda's not to be trusted. But I think there's something else going on here. Would you care to talk about it?" He sat on the bed behind her, watchful.

For a moment, Verve considered telling him the truth, that she did not want him controlling her and her magic. But would he understand her point of view and give her the freedom she needed? *Trapped*.

"Verve?"

Her focus moved to her breathing, her back to him, even as dread made her toes curl and stomach clench. If only Hel were here to comfort and advise her as to what she ought to do next. "Helena," was all she could muster, and it nearly broke her. Pushed aside was her fury at Fenn. Self-hatred and sorrow took over as she shook with silent sobs.

At once Fenn collected her into his arms and pulled her against his chest. "Is that what this is about?" he murmured into her hair.

Verve didn't answer but continued to cry. Grief tore at her, and she let it, allowing Fenn to comfort her…even though it made her loathe herself even more.

One hand held her close, the other stroked her hair. "I'm so sorry, Verve."

Silver tears ran down her face and landed on the floor, glowing faintly as they puddled at her feet. Soon she felt wrung out like a dishcloth, and that was when Fenn led her toward the bed and eased her down onto the mattress so she was sitting on its edge.

"Would you like me to make you some tea?"

Verve shook her head. "No, thank you." Her voice was nasal and ragged.

He lifted her chin and looked her in the eyes. "I'm sorry I upset you." Fenn leaned down and stroked her cheek. "We'll figure this out. I promise." After giving her shoulder a gentle squeeze, he conjured a blanket and draped it over her shoulders. "Why don't you lie down for a while? You've barely slept since we arrived here."

It was tempting, to let herself be taken care of and forget all that had happened. But if she was in fact the Fire Queen, there were many things Verve should know, especially since Tilda had been sent after her.

A memory rose in Verve's mind, one of a man and his books. *Dacre stood in his chamber, his hair rumpled and his expression barely composed as he sent a stack of books sailing onto his desk.*

Focus, someone seemed to whisper into her ear.

She closed her eyes and beheld several large tomes on First and Second Age prophecy, blood bonds, marriage bonds, and the Lands of the Dead. A tingle ran down her spine as she read the final title. Dacre's image flickered and vanished in her mind, but the books remained.

"Verve? Are you all right?"

Verve blinked her eyes open and wrinkled her nose. The air smelled strongly of her magic and ancient parchment. But when she looked around, there were no signs any magic had been performed, and Fenn seemed not to have scented it. "I'm all right," she said before Fenn could ask her again. "I think I'd like to rest awhile...if you don't mind." She looked up at Fenn, whose expression at once faded from concerned to relieved.

"Of course not." Fenn watched her as she lay down and closed her eyes. "I've put up extra wards and will be in the library if you need me." His footsteps moved toward the door. "Tilda can take care of herself, Verve. She's tougher than you think." The door whined shut, and Fenn was gone.

She waited a few minutes, just to make certain he wasn't going to change his mind about leaving her alone, then she attempted to return to the vision. Something felt important about it.

At once the image returned of the last book on the stack, the one about the Lands of the Dead. In her dreamlike state, Verve was aware of the smell of parchment and vanilla, but she ignored the residual bursts and continued to focus on the memory. It resisted her for a moment, but then the memory did something she did not expect. The book began to glow, flipped open, shuddered, and lay still.

Verve clung to the memory – though the longer she studied the book, the less certain she became that it was, in fact, a memory – and focused on the pages open in front of her. It was slippery to hold on to, the vision, and it took all her strength to make the words stand still. She read:

The Lands of the Dead hold many secrets. From spell-breaking and potion-brewing to the subtle art of managing one's own excess power—

The words began to fade, and Verve tried desperately to hold on, but it was no use: all grew dim, and the smell of parchment faded. With a sigh, Verve opened her eyes. Thunder rumbled in the distance, but soft light filtered in through the drapes, which were opened a crack. "Spell-breaking," she murmured. The book was at Dacre's mansion. "It must contain the curse Dacre performed and its counter-curse." Sudden eagerness to be moving overcame her weariness, and Verve leapt to her feet.

It occurred to her that perhaps the library here might contain a duplicate copy of the same book, but something inside told her otherwise. Did magical texts even *have* multiple copies? That was something to look into, perhaps. But was there time? She looked through the walls at Fenn, who was doggedly searching through the numerous books in the library. He seemed anxious. Verve gulped. *Will he forcibly control my magic? Will I hurt him if he doesn't?*

If Dacre's book also contained information about managing one's own power, then it would surely solve several of Verve's main problems. Unable to contain her excitement, Verve ran to the library, startling Fenn, who dropped a heavy tome onto the floor and threw up a protective ward around himself.

Breathing hard, Fenn lowered his defenses and frowned at Verve. "What's wrong?"

"I found it," she said, her hands trembling with excitement. "I found the book that can help me."

The crease between Fenn's brows smoothed out and his eyes lightened. "Where is it? Did you bring it with you?"

Verve shook her head. "No. I saw it in a vision."

Fenn stilled and the crease returned. "A vision? When?"

She grinned. "I had part of it earlier, but it faded, so I concentrated and it returned and – you don't seem pleased."

He took her gently by the shoulders and looked her in the eyes. "Normal visions don't work like that, Verve. They enter your mind and leave when they want, even though you can encourage them. You can't just turn them on and off again."

"What are you saying?" It felt as though she had been doused with icy water, and it took some self-control not to shake him off.

It was another moment until Fenn spoke again, and when he did, each word was articulated with sober care. "I might have let some magical wards drop in my eagerness to protect you against Tilda." He watched her closely. "Did you smell any residual bursts?"

Verve's mouth opened and closed a few times. She nodded but then shook her head. "I don't know. I mean, I smelled parchment, but the book was made of parchment." When he dropped his hands and paced, she took a small step back, suddenly unsteady on her feet.

"That magic that threatened you when we first arrived here…do you remember what the accompanying burst smelled like?"

"Not parchment," she snapped. "What are you getting at?"

He held up a hand. "It might have been an implanted spell, meant to be activated at a certain date, which would explain why I wouldn't have smelled the accompanying bursts. It sounds like someone is trying to lure you into finding this book, wherever it might be. I don't like it."

"But I smelled *my* magic, too."

The words seemed to do little to change Fenn's mind. His look was stern, and he spoke less like a husband and more like a teacher when he said, "Seeking that book is out of the question. We'll find something here that works." He gestured around at the many rows of books, and Verve's heart sank.

As tempting as it was to protest and fight back, she knew Fenn well enough to believe he would act on what he thought to be her own best interest…even if it made her unhappy. If she lost her temper now and her magic caused a catastrophe, Fenn would surely force mastership magic on her. She took several deep breaths and stilled.

For a few minutes she looked around the room, barely seeing anything through her furious tears. Then a cold certainty settled upon her like a morning's dew: she needed to leave. She needed to leave *now* before he stopped her.

CHAPTER FIVE

Verve forced a small nod and wiped at her nose, her ears ringing. Whatever Fenn said to her, she couldn't be certain. All her focus was on the door behind her.

Without having to look, she knew Tilda was in the room they had left her in, legs hanging off the edge of her bed and a troubled look on her face. In Verve's mind's eye, the she-fae rose and began to pack her bag.

I need to make a gateway to Dacre's estate, Verve thought as Fenn squeezed her hand and spoke some reassuring words that meant nothing to her. *The trees are too afraid of me. I need help*. She nodded absently while Fenn returned to his work on the shelves, directing one last longing and regret-filled look at his back. She turned and moved as quickly as she dared to her room.

There was no cloak, only shoes to be worn. Verve hastily tugged them on before running down to the kitchen. In a cupboard she found some bread rolls and dried meat, which she bundled up in a napkin and carried at top speed up to the barrier Fenn had created between her and Tilda. She needed to move fast; Fenn's cousin was at the front door even now.

Verve took a deep breath and tested the magical boundary. It had reacted when Tilda had sent over a piece of paper, but would it alert Fenn if she stepped through? Knowing nothing about how complicated spells like that worked and having no time to study up on it, she knew there was only one thing to be done. She sucked in a deep breath and charged through the barrier, which tickled and pulled at her but did nothing else to stop her. Verve did not remain long enough to see if Fenn had been alerted.

Tilda had left the house and was nearing the gate.

"Wait," Verve whispered.

The she-fae did not pause or turn as she disappeared through the gate.

Frowning, Verve pushed herself to her greatest speed, rushing through the gate so quickly it rattled. "Tilda, wait!" She looked around her, but the woman was nowhere to be seen using normal sight. Verve was about to use her magic when she heard someone clear their throat from behind her. Hairs standing on end, Verve spun around and automatically erected a shield around herself, something she had only rarely done on instinct.

Tilda's teeth were bared, but only for a moment. Soon she wore a look of surprise. "Does Fenn know you've left the estate and its protections?" Tilda readjusted her bag over her shoulder.

Verve fancied she could see fear radiating off Tilda, but as soon as she had read the emotion, it vanished. "There's no time. I need you to help me make a gateway to somewhere."

Tilda's eyebrows shot up. "You can surely manage yourself." She stepped around Verve, who followed on her heels. "Listen, my cousin will be more than cross with me if I go against his wishes. Goodbye."

"I'm my own person," Verve snapped. "My wishes matter as well."

"Then make a gateway yourself and go your own separate way from Fenn. But be warned: he will come after you. He can't help it." She threw a smirk over her shoulder and picked up her pace.

After drawing in a deep breath, Verve said, "The trees are afraid of me."

Tilda paused, listening apparently with some interest. She said nothing.

Verve continued. "They retreat deep within themselves and sort of – I don't know, play dead unless I threaten them. And I've been told you don't want to make enemies of trees, so I could really use your help, Tilda. Please." The moment that passed as Tilda turned, her expression thoughtful, seemed to last forever. Every noise in the distance could be Fenn searching the house for her, storming through the gate, coming to drag her back.

Finally, Tilda sighed and nodded. "All right. But we'd better hurry." She beckoned Verve to follow her, and took off at a quick walk. It didn't take them long to find a hawthorn, and when they did, Tilda startled Verve by producing a knife, slicing her hand, and then stabbing the tree.

"Why did you do that?"

The she-fae smirked. "Where do you want to go? The hawthorn here is waiting."

It took a split second for the shock to wear off, but Verve swallowed and quickly said, "Dacre Starside's summer estate."

If Tilda was surprised by this answer, she did not let on, but turned to the tree, which wasted no time or words before forming a gateway that led into the woods on Dacre's land. She gestured for Verve to go ahead of her, and it took all of Verve's will not to change her mind.

The last time Verve had been on this land, Dacre had attempted to transform her into the Fire Queen...by drowning her. Without a backward glance, she screwed her courage to the sticking place and stepped into a land shrouded in mist and silence. Just as Tilda closed the gateway, Verve could hear Fenn in the background, shouting her name. A brief twinge of guilt made her want to return, but she knew no good would come of that. She would find the book, get her powers under control, and maybe even break her curse, all in time for late afternoon tea. To her confusion, Tilda had followed her through.

When she saw Verve looking, she shrugged. "I cannot remain with Fenn. He'd hound me until I told him where I sent you. And seeing as I have nowhere pressing to be, I think I'll follow you for a while."

Verve raised her brows. "Oh?"

Tilda smirked. "That and I want to keep you out of trouble. If I ever want Fenn to speak to me again, I had better make certain you return to him whole." She made to move around Verve toward the house – wherever it might be in all the mirk surrounding them – but Verve stopped her by placing a hand on her shoulder, careful not to make skin contact. Tilda cringed but did not shake off her grip. "What? I know where the house is and can feel my way through trees and bracken."

"We need to be quiet. Someone's at the house."

The two women looked at each other. "Of course there is. This *is* his summer home."

"*Was* his home, you mean," said Verve with some self-loathing and yet some self-satisfaction at the same time. "There are three heartbeats. Do you hear any more?"

A small choking noise came from Tilda, and now she did move a-ways away from Verve. "You can hear and discern that all the way from here? We're six miles from the house." The look she gave Verve was beyond terrified. "Just how powerful are you?"

Verve scoffed. "Fenn can probably hear more than I can."

"No, he can't," Tilda said. "Smell that far, yes, but *hear*?" She rubbed her arms as though she was suddenly freezing, and when Verve started forward, she hesitated for a moment, groaned, and followed several paces behind.

Verve picked through the mist with little difficulty, as she could clearly see a path in her mind, though her eyes showed only a hazy blur. Distracted by what she could physically see, she closed her eyes.

Behind her, Tilda was moving at a much slower pace and was louder than Verve would have liked. "What are your plans once we arrive?" *Crunch! Crack! Crunch!* Her feet trod over so many twigs and sticks, Verve found herself getting annoyed as though Tilda had done so on purpose.

"I'll incapacitate whoever's there, get what I need, and leave." As she said it, Verve realized how weak a plan it was and that perhaps she was acting too hastily.

Tilda swore as she stumbled and righted herself. "Could you perhaps move more slowly? This pace is punishing."

Irritation flared within Verve's breast and she found herself clenching her fists, magic gathering around her, and she hastily put a damper on it. She did not, after all, want to frighten Tilda or alert the household of their approach. With reluctance, she slowed her steps. The mansion was a mere ten yards away, and she put a finger to her lips.

"I hear one heartbeat," Tilda whispered as loudly as a gunshot.

Verve shook her head and her lips formed the words, "There are definitely three." Though whether or not Tilda could see what she said through the fog, it was uncertain. She rounded the house on silent feet, barely allowing herself to breathe, though she knew her frenzied heartbeat would alert those within of her approach.

One beating heart was on the upper floor of the ever-changing house; the other two were lower in the earth, making Verve wonder if they were in the den she had entered her first day of captivity. But when she turned the knob to the door, which was mercifully unlocked, unbolted, and unmagicked, she knew at once no one was there waiting to greet them.

There sat the chairs by an empty grate. There was the spot where she had collapsed after Dacre had wounded her. A set of steps leading up to the upper floor appeared, and Verve tried and failed to calm herself. *Trapped.* She hadn't had an attack in ages. It would not do for her to collapse in a miserable heap right now. She needed those books. *But what if I get caught?* With a shudder Verve reminded herself Dacre was dead and could no longer trouble her. Anyone else should be easy enough to overpower, what with all the magic she now had at her disposal.

Verve prepared to summon her magic to create a shield of protection around herself as she had done with Tilda, but thought the better of it. Her magic had a potent smell and would alert the household to her presence. So, feeling naked and exposed, Verve crept up the stairs with the far noisier Tilda on her heels.

"Hello?" called a feminine voice Verve did not recognize. "Is someone there?"

Verve smelled a hot metallic odor, the typical residual burst Dacre's household staff was known for. Uncertain of how to proceed, she hesitated and was surprised when Tilda brushed past her. Verve reached out and grabbed her husband's cousin, who turned and glared at her, her lips forming the words, *"Trust me."*

Wary, Verve released Tilda, who shook out her arm as though it had gone numb. *She'd better not ruin this.* It was too late to stop her now; Tilda had already opened the door leading to the upstairs, revealing a servant who had raised a magical shield around herself.

"Who are you? How did you get inside?"

Of all things, Tilda let out a sob and moved forward, effectively blocking Verve from the servant's view. "Oh, thank mercy you answered. My horse has thrown a shoe, and I cannot get him to walk. I hope you don't mind my intrusion, but the door was unlocked and I thought you might be hospitable and send someone to help me." Behind her back, she gestured frantically at Verve.

Verve frowned, uncertain of what exactly she was expected to do. After a moment, the smell of hot metal dissipated, and Tilda's waving ceased.

"You couldn't fix it yourself?" the servant demanded, not leaving her spot.

"I'm unable," said Tilda hesitantly. "I'm only a half-elf."

The servant sighed and stepped aside. Tilda followed, closing the door in Verve's face before she could be seen.

"Thank you so very much. I believe my luck is finally turning."

"Yes, well, being a quarter-elf myself, I know how these things go. 'Tis only me and the jailer in the house, and he's half-fae, so you needn't worry about hiding your true identity here, miss."

After several minutes, the voices faded, and Verve knew them to be on the other end of the house as Tilda asked for a glass of water. Satisfied she wouldn't be caught, Verve opened the door with care and crept her way down a hall, trusting her memory of when she had first been brought here.

Nothing had much changed, save for the now-gray walls and wood floors bare of any rugs. Verve hastened toward the staircase, which seemed larger than she remembered in her worried state, and she took the steps two at a time, her feet making nary a sound on the wood. At the top of the stairs she paused to listen once more, in case she had missed any sounds and the servant was lying about who was in the household.

In the kitchen, Tilda and her quarter-elf host were discussing the weather and local politics. The two other heartbeats came from far down below. One sounded fae – a slower, gentler beating – but the other was distinctly human. *There aren't said to be many humans in Letorheas. Perhaps I ought to check on this person before I make my getaway.* Verve passed the red room where she had been forced to stay, and rounded the corner where she was met with a set of spiraling metal steps. These she took with some dread and hesitation, though she knew the master of the house would not catch her. At the top of the stairs, there was an empty landing, but for a blank, white wall that would seem ordinary to the mortal eye. Now Verve could easily see the faint outline of a door and, drawing a deep breath, pushed her way inside.

The room was every bit as messy as she had witnessed in her vision all those months ago. *He left in a hurry to find me. I hope he didn't take the books with him.* At the thought, her heart began to race and her palms grew slick.

A quick examination of the bookshelf revealed the books' absence. She looked at each title twice and moved on to the desk against the far wall near the window. There were stacks of books on it, and Verve at once found the five she had been hoping to see, all of them covered in a thin layer of dust. She snatched them up and tucked them against her chest before taking one last hasty look around to make certain there wasn't anything else she might need. Seeing nothing, Verve gladly left the room and shut the door behind her as quietly as she could manage.

In the kitchen below, the voices had grown silent. Verve paused, listening. There were no heartbeats, no breaths, nothing to indicate the two women were still even in the house. She focused and realized they had, in fact, moved outside and were walking away from the house. *Tilda did lie and say her horse had thrown a shoe.* All that remained in the house were three heartbeats, the inhuman one and human one, plus her own. There was also a great deal of snoring.

Verve wasted no time in racing down the stairs as quietly as she could, her feet barely touching the steps and the floor of the grand entryway as she went. From there she followed her ears at a slower rate, doubling back a few times when she thought her hearing might be deceiving her.

The snoring continued, even as she dropped the books and scrambled to pick them up again. She had found a door down at the end of a long hall with no colors, no decorations, and no other ways of leaving or entering it. As she reached out to take the black metal door handle, a sense of foreboding overcame her, and she reared back, saying to herself, *I should not have come this way.* Trembling, she turned, only to have curiosity dominate all other feelings, as it was usually wont to do. The terror remained, but she regarded it as one might a bumblebee that had stung and now lay dying on the ground, powerless.

Dacre did not want anyone uninvited going down here. Smug satisfaction dulled fear further, and Verve turned the handle with gentle care. The door creaked on its hinges, and the snoring below stuttered and then ceased entirely as Verve's feet took the first step into oppressive darkness.

"Marigold? It's lunchtime already?" called a male voice that tickled at Verve's memory.

It took her a moment to place it, but she remembered the voice as belonging to a fae she had once heard interrogating...someone. Even as she tried to grab the memory, her thoughts attempted to slither on to something else. *Curse whoever tampered with my mind.* Verve trod down the remainder of the cold stone steps, straining her eyes and using her other senses to compensate for her lack of sight.

"Mari?" the man asked again. "It doesn't sound like you." He let out a great sniff. "It doesn't smell like you either. New perfume?"

Verve suppressed a sigh. The second, faster heartbeat was near the man's. She would have to get past him to make certain he wasn't keeping a human prisoner.

Turning a corner, Verve was suddenly met with a near-blinding burst of light, and she stumbled out of the way, just as a bolt of violet fire was flung at her. The jailer's magic hit the wall next to her, causing it to partially crumble.

"You weren't supposed to come down here!" the man cried, throwing one shot after the other at Verve, who dodged them easily.

She quirked a feral half smile. "I wasn't? Well, it's too late for that now, isn't it? Besides, I never was one for living up to expectations." She raised a magical shield around herself, her residual burst clashing badly with that of the half-fae.

"No one said you would come down here." The tall, pale man's face paled further still, and he drew back against the cell he was obviously meant to guard, putting himself between Verve and what she wanted. "Please don't harm me, milady. I had nothing to do with any of this."

Verve frowned at those words, uncertain as to what he meant, but continued her slow approach. "Who else is down here?" She attempted to look around him, even as his shield flickered and he attempted to lob a fireball at her.

"Get away from me!" the guard cried. "I've got a family. Two bairns to feed. Have mercy, milady." With each word he spoke, the pitch of his voice rose and his words grew louder. He dropped to his knees and his fireball fizzled out and he bowed his head, trembling.

Heart racing, Verve cleared her throat and took another step closer to the fae, who swayed on the spot and promptly fell onto his side. "Um," she said and tapped him with a tentative tip of her boot. The jailer didn't stir, and for a moment Verve feared he might have died of shock.

"Leave him," said a croaky, ancient voice from the dank cell the man had been guarding. "He isn't dead, just fainted, Miss Verity."

Verve took a wary step forward, squinting to adjust her eyes to the newfound dimness that had arrived with the man's passing out. There was light coming from ahead, as though someone had lit a candlestick. "How do you know my name?" Her frown deepened as she beheld a wizened old crone with matted gray hair hanging down her back. Her clothes were soiled, her skin sallow and paper-thin, and Verve found herself wondering how long this poor soul had been kept down here. She listened. The heartbeat was quick, if a bit unsteady. Her breathing was slightly labored, and Verve scented fear mingled with dread. Verve repeated her question as the crone approached the iron bars.

"I was your caregiver upon your first arrival here," said the crone. Her breath and body smelled of rot, and Verve fought the urge to pinch her nose. "I am known as Olive, though that is not my true name. Names, as you know, have power, Miss—"

"I don't remember you."

The crone shook her head. "His lordship must have erased me from your memories."

Verve's insides churned at the mention of Dacre, and she clenched her free fist to prevent fire from forming in her palm. "Why would he do that?" She regarded the woman carefully, deciding to withhold judgement until she heard what there was to be learned.

With a sigh, the woman retreated a step back in her cage, her eyes on Verve, alert and wary. "Probably because I killed two elves in front of you and he thought you might find the memory unpleasant."

Something inside Verve stirred at that, though the feeling was weak and fleeting. "Were the elves my captors?"

The crone, Olive, nodded. "But so was I, Miss Verity."

She's laying her cards out on the table, Verve mused as Olive lowered herself onto a rickety wood bench. Aloud she said, "Did you ever help me?"

There was a moment's hesitation ere Olive spoke again, and when she did, her voice was kind and yet proud. "Your first night here, you had a fit. I comforted you until you could fall asleep. Not to mention waiting on you, taking care of you, and preventing his lordship from pursuing you as vigorously as he wished at first." The last part of her declaration rang false, and Verve hissed through her teeth.

"Really? That doesn't sound right."

Of all things, the old woman laughed. "So, you can sniff out half truths now, can ya?" Her head turned and she eyed Verve as though seeing her for the first time, and winced. Then a slow frown turned her lips. She squinted. "How did his lordship make a creature more powerful than himself out of his own blood? I wonder."

So, no one had told her what had transpired. Verve wasn't about to enlighten someone she didn't know – even if they had truly met already. "Are you the only human down here?" She was mindful that at any moment now, the elfin servant might figure out Tilda did not, in fact, possess a horse in need of assistance. Though she wanted to hear if they returned, Verve wasn't certain she was so able. All sound down here was muted and strange, and she did not wish to remain any longer than she had to.

"I am the only former halfling or human in this cursed place, Miss Verity."

Verve blinked in surprise. "How do you mean?"

A shadow crossed Olive's face, and she shook her head. "His lordship took his magic back, leaving me a shell of a person. I've aged ever so many years since he sent me down here." With a grunt, she attempted to sit up straighter, only to cringe in apparent torment.

Verve's heart thumped painfully for the woman. "The dampness of this prison can't help."

Olive snorted and gave Verve a dismissive wave of her right hand. "Is that why you came down here? To spoon pity down the throat of whomever you might find?" She watched Verve from the corner of her eye; a slight smirk rose across her face.

At once Verve had to stamp out her irritation at the woman's words, and she succeeded...barely. Her hands glowed a vibrant red, and she had to quickly hide them under her books, but not quickly enough for the crone not to notice.

"You still have your temper, I see. And, goodness, it's tied to your magic, is it?" She clucked her tongue. "Someone as powerful as you with that sort of magic will be dangerous, no doubt."

"Who says I'm powerful?" Verve said coolly.

Olive looked incredulous as Verve reached down for the jailer's keys, nearly dropping the books in her arms. "Lass, I'm fully mortal and even I can see you are something unusual." She frowned as Verve thrust the key into the lock and turned it. "Sure you want to be doing that?" The woman pulled herself to her feet with some difficulty and hobbled toward the now-open door to her cell.

"Why wouldn't I? You've done me no harm. And besides, no human deserves to be locked up in this strange land," said Verve. Concentrating, she magicked a pair of long gloves onto her hands, and held out her right arm for the old woman.

At that Olive snorted. "If you knew half of the people I knew before coming to Letorheas, you wouldn't be saying such things." Still, after a moment's hesitation, she took Verve's hand and allowed herself to be helped past the unconscious half-elf and up the cold stairs. She leaned on Verve heavily, though the latter did not mind, making certain their skin did not touch.

Soon it became obvious Olive would not be able to make it far from the house without having to stop to rest, and that just wouldn't do. Even now, Verve heard the jailer waking. If he were to pursue them....

"It's no use, Miss Verity. You're going to have to leave me behind."

With a curse, Verve steadied the woman and began to lift her with one arm, stopping when the woman backed away. "This is ridiculous. You can't want to return to that cell."

Olive huffed. "Of course I don't. But can't you see I am going to be naught but dead weight? He will pursue me. I know too much about things I ought not."

"I can take care of him," said Verve, jerking her head back in the direction of the jailer.

"That's not what I meant." Olive cringed as Verve lifted her under one arm and bore her up the remainder of the stairs. "You also forget I killed two elves."

"Yes, well," said Verve, "I killed the king and Dacre, so neither of us has clean hands."

Olive stilled as Verve rushed her through the halls, taking her out the back door, as she could not find the entrance she and Tilda had used; it seemed to have disappeared. *Perhaps it is only accessible from the outside. I remember this house to be ornery like that.*

"Killed his lordship? That's not possible," said Olive as Verve carried her toward the woods. "Miss Verity, please. I beg you. Put me down this instant. You and I need to talk."

Even though she was strong beyond reason, Verve was losing her grip on the books and the crone herself was proving cumbersome. So it was with some relief that she set Olive on her feet and readjusted her grip on the tomes. "What's wrong?" Had she gripped the old woman too tightly? She looked as one in pain.

"When do you believe yourself to have killed Lord Dacre Starside?"

Verve blinked. "I killed him at least fifteen months ago. Why?"

Olive started counting on her gnarled fingers, her lips moving, and a distant look in her eyes. At length, she reached a number and studied Verve with intense concentration. "Etterhean or Letorhean months?"

"What does it matter?" Verve asked. "I killed him. He's dead, and I'm rid of him."

"The timing is crucial," said Olive, shaking her head. "Tell me as accurately as you can, what phase were the moons in when you last saw his lordship alive?"

With a snort, Verve backed away from the now grim-looking woman. “Why?”

A sad, pitying smile spread across the old woman’s face and she sighed. “Because I saw him, alive and well, not three Letorhean weeks ago.”

CHAPTER SIX

At first, Verve stood there, swaying on the spot as she tried to take in what the woman had just told her. "That's not possible," she said, though doubt clawed at her insides. "You weren't there. I dealt him a fatal blow with my magic."

Olive shook her head. "My dear—"

"I saw the light leave his eyes. You have to be mistaken. That or time moves more strangely here than I first realized." Yes, that had to be it. Dacre couldn't be alive. He would have made himself known by now, attempted to exact revenge upon Verve for attacking him so violently.

"It didn't make sense at the time, but now I see what he meant," said the crone. "Lord Starside said, 'She has it, and there is no taking it from her...yet.' Then he muttered something about death and farce, but I could not quite make it all out. But, goodness, you're trembling. Are you all right, milady?"

Verve shuddered. "Don't call me that." She leaned over into the bushes and was violently ill. Great tremors wracked her body, and Olive held back her hair and patted her on the shoulder until the worst of it subsided.

"Here, Miss Verity. Sit down a moment and compose yourself." Olive, though apparently weak herself, took one of Verve's gloved hands and tugged her away from the puddle of sick. "Do you have any water?"

"No." Verve lowered herself to the ground and rested her head in her hands. "It can't be."

The old woman sighed. "You don't love him, then?"

Incredulous, she looked up at Olive. "How could I?" The mere thought brought on another wave of nausea. "I should have never left without Fenn." *How worried he must be!* Well, though the news of Dacre was unwelcome, at least she now had it...along with the books, which she only just realized she had dropped. Verve retrieved them, still unsteady as her breaths came in deep gasps.

"Fenn?" Olive cried. "But he's the one you ought to hate. He has tried to kill you ever so many times, Miss Verity."

Verve laughed without humor. "That is what you've been told, Olive, and nothing could be further from the truth." She shook her head as she heard hurried footsteps in the distance. "I've stayed here too long." Quieting her breathing, Verve could make out it was Tilda running toward them and not the part-elf servant. "Do you wish me to take you back to the mortal realm?"

True fear shone in Olive's eyes and she drew back a half step. "No, Miss Verity. I beg you not to return me there. I've not set foot in Etterhea for nigh sixty years now, I reckon. There's no one and nothing left for me there." She slumped, her eyes downcast. "In fact, there is nothing left for me *here*, either."

"Don't say that," Verve said, attempting to sound kind and not as impatient as she felt.

"No magic," said Olive, "no home, no person to care for...or care for me in return." She sighed. "Might I ask one last favor of you, Miss Verity?"

Verve nodded, her thoughts churning. "Of course. But then we really need to get out of here."

Olive drew in a deep breath. "I want you to kill me." The two women watched each other for a moment as one took in what the other had said, tension sparking between them.

"You can't mean that."

"Do it now. Quickly. If he finds me, he'll lock me up again."

Her tone was so desperate, her expression so pitiable, Verve couldn't help but be moved. But her conscience overrode those feelings at once and she said, "I can't kill you."

Olive blanched. "Then at least give me something by which I might do the job." She looked around and seemed to realize someone was fast approaching them. "Please. I beg you." She sank to her knees, which creaked beneath her gaunt frame. "Don't let me continue like this." With a sob she grabbed at Verve's shoes.

"Don't ask me to be responsible for another human's death. I can't and I won't."

Tilda came into view and slowed her pace considerably, her expression confused as her eyes met Verve's. "Is everything all right?"

Olive cringed at the sound of the she-fae's voice. "If you will not end me, then feed me but a crumb of your power and I shall live the remainder of my life out in contented exile."

"What's going on?" Tilda demanded, drawing a wicked-looking blade from the sheath at her side. "Who's with you?"

Verve held up a hand, and the she-fae hesitated. "Just a moment, Tilda."

"Let it be a quick moment, then." Though frowning, she replaced her knife and folded her arms across her chest. "I sent the house staff on a wild chase, but they will soon figure out someone housebroke. We have five minutes, seven minutes at the most, before aid is called for and we are pursued."

The old woman bowed her head. "Please, if you won't share but a mite of your power, end me."

Tilda tensed. "Why is this human asking you for power? Don't you dare give her a drop of it. Humans aren't to be trusted."

Verve scowled at her husband's cousin, her own muscles tensing. Perhaps she had been planning on giving in to the woman's request, or maybe it was the way Tilda had dared to order her not to, but Verve almost unthinkingly found herself drawing from the store she had taken from the Cunning Blade. Power beaded like a glowing drop of silver blood on her gloved fingertip and she told the crone to lift her head.

At once the old woman did so and her mouth opened, ready to receive the magic.

"No!" Tilda cried.

It was too late. The power dripped from Verve's finger and landed on Olive's tongue.

"What have you done?" Tilda had moved toward Verve, her face pale, but Verve at once cast a shield around herself and the crone. The she-fae took a step back, her eyes fixed on Verve's face.

Tears formed in Olive's eyes, and she took Verve's hand and kissed it. "I won't forget you for this, Miss Verity. It's more than I deserve."

As soon as the shield dropped, Tilda was in front of Verve, shaking her. "What are you thinking? You can't—" She let out a shriek as Verve forgot her own strength and threw the she-fae off, nearly sending her sailing into Olive. With a loud *thunk*, Tilda struck the tree opposite them and leapt to her feet, dagger in hand.

Fenn's words echoed in Verve's mind, *"She will harm you if given the chance."* Snarling, Verve drew fire into her hands, and the gloves shriveled with her magic.

Tilda replaced her knife in its sheath with apparent reluctance.

"We must leave at once," said Olive, rising fluidly, as though no ailment of old age now bothered her. "The nearby estates will have been drawn to that disturbance you two made, and it would be imprudent to tarry long." She stepped past Verve, who was only just in control, and placed a hand on the hawthorn tree there. "I need a blade."

Attempting to calm herself and extinguish the flames, Verve imagined the fire retreating beneath her skin as she reached for a feeling of peace within herself. It was hard to come by, but soon the flames were absorbed into her flesh, which glowed as a warning, her anger and fear a dull prickle in her wrists.

Tilda broke eye contact with Verve and stepped wide around her, approaching the tree from the side. "Let me." She drew her knife, slit her thumb, and stabbed the tree, which began to weep watery sap.

It physically pained Verve to watch the hawthorn suffer, and she decided that next time she would demand that the she-fae negotiate rather than threaten. She stepped forward as a gateway formed and an unfamiliar land came into view through it. "Where is this?"

"A safe place."

Verve grimaced. "Take me back to Fenn."

But Tilda shook her head. "You do that yourself. I'm not going anywhere near my cousin again for at least half a century when he's more likely to have calmed down." She eyed Verve sideways, as shouts were taken up in the distance. "Ah, seven minutes have come and gone. You would be wise to follow me now, *Verity*."

Verve scowled at the sound of her name on the she-fae's tongue and was about to argue, but the voices were getting closer with every breath. Not wishing to deal with the ten fae she heard approaching, Verve swore and threw herself through the gateway after Olive.

Tilda was through a second later, and the gateway snapped shut behind them. "Come. We don't want them to torture the tree and learn our location from it. We'd best put as much distance between us and it as we can."

Indeed, Olive had already taken off at a brisk walk, barely bothering to look over her shoulder. "There are several other hawthorns over here. Perhaps we ought to make a gateway somewhere else."

"Let me," said Tilda, pushing ahead of Olive. "I have a hideout in the northern territories."

Olive stiffened noticeably. "Those lands are full of monsters. Who in their right mind would keep a hiding place there?"

Tilda's ensuing grin was all teeth. "Someone who doesn't like to be found. Do you need one of us to carry those books for you?" She nodded at Verve, who was following at a hesitant pace.

"No, I can manage, thank you." Something was nagging at her, but she couldn't put her finger on it. Verve had been eager to forgive Tilda for her threat. The she-fae had been, after all, under someone else's control. *Is she still?*

Tilda stabbed a young tree and mingled her silver blood with its sap.

Verve blinked. "Olive, can you make a gateway to…." For a moment she frowned, realizing she didn't know the name of Fenn's family estate or how to instruct Olive or a tree to take them there.

She looked at Tilda for help, but the she-fae had already disappeared through the gateway and into the mists beyond.

"Miss?" asked Olive, her brow furrowed.

"Bother," said Verve, hurrying through so she wouldn't be left behind.

Olive was fast on her heels. "We need to stay close." Olive startled Verve by taking her arm in her hand and tugging at her to make her hasten her pace. Thankfully, she had just touched her sleeve.

Verve jerked away. "Don't touch my skin. I'm cursed."

Olive frowned but did not comment. "If this friend of yours knows a safe place, my guess is it's a-ways from any hawthorns." She sighed. "We must have a bit of a trek ahead of us." Her tone was low, and her gaze darted to and fro, as though she was expecting to be attacked.

Verve listened. The closest noises she could hear were three heartbeats and three sets of steady breaths, and that was the most for five miles. "There's nothing for a few miles, Olive," she said as they caught up with Tilda. "You don't have to worry."

"For now," said Olive darkly.

One mile passed and then another, and Tilda led them at a relentless pace. Verve had no trouble keeping up, but she worried for Olive, whose powers she knew did not equal either Tilda's or her own. But the old woman did not complain and managed to remain in stride for the first five miles.

It was when they had been walking for half an hour that the terrain became more treacherous. Briar and brush seemed to rise up to meet them, snatching at the hems of Tilda's and Olive's skirts. Tendrils of these plants reached out toward Verve, came within an inch of her shoes, recoiled with a hiss, and retreated into the mists beyond. The women's pace now had slowed considerably, and feet, Verve's included, began to squelch and sink somewhat in the muck and mire.

"How much farther?" Olive surprised Verve by asking. They had been walking silently for what felt like hours now, with no signs of civilization…or monsters, thankfully. Verve wondered about the latter. She knew precious little about Letorheas and what sorts of creatures it held.

Tilda grunted something unintelligible and continued to trudge forward. The sun had reached its highest point in the sky an hour ago and was now quickly on its descent. If they were caught out in the dark, and there really were dangerous animals about, Verve knew her company would not want to make camp.

"You need to either communicate with us, Tilda, or help us find a hawthorn," Verve snapped. She magicked herself another pair of gloves and then steadied Olive, who had lost momentum and was stumbling into her, causing Verve to nearly drop the books in her arms.

The she-fae shot Verve a dirty look over her shoulder. "There are not any hawthorns for at least seventy miles. You won't reach any before sundown with your human in tow."

Verve shared a look with Olive, who said, "We can't go on like this."

Tilda stopped suddenly, and Verve almost ran into her. "Just a mile or three more. Keep your human's maw shut, Verity, or goodness knows what sort of creature she'll attract." She looked Verve up and down with a sneer. "And try to put a damper on your magic. It's giving me a headache."

Maybe I should have let Fenn blast her to the next world, thought Verve grimly. Taking pity on Olive, she stopped the old crone and squatted in front of her. "Climb on. And don't touch my skin."

Olive did not protest or hesitate but at once situated herself on Verve's back. "You're too kind, Miss Verity."

"Maw shut," said Tilda.

Verve would have shouted something back at the ornery she-fae, but the wind changed direction and she could hear it, the distant cries of what sounded like a pack of wolves. The creatures were more than two miles off, if she was judging correctly. It was hard to tell, what with her hearing being so sensitive.

"Five miles." Tilda took a shaky breath. "Dire wolves are fast and have excellent hearing, so be quick and be quiet." She picked up her pace, and Verve followed suit.

The land quickly began to slope upward, and at the top in the distance, shrouded in mist, sat a ramshackle manor house surrounded by magic that Verve could feel prickling at her from yards away.

Tilda took off at a run, and Verve also ran. There were more howls now, coming from all directions.

"Make haste," said Tilda, no longer trying to keep her voice lowered.

Verve tried to move forward, but she slammed into an invisible wall, which jostled her and nearly threw Olive off her back. Voices filled Verve's head, wicked hisses and chirrups that made no sense at first, but as they grew in volume and in strength she heard hateful words about a Fire Queen and destruction.

Ice-cold sweat trickled down Verve's back as she tried to push forward. She made some progress, but not enough. The dire wolves were closing in. "What is this?" she demanded.

Olive slid off her back and ran through the invisible barrier without any apparent difficulty. She paused to watch Verve, her posture tense and her eyes horror-filled. And then, perhaps sensing Verve's was a lost cause, she turned around and ran toward the foreboding house at top speed.

Gray wolflike creatures with overly long snouts shot out of the mists. They snapped their yellow teeth, snarling and drooling in excess as they circled in toward where Verve struggled.

At once Verve abandoned her attempts to break through the barrier. Tilda turned to watch her, face pinched and mouth forming words Verve could not make out over the howls. A shiver ran up her spine as the creatures came within ten yards of her, then nine, soon six. *Do we know if I really am immortal?* She wasn't about to stand around and find out.

Verve reached for calm within herself, as Fenn had taught her to do, in hopes of pushing those emotions into creating something useful such as a sword, a fireball, a mace, a shield, anything to ward off the monsters. But her power was mostly found in her rage, and now there was only fear and it shut down her other emotions entirely.

It would seem hope of creating anything useful was lost. Trembling, Verve threw her free hand out, as though that would stop the dire wolves. The air filled with the aromas of burned sugar and vanilla, a weak flame flickering from her fingertips.

The wolves hesitated. One sat. Two of the sixteen bared their teeth, while others still pawed at the ground. As one unified front, each creature bowed its head, whines slipping out through their open mouths and over their lolling tongues. Then they turned tail and ran off, howling and yipping as though they had just had great fun and were now off to hunt something more appetizing than a scrawny she-fae – or whatever Verve was.

Breathing hard, Verve lowered her hand and collapsed to her knees.

"That was interesting," said Tilda, coming up behind her. "Why couldn't you form a shield? You had no trouble warding me off at the estate."

Verve glowered at the she-fae. "I don't know."

"Hmm. Well, lucky you, they must have been someone's pets at one point." She held out a hand for Verve, who conjured gloves and rose to her feet.

"You can't tame dire wolves," said Olive, climbing out of a tree midway up the hill. "Goodness knows his lordship tried." She nodded to Verve, her expression pained. "The real question is: why couldn't she cross through your wards?"

It took Tilda a moment to answer, and when she did, she sounded sheepish. "I set up the wards when I left, and they were meant to keep out enemies. I'm sorry, Verity, but they must think you're untrustworthy." She placed her hand on the invisible wall, and it shivered silver and dissolved entirely. "There. I'll put it back up once we're all inside. Come."

Weary, Verve gave the retreating creatures one last look and passed through the space where the ward had been moments prior. The air stank of ginger and clove. Up the remainder of the hill she went, barely taking in her surroundings. The ghost of a house was lit within. Rosebushes bursting with blue blossoms wept onto the balding lawn, unfurling as the sojourners neared, only to rear back at Verve's approach. If she had been less emotionally spent, she might have been offended.

Tilda threw out her arms in front of the faded crimson door, and the house shuddered open and spilled an eerie light onto the stone slab that sat in front of it. "I didn't expect to return with company, so please do excuse the mess."

Verve smiled halfheartedly. *Fae aren't so different from humans*, she thought, amused. But when she stepped inside and the door closed and barred itself behind her, Verve saw the she-fae had not been exaggerating the state of affairs. Broken crates had been haphazardly set around the small entryway. Cobwebs floated in the air, and their makers sucked noisily on their catches. Verve shuddered and hastened after Tilda, and Olive fell behind her in deference.

The paint on the walls – was it gray or perhaps blue once? – had peeled in many places, and flakes of it like dust motes swirled around light sconces as the trio passed. "Oughtn't you restore your wards?" Olive inquired. She ran a hand over the wall and then examined her fingers, which were thick with a layer of oily looking grime, and pulled a face.

"I've already done so, Miss…?"

Indeed, Verve heard the wards humming in the near distance. Clove was the predominant scent in the air, and it seemed to fill Verve's lungs. She gagged once, twice. Then she resolved to breathe through her mouth.

"Everyone calls me Olive," said the crone. "And *your* name is…?"

Tilda smirked but didn't answer. "There's plenty of food to be had in the pantry, so feel free to see to your needs. I'll build a fire and put a kettle on." She gestured toward the small kitchen in the room beyond them to the right, stepped in, and headed straight for the fireplace. The she-fae bustled around, throwing logs into the grate and casting fire in after.

Was Fenn out there looking for them now? How angry he must be.

"Don't be so gloomy, Verity," said Tilda, thrusting an iron pot at Olive. "Here. Fill this up to the brim, Olive."

Wishing to distract herself, Verve set her books down on a side counter and took the vessel from the crone. "Where is the pump?"

Tilda waved her hand and knives jumped to life on the middle counter and began chopping carrots, potatoes, and onions. "Just through there. But that's servant's work." She jerked her head at Olive, who seemed unoffended by the title.

"She's no one's servant here," said Verve and then took the pot through the back door Tilda had indicated. Breathing hard, eyes blurring, Verve stumbled toward the pump and began filling the pot. Up, down, up, down. Weariness settled on her like a cloak as she took in the events of the day and whispered to herself, "What have I done?"

CHAPTER SEVEN

Supper was a somber affair. No one had spoken much while the soup was boiling – Tilda had no qualms about eating meat as some fae had, for which Verve was grateful, so venison had been added to the pot – and the silence continued as they ate.

Outside the skies were growing dark. Two full moons shone down on the large house without clouds to block them. Verve picked mold off the bread she forced herself to eat, even as her stomach roiled in protest at being fed at such a time as this.

Finally, after they had supped and were satisfied, Tilda produced three lanterns, lit them, and passed them around. "There are two bedrooms upstairs and a sofa down here in the parlor. The latter is probably moldy and needs a good airing." She looked at Olive pointedly.

Verve thought of Olive alone in that hard, cold cell and said, "That sounds lovely. I'll sleep there."

Tilda raised her eyebrows but did not push the issue. "It gets cold at night here. But you have fire, so you'll be able to start a blaze in the fireplace easily enough."

Olive looked at Verve with interest. "You've fire, eh? Like his lordship."

Inwardly, Verve cringed. "Yes, I should be fine. Thank you."

"My pleasure." The way Tilda said it convinced Verve she was not quite sincere. She picked up her bowl and plate, collected Verve's as well, and bore them away. Over her shoulder, she said, "I wouldn't advise leaving the premises, especially at night. My wards won't let you back in, and there are worse things than dire wolves to contend with."

"Like what?" Verve asked as she picked at a loose thread on her trousers.

When Tilda failed to answer, having left the room, Verve turned to Olive, who took a deep breath and said in a hushed voice, "Nothing you want to tangle with. Bog sprites – shape-shifting man-eaters. I believe you've encountered one already. Then there are the Unnamed, which are little more than vapors that will strangle you in the dark. And Astrals that project pictures of dry land where there really is water. They lure you out into rivers, ponds, or lakes before they drown you." She stopped when Verve shuddered. The look she gave her was sympathetic and she veered the subject away from water. "You don't have any plans to leave here this night, I hope, Miss Verity?"

Verve shook her head. "It sounds too dangerous." She moved toward the fireplace and threw in a few logs from the stack that rested next to the sooty hearth. "In the morning, though, will you help me find a hawthorn and make a gateway somewhere for me?"

If Olive was curious as to why Verve could not do so herself, she didn't say. "I'd be happy to, Miss Verity."

"Please, just call me Verve." Verve removed her right glove and studied the grate. Next she tossed in a handful of kindling, drew on the dormant anger sitting in her belly, and threw her feelings at the logs, which at once caught fire. The air filled with the scents of vanilla and toffee.

"You ought not give your name away so freely, Miss Veri— Verve. Names have power."

"That's an old wives' tale," said Tilda, sweeping into the room and scooping up her own lantern. "Superstition is the way to madness."

Olive made a face but did not argue. "Will you be needing anything before I retire?" The crone rose and picked up her lantern, which bathed her face in an eerie green light.

Verve yawned and shook her head. "No, thanks, Olive. Sleep well."

"I will, thanks to you." She paused as Tilda left the room and could soon be heard noisily ascending a set of creaky stairs. "I owe you not one but two life debts, you realize."

Verve stared at her. "How do you mean?"

The lantern bobbed as the crone approached and hesitated a few feet from her. "You freed me from my prison and gave me more than an ample amount of power. I am in your debt." She did not seem to relish the thought. "I will serve you faithfully until I can repay in kind."

"You don't need to do anything."

It would seem Olive could not be swayed. She did not insist but she did not concede, her eyes glittering in the semidarkness. "Sleep well, Verve." And with that said, she followed the path Tilda had taken and left Verve to her thoughts.

After listening for the telltale footsteps that assured her she was alone, Verve set her lantern on the table next to the sofa. In one swift stroke, she lifted the sheet from the dusty sofa and sat upon the cushions with the books she had pilfered.

She hefted the first one into her lap, a book that told her it was not a conveyable text before she had even touched it. *First Age Prophecy: A Guide to What Came in the Great Before.* Verve put her nose to the page and breathed in the heady aromas of decaying paper, which always smelled like vanilla and tobacco to her. She reared back instantly as her nose perceived clashing metallic and chocolate notes. Coughing, she set that book aside and reached for the next, a velvety black one with gold lettering on the front cover. *Second Age Prophecy: A Comprehensive Guide to What is Yet to Come.* This one she did not smell. With care she turned the fragile-looking pages but soon lost patience, set the book aside, and went for the book that had her interest the most, *Traversing the Lands of the Dead.* This she regarded a moment in silence, and then opened with care.

The pages were brittle. Bits of book debris wafted around in a cloud, and Verve sneezed. After rubbing her nose and blinking her watering eyes, she carefully turned the first page. Something deep within her tingled, a warning that this book was not all it seemed. It did not frighten her as she knew it ought; rather, Verve found herself intrigued and turned one page after another, until something caught her eye and made her stop.

It was a black dot, no larger than the tip of her little finger, and it sat innocently in the bottom corner of page thirty-three. Verve regarded it, her fingers itching to run a hand over it. Yes, there was something purposeful about the dot, though she didn't know what made her think that, other than the tug in her breast, where her heart had doubled its pace. This was the page she had wanted, the reason she had run away from Fenn to find this book. With difficulty, Verve managed to tear her attention away from the dot and scanned the words.

Deep in the bowels of the other world lies the Fount of Severing and the Founts of Gain. Within the former's murky waters is believed to lie the secrets to souring your enemies' relationships, killing high fae, and breaking curses.

Verve's eyes roved across the page, searching for more information. Finding none, her attention returned to the dot. It was calling to her. As one dreaming, she traced her pointing finger down the page, hesitated a moment, and let her nail touch the ink first. Nothing happened for a moment, though Verve thought she heard the distant calling of her name. Then, as though drawn by a magnet, her whole finger slammed down on the page and the room was swallowed up in darkness.

Ah, there you are....

She blinked, testing her eyes against the blackness that engulfed her, but nothing would come into view. Her body tingled with the awareness that somewhere, someone was watching her. With a grunt of effort, she pried her finger from the page and lay back, panting as light flooded back around her.

"Hello?" she breathed.

No one answered. The voice she heard had been distinctly masculine and familiar though muddled somehow, obscuring its origins.

Verve was about to turn the page, but paused for a moment when she realized the dot had disappeared. *Well, that's strange.* She ran her right hand over the gooseflesh on her left arm, and stared into the blaze in the grate.

Weary suddenly, Verve closed the book and set it down with care on the side table. She covered herself with the dust sheet and fell into an uneasy sleep.

* * *

For the first time since her transformation, Verve slept the full night through, though it had been riddled with nightmares. She dreamt of the biggest hawthorn she had ever laid eyes on; at least, she *thought* it was a hawthorn. The bark had been pitch-black, not the silver she was accustomed to seeing. And when she had touched it, the tree had grown to fill the sky before splitting into a gateway that led to the bowels of the earth, shrouded in an impenetrable mist. The nightmare repeated itself, and when Verve awoke with a gasp, she had seen the tree grow over fifty times. Only, the last time ere she woke, it had exploded into a cloud of bats.

Sitting up and blinking her eyes furiously, Verve swore she could still hear their wings fluttering around her head. Something brushed her cheek, and Verve shot a ball of fire at it, filling the air with burned toffee smells and a whiff of smoke.

"Ouch!" said a familiar voice.

Verve looked around her desperately for the source of the voice and was relieved to find Olive standing there, right little finger in her mouth. "Sorry. Did I get you?"

Olive nodded. "Singed the hairs right off my wrist, and my skin's as pink there as a rose petal." She quirked a thin eyebrow at Verve. "Bad dreams?"

Already the night terror was receding from her thoughts. In its place, the ink spot on the book page the night previous. With some difficulty, Verve untangled herself from the dust sheet and got to her feet. "I touched a spot on a book last night."

"Hmm?" Olive turned from Verve and began feeding kindling to the dying embers of the fire.

"It was calling to me – the ink spot in the book I opened last night."

Olive stilled. Slowly she turned, her eyes narrowed. "And you touched it?"

Verve nodded and absently smoothed her hands down her trousers. "It was like I had to." She watched the crone, who left the fire and took to pacing.

"What happened next?"

With a sinking sensation in her stomach, Verve explained how the world had grown very dark, that she had heard a voice, and then fallen into a deep, terrible sleep. When she relayed, at Olive's request, what the voice had said, the crone stopped pacing and at once went for her shoes, which sat by the door.

"Pack what you need to, Miss Verity. We need to be far away from here within the hour."

"Someone's looking for me?"

Olive leveled a look at Verve that turned her insides cold. "I believe you activated a tracking spell."

"Dacre knew I would find these books, didn't he?" At once she felt like flinging them away from her into the fire.

Olive gave one curt nod and rolled up her sleeves. "You haven't broken your fast, but I imagine we can do so on the road." As she spoke, her voice simmered down to a soft whisper, which Verve had no trouble deciphering, but wondered why she was using...until Olive looked meaningfully at the ceiling.

"You don't think—"

Olive hushed Verve and her lips formed the words, *"Better safe than sorry."*

Morning's light had yet to invade their sanctuary, though in Verve's mind's eye it was fast approaching the horizon. There was next to nothing to pack, just a few bits of food in the kitchen, which she bundled up in a napkin, and the books, which she tied up in the dust cloth she had slept under, and carried them slung over her shoulder.

Judging by the deep, rhythmic breathing coming from above them, Tilda was still sleeping. Uncertain as they were as to where her true loyalties lay, it was best to leave without her following them. The fae did not wake as Verve followed Olive from the house, both taking great care to remain as silent as possible. But when they got to the point where Tilda's ward began and ended, Olive held out a hand, effectively stopping Verve in her tracks.

Olive gave her a curious look and stepped through the ward herself. She waited for Verve on the other side, pulling her right hand back and forth through the red, shimmering force. "It should let you pass, Miss Verity." It seemed Olive was unable to remember to call Verve by her preferred name, but Verve didn't press her. "But once you've passed out of it, you won't be able to go back in without her dropping the ward altogether."

That made sense. Verve nodded but hesitated a moment, testing the ward with her gloved little finger. To her surprise, once her appendage had passed through, Verve was unable to pull it back, so she hastily removed her entire person from the enclosure of the ward and set off with Olive down the hill whence they had come the day previous.

"We'll need to keep our wits about us until we can find a hawthorn," Olive murmured, her gaze darting to and fro. "Have you any weapons?"

Verve frowned. "No." She tried to restrain her pace to match Olive's slower one, which stoked her impatience and temper. She would need to watch both if she did not want to provoke a sudden, dangerous display of magic.

"Well, at least you're powerful enough to get us out of any dire situation, should one arise." Olive snatched the cloth carrying the food supplies out of Verve's hand and fiddled with the knot. "Keep watch while I ration this." Grunting, Olive thrust a hunk of cheese at Verve and took an apple for herself. When she caught Verve staring, Olive made a face and said, "It won't do to have either of us fainting from want of nourishment. I don't know about you, but that stew last night did nothing to satisfy my hunger." Once they had walked a bit farther, Olive took a tentative bite of the green apple.

After ten minutes of their half running, half walking, the sun broke over the green hills to the right. Up ahead, the trees were but pinpricks on the horizon, and Verve had trouble calculating how much time it might take them to reach any woods.

"Just because it's light out it doesn't mean we can drop our guard," said Olive, holding on to the remains of her apple instead of chucking them aside.

"Tell me of tracking spells," said Verve. Her thoughts had strayed back to the spot on the book.

Olive's shoulders heaved. "It will still take his lordship some effort to find you, as those sorts of spells are oft made in haste and do not lead to the exact location of the one pursued." She rubbed at an apparent pang in her side, and Verve discreetly slowed. "When you touched the spot, it informed the maker of the spell that you had the book in your possession. My guess is he first checked his estate, as that is where he had kept the book." All the while she spoke, Olive kept her voice lowered to a whisper and her eyes continued to scan the land around them.

Verve could neither see, hear, nor sense any living presence within four miles of them, and she told Olive so. "Dacre must have sent me the vision of the book somehow." When Olive gave her a confused look, Verve explained what had transpired at Fenn's estate regarding the vision she had experienced.

Olive shook her head. "The residual burst sounds wrong, but the action sounds like his." She gave Verve a dark look. "He must have more allies than I first realized. Parchment-scented bursts would be the Wetherfolds."

"Who?" Verve steadied Olive with gloved hands.

"The Wetherfolds of these northern lands. They're nigh-feral and mostly made up of half-elves." Gently she extricated herself from Verve's grasp. "He'll be looking for the hawthorn you used to transport here soon, if he hasn't already found it. We should veer east." Abruptly she changed course, and it was Verve's turn to lose her footing.

"What do you think his purpose is?"

Olive didn't answer at first but continued plodding toward the hills that had been on their right and were now straight ahead. There were no trees for miles it would seem, but if they did not wish to run in to Dacre, then this was the best course to avoid him. "He'll be wanting your power, for one thing. He believes it should be his." The old woman nimbly leapt over a crevice, and Verve followed suit.

"What is the other reason?"

The laugh Olive let out was one void of humor. "Well, love makes men do strange things."

Verve groaned. "Not that nonsense again." She slowed once more to accommodate her traveling companion, kicking a rock out in front of her with such force, it skipped several hundred feet and rolled to a stop on the grass way ahead.

"Like it or not, his lordship has fallen in love hard and fast with you."

"But I killed— well, I *tried* to kill him."

Now Olive's laugh was more sincere. "Don't think that'll put someone as fiercely passionate as him off. When a fae falls in love, it's forever."

Thoughts of Fenn entered Verve's mind, and her blood warmed. Perhaps he would be more forgiving of her leaving him than she had first thought. *Or maybe it only hurt him more greatly.* To distract herself from the alternating pleasant and guilty ideas floating around, she cleared her throat and changed the subject. "But why was I unable to kill him?"

"Hmm?" Olive crested the hill and waited for Verve, who had lagged behind momentarily.

"Dacre. The magic I threw at him should have been fatal. It *was* fatal…I could feel death in it."

Panting, Olive reached for the canteen hanging from her side, took a short swig from it, and offered it to Verve. "No one can kill a high fae." She looked at Verve and took the canteen back.

Verve blanched. She had not told Olive of what had happened to her with the Cunning Blade, how she had absorbed its powers. And she wasn't going to. Still, she was curious. "But what if someone *could* kill one?"

"Well," said Olive after some time, still catching her breath at the top of the hill, "then that someone could not have their would-be victim's magic flowing through their veins." She gave Verve a pointed look. "It would rebound on the attacker or simply fade. Magic knows its master and won't allow them to come to harm."

Verve thought on this. If what the crone said was true, she couldn't thwart Dacre and whatever plans he had for her. She might be more powerful than he, but he couldn't be harmed or waylaid by her magic. Raw power rippled beneath Verve's skin as the thought ate at her. It caused her to glow, and Olive took several none-too-subtle steps back.

"You'd best put a leash on that, Miss Verity, if you don't mind me saying. We don't want to attract any creatures…or fae, for that matter."

The heat in her ire cooled somewhat as she tamped it down, but her skin continued to pulse with pent-up power. "Is there no other way?" Verve took in a slow, deep breath and closed her eyes, willing the magic to go to rest.

"No other way to what?"

Verve opened her eyes. "No other way to defeat him." She readjusted the sack of books hanging from her back and started down the hill, Olive close on her heels as she broke into a run.

"You'll have to untie your magic from his so he can't control it or you. Or…."

"What?" Verve looked expectantly over her shoulder.

Olive shook her head. "Or *you* will have to find a way to take control of *his* magic, that which lies within you and that which lies within him."

"I don't want to control him," said Verve. "As much as I hate Dacre Starside for what he's done, I don't want to be anywhere near his magic." She grunted as they reached the bottom of the hill only to be met with the beginnings of another, steeper one. At this hill she slowed, making certain Olive was able to keep up with her.

They were quiet for a while, running side by side, their steps growing slower and more uncertain as they neared the pinnacle. Soon Olive was panting again and had to stop to take another swig of water. When she passed the canteen to Verve, Verve refused it. She did not need as much as she once had, and what they had was running low besides.

"Is it possible to rid myself of his magic?" Even without squinting or using her superior sight, Verve made out a forest up ahead and knew they could reach it within the half hour.

"What is in those books of yours, I wonder?" Olive prodded the makeshift sack dangling from Verve's back. "I saw you had one on Second Age prophecy. That would little concern you, unless you're the Fire Queen."

Verve laughed. "That isn't possible."

"Isn't it, though?" The look she gave Verve was a knowing one. Mercifully, she changed the subject. "And what of the others you stole? I did not see their titles."

"First Age prophecy."

"Useless." Olive nudged a pebble with the toe of her right boot. "What else?"

"A book on the Lands of the Dead."

Now Olive grinned, exposing her yellow-stained teeth. "That is most interesting and no doubt quite useful. Ha." She wiped a hand across her sweat-flecked brow and started down the hill.

They remained silent as they descended and the land opened up onto a boggy plain. The smell of decay and sulfur hit Verve full force, and she retched once and then took several deep breaths through her mouth. "Should we go around?"

"If we don't want to wind up fodder for quicksand, then yes. What do you see?"

Verve looked to the left. The bog seemed to go on for miles in that direction, so she peered to the right and shook her head. "At this rate, it might take us 'til dark to go around."

Olive cursed. "We can't be caught in the open when night falls."

"I know," Verve snarled, sparks flying from her fingertips. "We'll have to go back and hope Dacre hasn't already made a gateway here."

Olive watched her with interest. "Do that again."

"What? Dissolve into a fit of worry and despair?" She snorted, and Olive's eyes twinkled.

"How much control do you have over fire?" Without warning, she stepped into Verve's space and snatched away the sack of books.

"What are you doing? I need those." Verve reached for them, and Olive slapped her hand away. The blow did not hurt, but it stoked the flame that always kindled in her blood and brought it to the surface. Again she started to glow. "Are you *trying* to make me incinerate you?"

Olive studied her. "Not much control, then, but you have a lot of fire in you. I wonder what you could do if truly provoked."

Verve scowled and backed away from the old woman. "Give me my books back."

Olive hoisted the pack over her shoulder and shook her head. "You don't need 'em right now. I'll be fine carrying the load as you make a path for us."

"I don't think—"

"Don't worry about thinking. It's *feeling* we're concerned with at the moment." Olive gestured at the wasteland in front of them. "Go ahead, move right to the muck's edge and wait for my instruction."

With a roll of her eyes, Verve stepped to the border of the bog and stared down into the murky waters. There were cattails everywhere. Dead birds littered the surface, their feathers appearing to have been tarred. Pity swelled inside of Verve, and the sparks from her fingers faded.

"No good. Think of something that makes you irate."

In the distance behind and to the right of them, Verve heard a tree groaning as it split into a gateway. The fire died completely. "He's here." Shaking like a reed, she stepped back from the water and walked toward the south in hopes of putting as much distance between herself and the gateway as possible.

Olive caught her by the sleeve and steered her back toward the waters. "No, m'dear, there's no time. You need to get properly furious, and you need to do so now."

Verve glowered at the woman. "You are not helping."

"Well, that's tough luck. You know what else isn't helping?" Before Verve could shoot back an answer, Olive sneered at her. "I'll tell you what isn't helping anyone, your complete lack of spine concerning the man who is trying to claim your powers. The magic you have is truly wasted on someone so useless they can't even make a tiny spark on purpose."

"I know what you're doing."

Olive smirked. "Then let it work, you frail, useless, fainting violet."

At the words, Verve's fingers grew hot and several sparks shot from them, igniting some grass. Fear waned within her breast. She welcomed and embraced the heat. Closing her eyes, she stepped forward into the muck and mire, fire rippling forth in tentative waves from her body. The first step found her stuck in mud, but she fought the panic and tapped into her rage, kindling it into a deadly fire.

Heat swept out in front of her and to the right and left, and she knew without having to look that the ground ahead and beside them had lost most of its moisture. "I'm doing it," she breathed.

"Don't just stand there. Move," said Olive, fast on her heels. "Keep your focus, Miss Verity. Push your feelings outward."

The initial terror and hesitancy were replaced with a giddy sort of glee. Her pace increased and she opened her eyes to find the way ahead of them as dry as a desert, flames licking at the corpses of dead things. *What else can I do?*

Stride by great stride, they had moved miles within minutes. Behind her, Verve could hear Olive panting. Guilt made the flames falter. She shouldn't have kept such a punishing pace for the aging woman.

"Keep going. I don't have your keen senses, but even *I* know someone is behind us."

The fire died entirely. It did not matter, however, for her blaze had dried the land in the near and far distance, and as they ran, dust kicked up behind them.

Not a minute after the flames had left her, the pair reached the wooded area, and Verve looked around frantically for a hawthorn. "Do you see anything?" Her eyes scanned the scant gathering of trees but she was having trouble finding a suitable one with which to make a gateway.

In the distance behind them, Verve heard the slow beating of a fae heart. She did not pause in her searching to discern who approached, and nearly jumped out of her skin when Olive tapped her on the shoulder.

"Take this," said Olive between great gasps for air. She thrust the sack of books at Verve and bent over, breathing hard. "Do you have water?"

"You're carrying the canteen," Verve reminded her.

Olive shook her head. "That's not what I meant." She looked up and met Verve's eye. "Can you flood the plain behind us? Turn it into a swamp again?"

A dull pulse of pain formed behind Verve's left eye, which began to twitch. "You can have both?"

"Of course you can have more than one element. And if you have as much power as I think you do, there's got to be water in there."

Footsteps moved up the second to last hill they had climbed. "What do I do?" Verve wailed.

"I never had water, so I can't help you there. Think watery thoughts and I'll keep searching for a hawthorn." She left Verve standing alone, trembling.

Dacre would take her. He would trap her and control her and she would never be free again. She shivered as silver tears streamed down her face, freezing to her cheeks as they rolled to her chin.

The air had grown cold and Verve's breath fogged in front of her. A mist rose from the ground that had been scorched moments earlier, obscuring everything for miles. *Breathe, you silly woman,* Verve chided herself. But her body wasn't listening.

Snow fell from the heavens as dark, rumbling clouds rolled in, turning the early morning sky black and throwing the mists into shadow. In the near distance, Olive cursed beneath her breath.

"Well, that's one way of doing things," she said. "No one will find us in this fog…but we're not going to find any hawthorns in it either. Would you care to try something else?"

But fear had its talons in Verve and she couldn't shake its mighty grip. Instead of letting it root her to the spot, however, Verve forced herself to move, her breaths coming in pants as sweat trickled down the nape of her neck. She moved without seeing, her other senses taking over as her vision blurred.

The mists continued to thicken. The snow still fell in great flakes, and a wind tore at Verve's hair. Twice she nearly dropped the sack of books from her shoulder, but some sense remained in her. *You need the information you carry. Hold on to it.*

The third party, Dacre or whoever they might be, had moved farther away from them, perhaps lost in the fog. No voice called out to them, raising Verve's suspicions further still, and she tried in vain to quiet her breathing.

At last, after she had woven her way blindly through the wood, Verve's hand flew up in front of her and smacked against the smooth bark of a tree. Beneath her touch, the tree trembled, and she knew without having to see it that she had been drawn to a hawthorn. "I've found one." Her voice was barely above a whisper, her lips trembling. She tried again. "I found a hawthorn, Olive. Please hurry." The winds continued to tear at her hair and clothing, and Verve knew she needed to calm herself. She closed her eyes and counted backward from twenty.

"Where are you?" Olive called out more loudly than Verve would have liked. "My goodness, it's like trying to see through molasses. Can't you lift it for a moment so I can find you?"

"I'm working on it," Verve said.

Snip, snap, crack, crunch! Olive was making enough noise to wake the dead.

As if in response to the commotion, the third party in the distance moved closer. They were perhaps two miles away now, and Verve knew she had to do something quickly.

She thought of the clouds of mist moving away from her and forming a great wall between her and the one who pursued them. Then she reached deep within for a feeling, alighted upon sadness, and pushed the emotion and her magic together at the mist. It took a moment, but as soon as it began to move away from them and toward Dacre, Verve took her first even, calm breath in an hour.

Olive stood several yards away, and as the mist revealed her form, her shoulders heaved in a great sigh of apparent relief. "Well, that was interesting. You found a suitable tree, you say?"

Numb, Verve nodded without speaking a word.

"And you need me to make the gateway?"

Verve closed her eyes, sighed, and removed her hand from the tree, which seemed relieved as well. "They're too afraid of me."

"Hmm." Olive came up beside her and placed a wrinkled hand where Verve's smooth one had been moments prior. "You've been taught the compassionate way. You might have to start using force." She gave Verve a searching look before holding out a hand, palm facing upward.

"What?"

"You've a knife on your person or something I might pierce the tree with?" When Verve made a face, the old woman shook her mane of tangled hair. "If you can't or won't produce one, we'll do it your way…even though his lordship very well might be on our heels."

Olive's words made Verve's eye twitch, and she could barely focus on the world around her. "Hurry, please." Her hands trembled as she plucked a blade of grass from the earth and fed calm feelings into it, and transformed it into a knife.

Olive snatched the blade from Verve and sliced the palm of her own hand, which beaded with crimson. "The trees will answer to the stabbing pain of a knife but not your brand of magic, eh?" At the word 'knife', the crone plunged the blade into the tree, which at once began to plead for mercy. "Did you ever wonder why that is?"

Over the hawthorn's keening, Verve said, "Not really. Can't you just—"

"I'll need a destination, Miss Verity."

Verve sifted through her memories, trying desperately to grasp on to the name of Fenn's family estate. All she could think of was his family name, and perhaps that would suffice. "Larknott estate."

"What? Where is that?"

"The Larknott family estate in Letorheas. That's all I know."

Olive turned to the tree, which burst apart with a shriek and formed a gateway to a great wood. "Does this look familiar? Miss Verity?"

"I-I don't know." The fog was lifting, and Verve heard their pursuer fast approaching. Without another thought, she threw herself through the archway, Olive fast on her heels as a laughing voice called out,

"You can't run forever."

CHAPTER EIGHT

Taking Olive by the arm, still careful not to touch her flesh, Verve led her quickly through the trees, hoping and praying she had brought them to the right place. The woods seemed to never end as they ran. After twenty minutes of this, Verve knew the crone could no longer keep up and took pity on her. They stopped running, and Olive drained the rest of the canteen.

"You said Larknott," Olive said at length. "That would be the Rogue Prince's family." The words came out with a shudder and she shook her head in wonder. "You mentioned returning to Fenn. What have you got to do with the likes of him? Is he the one who cursed you, as you say you've been?" She waited, her eyes wary.

Every sound to Verve's ears was a gateway opening, every stir of wind, a hex thrown at her back. "No. We should keep moving. Dacre will have found our hawthorn by now." She held out her gloved hand for Olive, who shook her head.

"Can we slow down?" When Verve made a face, Olive held up a hand. "You gave me plenty of power, but I don't know if you realize how fast you've been driving us. Your form is a blur sometimes. And you've been dragging me most of the way."

Verve bit her tongue and tasted blood. "I'm sorry." She stepped forward. "Will you let me carry you?"

Olive hesitated. "Are you able to carry both me and the books?"

"Yes." She turned her back to Olive and crouched, waiting for the crone to climb onto her back. "But remember, don't touch my skin."

"This isn't dignified. But then again, neither is rotting in a cell." Without further ado, Olive scrambled onto her back and loosely wrapped her arms around Verve's neck, the fabric of her sleeves protecting her arms and hands. "Is this too tight?"

Without answering, Verve straightened and took off at top speed. She used through-sight, casting her gaze around in different directions, and sighed in relief. They had arrived in the correct part of the world, but she was heading in the wrong direction, so she veered to the right and corrected their course.

Olive swore and held on more tightly. "Next time, dear, warn me when you do that."

Verve had spied the gate around Fenn's family estate for but a moment and shut her eyes, returning her vision to normal. In that short moment, something had seemed not quite right, but she wondered if it simply had to do with her own nerves. Running as she was, it would be imprudent to lose focus on the task at hand. She would see the mansion when they arrived there.

At one point, Olive's grip slipped and Verve had to stop so the old woman wouldn't fall to the ground or worse, into a tree. Carefully she put Olive down. "You can walk the rest of the way, but make haste: we're near, but Dacre can't be far behind." Without waiting for Olive to recover, Verve set off again at a quick walk, scanning the trees around them for danger. All was calm, all was silent. Too silent. Verve broke into a run.

The smoking remains of Fenn's estate came into view, filling the air with the stench of burned parchment. Verve clutched her mouth, a silent scream building on her lips.

It was all ruin and ash and piles of rubble behind the magical gate, which seemed to still be working. Coming to her senses, Verve launched herself through the gate and into the mess, screaming for Fenn.

At the sound of her voice, scavenger birds screeched and soared into the heavens and perched on nearby trees, regarding Verve's progress through the piles of stone with beady eyes. She did not want to think of why they might be there.

Soon Verve was heaving giant blocks of crumbling rock into the air and throwing them aside so she could make certain her love wasn't trapped beneath. She sensed rather than saw Olive approaching and called out a warning: "The gate won't let you through. You have to share a blood bond with the master."

Olive let out a low string of curses as she stopped beyond the gate. "Then how was it blown apart from within?"

Verve's head swiveled to look at her so quickly, her neck made a loud cracking noise. "What makes you think it was blown apart from within?" She continued digging through the ruins.

"Look at the way the stones fell: outward. Also, note the patterns of the scorch marks. Someone definitely did something to the building from within. Do you know who would have—"

"Fenn!" Verve cried again. And again there was no response.

Olive took a few tentative steps closer to the gate. "Think, Miss Verity. Can you feel anyone here?"

Verve shot Olive an exasperated look. "I don't know."

Olive rolled her eyes. "Can you hear anyone breathing? Or hear a heart beating?"

A sob tore itself from Verve's chest. "No."

"And you say the Rogue Prince was the master of the estate and was in there when you believe this happened?"

"No. I mean, yes. I don't know." Her voice had grown shrill, and red lightning flashed in the sky.

Olive took a wary step backward. "All right, easy now. All I'm saying is this is a very powerful magical being we're talking about. He's not in the rubble, Miss Verity. You can stop searching."

Blindly, Verve stumbled onward and began throwing more boulders around. "I have to be certain."

Olive said nothing at first and watched her. Her hands fluttered as if to touch the bars only to think the better of it at the last moment and grasp her skirt in folds instead. After twenty minutes of following Verve's progress, it would seem Olive had had enough. "Miss Verity, I do not feel safe standing out in the open like this. You'll either need to grant me access to the property or send me on my way. I'm not going to stand here and wait to be captured." Her voice was hoarse with tension.

Verve sighed and turned from her labor, her blouse soaked in sweat. "I don't know how to let you through. H-he said only the master of the estate and those sharing a blood bond with him could pass through the gate unscathed."

"Blood bond, eh?" Olive smirked. "And how are *you* in there, I wonder?"

At that, Verve felt herself flush. "Well...."

Of all things, Olive laughed and slapped her thigh. "You and the Rogue Prince are mates, are you?"

"Spouses," Verve shot back.

That did nothing to abate Olive's merriment. She simply chuckled.

"I don't see what's so amusing."

Before Verve could stop her, Olive put her hand on the gate, which shivered beneath her touch, and stepped through, unharmed. "Oh, this is too much. He didn't want to *kill* you. I can't – I need to sit down."

Verve stared at her blankly. "How did you get through?"

"Easily," said Olive. "You share a blood bond with the master."

"And I gave you a drop of my magic. But that's not blood."

Olive shrugged. "Magic is in your blood, and blood is in your magic. You can't separate the two."

"Then my curse won't harm you. Which means...I could have given magic to my family and – and Helena would still be alive. She would have been able to protect herself from my magic." Her lower lip trembled and it took all her self-control not to slap herself. *I need to hold it together.*

Olive was watching Verve, her expression sad. "Not all take to magic so easily. It will kill non-middlings, if given as you gave to me."

"Helena was a middling," Verve snapped.

Olive raised her hands in placation. "But that doesn't mean she would have taken it well. Or would have wanted it to begin with."

Verve paused.

"Did *you* want the magic thrust upon you?" The old woman dusted off a block of stone and seated herself.

"This is different. She *died*."

Olive sighed. "As all mortals and elves have done or will someday do. That does not mean we can or should transform every middling that crosses our path. The change is hard to get used to, and not everyone adapts well to it."

A new thought occurred to Verve, one that propelled her away from the rubble and set her mind on fleeing. "What of Dacre? If I have his blood in me, his magic, can he pass through the gate?"

Olive put a hand on Verve's arm and stayed her. "He gave you his blood and magic, you did not give him anything. Yes, you share a blood bond, but it is of *his* blood, *not yours*. He has nothing of Fenn's in him."

"Then how did this happen?" Verve gestured to her surroundings, the ruins of the formerly great mansion. "It reeks of magic."

"*His* magic, though?"

That made Verve pause. She sniffed again. "There's someone else's magic at work here." Once again she poked through the destruction.

Olive frowned. "I wonder...." She rose and approached the pile of rocks that had once been the entryway and traced her fingers over the charred surfaces. "Yes, there was definitely an explosion from within. I'm thinking someone either used their magic directly to cause this devastation, or perhaps employed an incendiary package."

Verve's brow wrinkled. "A what?"

Olive gestured at the mounds around them. "Someone gathers as much destructive magic as they are able and stores it in an object. It can either be prepared to set off an explosion at a certain time or, with very powerful fae, it can be detonated from anywhere in Letorheas." The woman pointed at the sack of books lying all but forgotten near the gate. "You go through those books, Miss Verity. They might hold the key to freeing you from his lordship's magic. Only then can you have any peace of mind."

★ ★ ★

While Verve attempted to skim through the tomes, Olive was everywhere. She gathered logs for a fire – though how she managed to come across these, Verve couldn't say – and foraged for tinder. Soon she had a nice fire burning in a circle of rocks that Verve hadn't even noticed her gather and lay out.

Soon enough, however, Olive seemed to tire and brought the canteen to Verve, who was glad to hear its contents sloshing around. She drank her fill and passed the vessel back.

"Have you found anything?" Olive nodded at the text on the Lands of the Dead, which lay open on Verve's lap.

"Nothing that I think is helpful."

Olive leveled a stern look at her. "Have you studied it well?"

Verve swore. "Goodness, Olive, I've only been perusing it for half an hour now." Ire pounded behind her eyes and magic threatened to explode onto the unsuspecting woman sitting across from her.

"*Two* hours you mean, and you haven't perused more than a paragraph, I'd wager." She pointed at the ground. "Give your sore eyes and heart a rest. His lordship will surely allow you a fair head start before he finds a way through those bars." Her eyebrows rose to underline her sarcasm.

"Don't push me when I have burnable texts in my hands," said Verve.

But Olive was not done. "We only have so much daylight left, Miss Verity. We need to have some direction ere sunset, or else we'll be helpless as babes lost in the woods."

"I'm working on it." Verve's skin pulsed with a dangerous light, and the crone regarded her warily.

"I'll construct a shelter for us if it comes to it, but you need to—"

"I know." In front of them, the fire shot up as high as the treetops in the woods surrounding and turned a poisonous green. Within the blaze, what appeared to be great serpents writhed and slithered heavenward, causing Verve to shriek and fall backward off her perch.

"There's the temper," said Olive approvingly. "Now, put that into your research." Without another word, she rose and ambled over to a patch of spared grass. With a twist of her wrist, she pulled up a dandelion by the roots and studied it, giving no further looks at Verve.

She's not wrong, you know. Verve picked herself off the ground and dusted down her trousers with perhaps more vigor than was necessary. Once again she sat on the boulder and gently opened the book. "What am I looking for exactly?"

Olive didn't answer. Not that Verve expected her to.

Verve rubbed her eyes and stared at the page in front of her. She'd read it at least a dozen times over and now had it memorized...lot of good the contents would do her. The page was about a renowned potion-maker named Igraine, a half-mortal elf who passed into Ithalamore, the Lands of the Dead, when an experiment of hers had gone wrong. Legend told that her heart had been so pure that her spirit was allowed to move in and out from both worlds, dragging whatever she wanted back to the place from which no other returned. Verve turned the page, which went on to extol the woman's virtues. With a yawn, Verve flipped to the next page, scanning the lines for something useful. Her heart leapt when she alighted upon the final paragraph on Igraine:

Though a potion-maker, Igraine was no stranger to the world of curses and bonds. In fact, it is believed, shortly before her death, the elf was working on two coveted tonics: one to break curses and one to break blood bonds. Whether or not she succeeded remains unknown. Her work disappeared days after her demise, and some believe her spirit moved all her findings in order to hide those secrets from the world.

"This is good," said Verve as she moved on to the next page. She could hardly focus on the text in front of her as thoughts began to race through her mind. This Igraine was the only allegedly successful maker of these potions...and she was deceased. *Can she really move back and forth between the lands of the living and dead?* If so, would the elf help Verve – *could* she help Verve?

Olive startled her from her thoughts. "There's rain in the clouds. You'll want to find a way to protect those books."

As if responding to her words, the heavens rumbled. A cold raindrop pattered down on Verve's head and she looked up.

"Hurry!" Olive scrambled toward the books as lightning flashed and the land grew still. She dove at the tomes as though they were her own offspring and took shelter with them under some of the ruins. No sooner had she moved to safety than a great gust of wind swept down among the rock piles, tearing at Verve's hair and threatening to lift her from the ground.

Verve fought against the ensuing deluge and threw herself in after Olive. Lightning bathed them in an eerie green light for a moment as rivulets of water streamed into their shelter.

Olive swore and hefted the books into her lap after sitting. "Do you have any feathers? I fear I'm well out of my depth here."

With a frown, Verve plucked a blade of grass from the ground and studied it as she willed herself to calm. *Grow and become…oilskin cloth.* She closed her eyes and fed feelings of weariness into the grass and shoved her magic at it as well. The transformation took a moment, but when Verve was certain it had taken hold, she opened her eyes and found that which she had meant to create.

Olive snatched the weatherproofed fabric from Verve's hands and wrapped the books in them. "Best if one of us holds these in our lap." She grunted and passed the volumes to Verve, who rested them on her crossed legs.

Outside, the rain continued to pour and the wind beat against their shelter. Lightning flashed again and again, and the resulting peals of thunder grew louder and closer, making Verve believe the storm's eye was almost over them. "How long do you think this will last?"

Olive shivered and rubbed her hands over her arms. "Y-you do realize our weather is almost always manufactured, yes?"

Verve's eyes widened. "You mean weather-makers created this storm?" It was an unsettling thought, beings who controlled the weather. Then again, she reminded herself that her moods had shifted the weather at times. "Why would they make it storm today? And—"

A new boom of thunder shook the earth as the air lit up blue. Verve's hair stood on end. "Blast, that sounds close."

Olive blew on her own hands, warming them. Water continued to trickle in, soaking her skirts and Verve's trousers. "I believe it is for our benefit this storm has been made. Or, rather, it is meant to draw us from our hiding place." That did not sound good.

Will they flood us out? Verve drew in a slow breath. She needed her wits about her, if Dacre was as close as she believed him to be. "We need to leave here now. You as much said yourself Dacre will find a way through the bars. I won't wait for that, cowering in a hole as he tries to drown me." A hysterical laugh tore itself from her lips, and the look Olive gave in response showed she was questioning Verve's sanity.

"This is what he wants. To drive us out. We'll good as be handing you over if we leave now."

What was to be done? *Trapped.* Breathing heavily, Verve ducked out of the shelter and stood in the downpour. She listened.

There was Olive's heart beating fit to burst through her ribcage. Her knees creaked as she rose and stood in the entryway. "It's no good, Miss Verity. We're trapped."

Verve held up a hand for the woman to be quiet. She focused on her own heart's sluggish beatings for a moment and listened more carefully. Raindrops became thunderous to her ears as they pattered against her clothes and the ground, but she reached beyond into the wood surrounding and heard three heartbeats, all of them matching that of a fae. The air filled with the smell of parchment, oak, and patchouli. The three scents were as distinct from each other as the heartbeats, and Verve knew Dacre was not among them. She could have fainted with relief as she shook her head. "Olive, there are three out there. None of them are…him." She felt Olive moving nearer.

Then, using through-sight, Verve looked into the woods surrounding and found two she-fae with their hands raised to the heavens, directing the storm clouds toward the ruins. They were perhaps half a mile away and directly aligned with the front gate. Verve turned her focus to finding the owner of the third heartbeat and beheld a slight male fae who looked as young as Dav. He was a-ways behind the ruins and was waving his arms madly, and the heavens were responding with gusts of wind.

Her teeth clenched together and her eyes narrowed. Why would someone use a mere child to drive her out of her hiding place? "Enough!" she shouted, her voice echoing all around them.

The rain stopped. The winds died. Silence reigned.

"Well, that was civil of them," said Olive, moving to Verve's side.

Verve winced. She had a feeling the storm's sudden ceasing didn't have anything to do with the weather-makers.

"You said his lordship isn't among them?"

"Yes, but—"

"Well, then. It looks like we'd better flee while we have the chance." She reached for the books, but Verve shook her head. "Can you manage to fight off three weather-makers and hold those at the same time?" Olive asked.

Something told Verve she didn't have much choice; they were just too heavy for Olive to run with. "What if Fenn comes back and I'm not here?"

"So what if he does?" said Olive. "Not to be callous, but he can take care of himself. It's *you* we've got to worry for." She lifted her skirts and ran for the gate, her hand stretched forward, palm outward.

Verve hesitated. Perhaps Olive was right. *Besides, Fenn might not want to see me after I abandoned him like that.* That was not a happy thought, but it drove Verve to tuck the wrapped books against her chest and follow the crone out of the estate grounds.

There were still three heartbeats and some soft voices speaking, all confused and desperate. "Why did you stop?" asked one she-fae.

"*I* didn't stop. *You* did," said another.

The child wasn't speaking, but Verve heard him sigh as he trekked back to join the two women. If Verve and Olive weren't careful, they would cross paths with him; not that the fae didn't already know they were there.

Olive's lips formed the word, *"Run?"* The way she held herself suggested she was anxious to get moving though felt held back by not wanting to leave Verve.

Verve forced herself to not turn to look at the estate grounds. Fenn wasn't there, she reassured herself. There was no use remaining.

Out of nowhere a bolt of lightning flashed down from the heavens and struck the ground in front of them, throwing Verve and Olive backward. The air smelled of oak trees and burned things. Another bolt hit the ground between them as Verve scrambled to her feet.

Visibly trembling, Olive formed a shield of protection around herself. It was green and blue in places and looked like a soap bubble waiting to be popped. She nodded at Verve, who attempted to form one herself.

Another bolt struck the ground nearby, but Verve was ready this time and it did not throw her backward. She braced herself and darted through the trees, Olive in her bubble close behind.

"You'll want to get that shield up, Miss Verity!" Olive shouted as three bolts of light whizzed overhead.

"I'm trying." Panic rarely aided her magic, and today was proving no exception. A glowing fork of yellow light struck her in the back and she cried out in shock, falling to her knees and dropping the books.

"I've got her!" said a male voice.

The air smelled of parchment and patchouli, and Verve gasped for air as Olive continued running, only sparing her a glance. *So much for owing me two life debts.*

Three fae surrounded her in a blinking of an eye, nets of golden light gathered in their hands. "Easy," said one of the she-fae as Verve leapt to her feet. "We don't want to harm you."

Verve laughed without mirth. Instinctively she bared her teeth as they closed in. The air was filled with electricity, and Verve knew they were ready to strike her again if she did not comply. If only she could figure out how to create a shield like Olive had. She'd done it multiple times, but the magic was not coming to her now.

"Raise your hands in the air, milady," said the other woman.

When Verve did not obey, the male fae struck her with another bolt of lightning. It hit her in the side, and her blouse smoldered on contact. It did not, however, do more than sting and knock some of the wind out of her lungs.

"Elspeth will take you home to your mother if you do that again," said one of the she-fae to the male.

"How else are we supposed to catch her for the master?" said the male. He seemed eager to strike again. "The only thing halflings answer to is pain and terror." As if to illustrate his point, the fae threw another bolt at Verve.

Only this time, Verve surprised herself by reaching her hand out to meet it. The lightning fizzed at her fingertips for a brief moment, turning from yellow to blue as she mastered it. Shaking, she grasped the pulsing light and turned it into a whip, striking out at the fae who had meant to hit her with it.

"Does she *look* like a halfling to you?" the one named Elspeth said as Verve lashed the whip around the young man's ankle and raised him high in the air.

"Els, watch out!" The warning came too late.

Verve took the male fae and whipped him around wildly at the end of the lightning rope, striking the other two fae down like they were tenpins. The three groaned in a heap, but Verve did not wait for them to recover before summoning the dropped nets of golden light and casting them over her would-be captors. With a savage twist of her wrist, the nets tightened, and only when Verve was satisfied they would not escape did she pick up her books and flee into the woods.

It did not take long for her to find Olive, who was hiding in the brush a mile away. Verve scowled as she pulled the shrubbery aside. It was getting to be a bother, being promised help from this woman, only to have her run for the hills when trouble arrived. But Verve needed her to make gateways.

At the sight of her face, the crone shrank back a bit, muttering a sorry excuse for an apology and crawling out of her hiding spot. She followed Verve to the nearest hawthorn.

She could have made a gateway and left me entirely stranded, Verve reminded herself, though she did not feel like being so charitable to Olive in that moment. "The weather-makers won't be giving us any more trouble."

Olive cast a nervous glance at Verve and held out her hand, presumably for a knife. When Verve hesitated, Olive sighed. "The trees are so terrified of you because you can destroy them without batting an eye. They don't co-operate because they know you won't really harm them. Maybe you ought to disintegrate one or two. You know, to get your point across."

Verve stared at her. "They're sentient beings."

Olive shrugged. "It's your decision, however unwise it may be." She continued to hold out a hand until Verve told her she had left their one knife back at the estate and she didn't have the focus to create another one at the moment. "Bother."

"Could you please just do it the nice way? We don't have time for this."

"We hardly have time for *that.*" But Olive rolled up her ratty sleeves and pressed her palms against the hawthorn's silver trunk. After a moment, the tree stirred and demanded sunlight in exchange for their safe passage to a different land. Olive rolled her eyes. "Do we look like weather-makers to you?"

The tree was silent for a moment. *"Why won't your mistress help? She could...."* At once the tree stopped talking and quavered slightly, as though it had said too much.

"She could, could she?" asked Olive of the tree. Her eyes went to Verve's face. She frowned. "How about I have her incinerate you instead as an example to your kin, hmm?"

At once the hawthorn split into two parts, its branches winding and slithering to form a rather ornate gateway leading into a meadow with golden sunlight streaming down. *"Don't harm us. We meant no disrespect, Firstblood of No Land."*

Verve opened her mouth to ask where the gateway was taking them, but there was the sound of another gateway being opened in the distance. The wind changed, bearing with it the smells of coffee and chocolate. Without thinking, she grabbed Olive and pulled her through, thankful her curse did not extend to the woman.

"What's wrong?" Olive asked, instantly alert.

"Dacre's right behind us."

Olive's expression darkened and she moved back to the hawthorn, where the gateway had just closed. Then she hurled a fireball at the tree, which instantly went up in flames. Again and again she lobbed flames at the tree. "Help me!"

Verve stared. "What are you doing?"

"A tree that has formed a gateway with another tree is linked," she said between gasps as she continued her assault on the hawthorn. "If his lordship talks to the other tree, it will lead him right here. But if I destroy *this* tree, the one that brought us here will be destroyed also. So don't just stand there, get to work."

It was obvious the tree was already beyond saving. Guilt tugged at Verve's stomach as she drew sorrow and magic into her hands, giving them a mighty thrust at the tree trunk.

The hawthorn, which had begun shrieking, at once went still and shortly after dissolved into ash.

CHAPTER NINE

They walked through the woods for some time, trying to discern where the gateway had brought them. There were no other hawthorns in sight. In fact, as they walked, the trees quickly thinned, leading them to an open field.

Olive stooped and picked up a stray head of grain that had been chopped off and discarded. She sniffed it and frowned. "This could be from anywhere."

Verve scanned beyond the fields and beheld a large red barn. "What color are barns usually in Letorheas?" Without waiting for an answer, Verve moved through the muck and headed for where she smelled apples ripening on trees.

"Miss Verity, this could be a trap. We have no idea where the hawthorn sent us."

A quick search using through-sight told Verve they were alone in the great outdoors, where the light was beginning to fade. Wherever they had emerged, it was warm enough to be second summer and the heavens held no unusual clouds or signs. "We're in Etterhea," said Verve, relief filling her.

"In Etterhea, you say?" Olive moved closer. "This does not bode well. You're wearing trousers and look rather wild, if you don't mind me saying. There's no mistaking you for a normal human."

That made Verve laugh halfheartedly. "I wonder where the tree brought us. Maybe I'm not far from home." At the words, however, dread dropped into the pit of her stomach and sat there like lead. *You shouldn't see them again, Verve.* She gulped and trod more softly.

"Does this place seem familiar to you?"

Verve shrugged. "You know how most places in Etterhea look the same." They paused outside the orchard, their eyes on the house where several heartbeats could be heard and voices were raised in laughter.

"If one of them comes out and finds us...well, there are still witch burnings in the world of man, I assume." Hastily the crone dragged a hand down her face, filling the air with the weak aroma of brown sugar. Her face went from ethereal and perhaps frightening to humans to plain and gaunt, just like the day Verve had found her in a cell. She looked at Verve, watching her with wide eyes, waiting.

Verve did as Olive had done, dragging a hand down her own face until an oily film developed on her skin. She swallowed and then tamped down her magic. The air smelled of vanilla as she finished and went about plucking red groundlings, tucking them into the sack with the books.

"Apples won't sustain us long," said Olive.

"I know."

The look they shared was grim. They would have to scrounge for food, perhaps beg, if they were to be here long. That was, however, not part of Verve's plan. She took Olive's gnarled hand and led her out of the orchard and toward the barn whose door had been left open.

"We're going to get caught, arrested, and tried for stealing."

Verve shook her head and led Olive into the barn, whence came the odor of drying hay and alfalfa. It took her eyes a moment to adjust to the dim light, but when they did, she handed the sack to Olive and poked around for a good place to hide and sleep for the night. "We'll leave before sunrise and find a hawthorn to take us away from here." There were no suitable hiding spots on the ground, so Verve moved toward a ladder leading up to the haymow.

"But where to from here? Do you have a safe house in Letorheas?"

"No, I don't."

Olive's shoulders heaved and she handed the books and apples back to Verve. "In Etterhea?"

Verve thought on that a moment as she swung the makeshift pack over her back. "I have family scattered throughout the territories. Perhaps I can impose on one of them." As she said the words, however, she knew it was a bad idea. If word got out she was back in Etterhea, it wouldn't take Dacre long to show up at Maplehurst and start questioning her family. He wouldn't even have to threaten them to get a list of places she might go; Dacre would simply charm the information out of the women.

"Best not to stay with family," said Olive as she slowly followed Verve up the ladder. Panting, she reached the top and stepped into the haymow. "Family can betray you." The bitter tint to her words made Verve wonder what had happened in Olive's past, but she brushed those thoughts aside.

"Do you have any hiding places in Etterhea?" Verve set down her oilskin sack and stretched her limbs.

Olive sneered. "Anyone I ever knew here is probably long since dead or moved on. And any place I might have claimed as my own would have been discovered or is in such a state of decay as to be uninhabitable."

They both grew silent as men's voices mingled in the near distance. Olive opened her mouth, but Verve put a finger to her lips and settled down into the hay.

"You got it?" asked one man.

"Ya," replied a young boy's voice as footsteps headed in the barn's direction.

"Don't forget to lock the door."

The barn door groaned closed, pitching the she-fae into semidarkness. Verve tried and failed not to fret. How were they to get out the following morning before the household had awakened? She looked to Olive, whose expression was bleak.

Outside, a lock clicked into place and the voices moved away. Once all had grown quiet again, Olive let out a great huff and put her hands on her hips."What now?" she asked.

Collecting herself, Verve opened her sack of books and tossed an apple to Olive, who almost dropped it. "We'll find a way out."

Olive groaned. "What language were they speaking? It was ugly and brutal-sounding."

That made Verve pause and look up from her books. "It wasn't Common?"

"That's right. You've been blessed with a translation spell." She sounded bitter. Slowly she lowered herself into the hay and hissed. "This dratted stuff is painful and pokey." Emphasizing her point, the crone jabbed a blade of hay in Verve's general direction.

Verve tried to ignore Olive's griping and opened the book on Ithalamore. Though the light was dim, Verve's eyes were up to the challenge of discerning words in near darkness.

While Verve scanned the pages for something useful, Olive crunched away on an apple and looked around the haymow. The energy she radiated was nervous and tinged with bits of dread. So powerful were her feelings, Verve could swear the whole barn was filled with them, winding their fingers around Verve's throat and attempting to throttle her.

This would not do. With a gasp, Verve rubbed her neck and shot an accusatory glare in Olive's direction. "Are you using magic on me?" she demanded.

At these words, Olive's eyebrows shot heavenward. "No. Does it look to you like I would do anything of the sort?" Her words were calm enough, but Verve could smell her fear.

"We'll get out of here, Olive. You don't need to worry." She said the words as much for herself as for the crone. She had enough power to protect them from any mortals who might have ideas about what to do with strangers squatting in their barn.

Olive stared. "Who says I'm worried?"

It was Verve's turn to stare. Though faint, there was a darkness gathering around Olive like a shroud, prowling around her form and spiraling outward as though it meant to grab Verve.

"Are you not well, Miss Verity? You're glowing a bit green."

Indeed, when Verve looked down at herself, her body was pulsing with a sickly green light. It stretched out from herself and reached toward Olive's darkness, pulling on its edges like one might crimp a pie until, with a great shudder from Olive, the darkness unspooled from around her and clashed with Verve's green light. At once the glow separated from Verve's body and gathered the darkness before swallowing it whole and hovering in the air in front of her.

She couldn't explain it, but the light, which now pulsed more brightly, looked...appetizing. "What is it?" Verve asked, reaching toward the light as it reached toward her.

Olive yawned and lay down in the hay. "What's what?" She sounded calmer, more relaxed.

Verve's stomach rumbled and clenched. "That glowing thing. What is it?" Apparently the light could wait no longer but shot toward her at an alarming speed and poured into her mouth. At first it knocked the wind out of her and she choked on it; it was oily and sweet. Instinctively she swallowed, and the glowing ball disappeared down her throat.

It would seem Olive was no longer sleepy. She sat up with a start and stared as Verve licked her lips. "Did you just eat my terror?"

"No. Is that even possible?" A strange feeling overcame her senses. Her power, which she had tamped down, broke free of its restraints and lit up the haymow.

Olive swore and rushed at Verve. "Control it. We don't want the men returning."

At her words, the power within shuddered and pulsed once, dully, then faded altogether. Still, however, Verve felt energized and ready to explode. So this is what Dacre had meant, all those months ago. "It's true, then."

The crone seemed to breathe more easily now that the light had dimmed, and settled back down into the hay. "Gref-Etan," she said darkly.

"Grief-eater?" Verve said, her mind at once translating the word. "Dacre mentioned fae eating others' feelings, come to think of it."

"Not just any others. Mortals." A frown formed on the woman's face and she shook her head. "You shouldn't have been able to do that to me, since you made me into a halfling again." Her words were tense, and Verve could see the worry and suspicion pouring out of her skin. "What exactly *are* you?" The horror in the woman's voice was a cold, hard slap across the face and it distracted Verve from how much she wanted to pluck those feelings from the air and devour them.

Verve squirmed and returned her attention to the book in her lap. "I don't know."

"Humph." Olive folded her arms across her chest and settled down more deeply into the hay. "No one could ever tell me what type of creature the Fire Queen would be. Some said a half-elf made into a full-blooded fae. Others still told of a woman descended from the stars to walk among us." She gave Verve a shrewd look. "But I knew you when you were mortal. And I know his lordship turned you into a fae."

"Halfling," Verve murmured as she tried to return her attention to the text in front of her.

"Fiddlesticks. You are human, you are fae, and you are…other." Olive shivered and gathered hay with which to cover herself. "That makes absolutely no sense. You can be two things, but you cannot be three. It goes against nature. It goes against…magic."

Verve clenched the book so tightly in her hands, it was a wonder the binding didn't crack. With care she pried her fingers from the pages, which stuck to her dewy skin. Olive was observant…too observant. Perhaps Verve had made a grave mistake freeing her from Dacre's prison. She tried keeping her attention on the words she was meant to be reading, but she could feel Olive's unwavering gaze on her face, and it was unnerving. With a sigh, she looked up from the book and met her stare. "I need to find a way to get a hold of someone dead, and your obvious terror is distracting me." Verve tried to keep her tone calm, measured. The result made Olive flinch.

"You can't contact anyone dead. They go to Ithalamore, and that's that. No cross communication."

"Igraine doesn't seem to have that problem," Verve murmured, catching mention of the potion-maker's name once more on the page. This time it was simply a reference to her student and protégé, Imalkis,

Olive blinked in apparent confusion. "Who?" She sat up and leaned toward where Verve sat, squinting at the pages in the latter's lap.

It was distracting, the terror fading into curiosity. The tendrils of shadow turned poisonous green and swirled around the crone. Thankfully, curiosity looked a lot less delicious, so Verve was able to turn her attention away from it and return her focus to the book. "No one." When Olive continued to stare, Verve offered, "Someone to do with a fellow named Imalkis."

"I've not heard of Igraine, but I have heard of Imalkis," said Olive. "Some genius potion-maker that went missing several months ago."

That had Verve's attention. "What is he known for?"

Olive settled down in the hay on her back and looked at the ceiling. "Oh, nothing ground-breaking as far as his profession goes. He had theories of reviving dead halflings with a special elixir made of unicorn blood and dragon scales. Of course, he could never test the theory."

"Why?"

Olive looked at Verve as though she were daft. "Well, for one thing, no dragons exist in this realm. And for another, unicorns went extinct ages ago." She sighed. "From what I heard, Imalkis is all bluster and bumble." Olive grew quiet as the sun's light leaked entirely out of the sky, blanketing the haymow in inky shadows. "It would be interesting, though, to know if he found it."

Verve waited for Olive to finish, and when she didn't, she looked back down at her book. "Found what?" She scanned the pages for more of Igraine, but it would seem the woman had been restricted to those scant pages she had already gone over.

"The Gate of the Dead." Olive's slight frame heaved.

Verve closed the book. "Imalkis found the Gate of the Dead?"

Olive snorted before looking at Verve, her expression at once sobering. "That would interest the Fire Queen, wouldn't it?"

With a gulp, Verve smoothed her hands over her arms. "Imalkis knows where the Gate of the Dead is located, and he's recently gone missing?" This did not bode well.

"I've only overheard conversations, mind. No one thinks much of talking in front of a helpless human prisoner in her cell." She sounded bitter, and irritation warred with pity in Verve's breast.

"What might have some of these conversations been about?" Verve picked at a spot on her trousers and attempted to compose herself as Olive gathered more hay around her form.

"It would seem he had made some great new discovery, oh, many months back. Then he disappeared."

Verve stilled. "What had he discovered? The Gate of the Dead?"

Olive shrugged. "It was common knowledge, his claim to have located the Gate of the Dead, by that time. One of the guards mused he had made no new discovery, that it was a ruse."

Pieces of a puzzle swirled around in Verve's mind, some of them fitting together with a snap as others barely came into focus. "What if Dacre knew of this potion-maker—"

"Oh, it is more than certain he did. No one in Letorheas can go very far without eventually hearing his name crop up in conversation." Olive scowled. "Do you think he knew the man?"

"I was going to ask you the same question." Weariness settled on Verve as she turned the idea over in her mind. "'The Gate of the Dead has been opened. Run, little Firstblood, run.'"

Olive let out a sound somewhere between a laugh and a grunt. "You go around reciting prophecy often?"

Verve ignored her words. "I think Dacre heard rumors of this man, knew he was supposed to have found the Gate of the Dead, and wanted something there badly enough to take the potion-maker into his custody."

Olive clucked her tongue and sat up once more. "Now he's stealing other fae? You've got quite the imagination, child. What could his lordship possibly want from Ithalamore?"

"I don't know." Verve ran a shaky hand over the pages of the book as the remnants of day faded entirely. Here there was a new moon, and the sky was overcast, preventing starlight from shining down on the barn. With reluctance, Verve closed the cover and replaced the book in the sack with the others. "I'll need to study more to find out." She stretched her limbs and lay on her back.

Thoughts raced through her mind, none of them taking full form. Verve's eyes closed and once more she stood in front of a black hawthorn tree, ten times the size of Maplehurst. This time, the tree did not dissolve and rebirth itself as she watched, but it sat there, unmoving, giving no indication it was anything other than an ordinary tree.

Verve ran her hands over the bark. It was stone-cold to the touch, and its surface was as hard and sturdy as iron. Something was different about this tree. Like her, it was other. Unlike her, it was ancient. Power flowed through it, of that Verve was certain; it...called to her.

"Take that which belongs to you," said a low, feminine voice.

A shiver rippled through Verve's body, and for a moment, she forgot she was dreaming. "What are you? You're not like any hawthorn – no, not like *any* tree I've ever seen."

As if in response to her words, the tree pulsed beneath Verve's fingertips and lit up like the midday sky. It also grew unbearably hot, scalding Verve's skin, which became fused to the bark. She let out a scream, but the tree's roots rose from the ground and covered her mouth. *"Will you three take it ere he can? I wonder...."* The roots thinned and grew tendrils, which filled Verve's mouth and snaked down her throat.

The world went black as Verve's eyes rolled back in her head. She tried to pull away, but the tree was in full control of her movements now, rooting her to the spot as it crawled through her veins, pushing up against her skin as though it meant to rip her to shreds. Sweat beaded on Verve's forehead, ran down the back of her neck. Back in the real, waking world, she could tell her body was convulsing.

"The other two stand in your way, Firstblood. You must allow one to eliminate the other if you are to succeed." The tree stroked her face with a leafless branch.

Verve thrashed against the hawthorn, and awoke with a start when someone slapped her hard across the face. It didn't hurt, but it was a bit of a shock. She could still feel the tree crawling down her throat.

Swearing and flailing her arms about, Verve stumbled to her feet, leaned over the edge of the haymow, and nearly fell off. Olive grabbed her from behind and hauled her back to safety.

"That must have been some dream." Olive put a finger to her lips as Verve fell into a heap, her breaths labored.

The world was yet dark out, but sunrise did not feel far off. In the near distance, several voices spoke as they moved toward the barn. They were anxious, alert.

Olive's gestures said it all. *"Stay quiet and hide."* At once the crone lowered herself onto the hay with care and started covering herself with it.

It took Verve a moment to come to her senses and silence her breathing before she could bring herself to burrow deep within the hay. There were the sounds of a rifle being loaded, and the lock on the barn was opened.

"You saw the light from here, Alphonse?"

Verve closed her eyes and hoped she would not have to hurt these people. She did not relish the thought of using her power against anyone but Dacre and his allies, but she knew she would use force if it came to it.

"It was unnatural," said a youth. "Blue like a gem. And it flashed—"

"Was this before or after the woman screamed?"

The youth grunted. "Weren't no woman, Da. Sounded like an angel."

There was a pause, and the older man laughed. "And angels scream now, do they, Alphie?"

"Why do you reckon we neither heard nor saw anything?" said a third voice, belonging to a woman.

Three pairs of footsteps moved into the barn, and lantern light relieved the dimness. "We locked the barn last night."

"But the hands have the key. They might have opened it again."

The man sighed. "They would not have."

"And you always trust the hired hands, Da?"

There was the sound of an open palm striking flesh, and the youth whimpered. "Mind your tongue, boy. I trust those men with my life."

"See anything now?" asked the woman as the lamplight danced nearer still to the mow. "You were just sleeping."

"It awoke me from my dreams, the sound and the light."

Fear crept up on Verve and seized her. It took all her strength to keep from taking in the deep gulps of air she longed for. *You're not trapped. It's only hay on top of you. Once these people are gone, you can brush it off and get up and move. You're not—*

"What's this?" asked the father. The lamplight moved away momentarily.

Verve held her breath.

"An apple core? Alphie, you been stealing groundlings again with your friends?"

The boy's response was a quick and horrified, "No."

"Hmm."

The ladder creaked beneath someone's weight. One rung was climbed, and then another.

"Get down from there, else you'll break your neck," said the woman.

The creaking ceased for a moment. Verve allowed herself a slow, soft breath.

"Something moved up here!" the boy shouted.

There was an exasperated sigh from below, and someone else took the bottom rung. "You and your imaginin'. Alphonse, this is your last warning to get down from there, or so help me...."

Stillness came over Verve and she closed her eyes. *Go away. Just go away.*

The youth mumbled something about knowing what he had seen as he clattered down the ladder. When he reached the ground below, there was the sound of flesh striking flesh once more, and the boy cried out. "When your da says to come down, you must do so, ya?"

"Ya, Mum." The response was a whimper.

"Sun will be up in the comin' hours," said the man. His heavier gait moved through the entrance to the barn, followed by the mother's and the boy's lighter treads.

Verve did not allow herself to take a deep breath until the barn door whined closed and was locked once more. She took as much care as she was able to remain quiet, but her breaths were shallow and quick gasps, and her whole form shook as the world spun.

"Easy there, Miss Verity," said Olive, nearly startling Verve out of her skin.

Verve's fingertips ignited and Olive at once tucked them into fists, hissing as her own flesh burned at the touch. It took a moment, but soon enough the fire died down, Verve's breaths became more even, though her heart continued to gallop.

"Good, you *can* control yourself." Olive gave Verve an awkward pat on the shoulder and handed her the canteen. "Take a slow sip of this and then gather your thoughts and your things; we need to be out of here within the half hour. Can't have the barn burning down around us; it would only take a small spark."

There was no arguing with that. Verve closed her eyes and listened to her own breaths, willing her heart to slow, and after a minute of this, it did. Her disguise had slipped and she was glowing slightly, but with some effort, Verve managed to slip on a normal appearance and tamped her magic down. For her efforts, her head ached. *Get a hold of yourself, Verve.*

The man was not wrong: the sun was on the rise and would breach the horizon within the next hour and ten minutes. How Verve knew this, she couldn't say, but felt it with such certainty and dread that she rose and gathered her things and was ready to move on within five minutes.

At the barn door, Verve paused and listened to the world outside. There was a thin, frail heartbeat fluttering nearby, but not close enough for the two of them to be detected, Verve hoped more than believed. Any other human was most likely in the farmhouse or another outbuilding and would not hear Olive and her leaving.

"How do we get out?" Olive asked. "I hear you picked a lock belonging to his lordship."

Verve dried her palms on her trousers. "That was a door lock. This is a padlock, and it's on the outside. We'll have to use magic." On instinct, she placed her hand on the door and closed her eyes. There was a sense there, something that felt stern and watchful, and Verve assumed it must be the lock giving her those feelings.

"Don't burn the barn down."

That broke Verve's concentration, and she opened her eyes with a flinch. Her hand, still on the door, glowed orange, and the wood there smoldered and crumbled. Outside, the lock fell with a loud *thud* onto something metal on the ground.

A dog took up barking. Lights flickered to life in the house.

Verve did not waste an instant but yanked the door open, grabbed Olive with her non-glowing hand, and pulled her toward the orchard whence they had come the evening previous. Dogs were called, men shouted, but no one could catch them.

It was dim out yet. Coyotes howled in the distance, adding extra urgency to Verve's steps. But the punishing flight could not be sustained.

Roots seemed to have risen up out of nowhere, and though Verve flew over them with ease, Olive tumbled to the ground. There was a sickening crunch as she rolled, and the crone let out a yelp.

"Are you all right?" Verve asked. She ran back to Olive's side and cringed when she beheld her leg. "Oh."

Bone poked through flesh, and Verve felt as though she might swoon. *If only Helena were here. She is a wonderful nurse and would know what to do*. She swayed and closed her eyes. The dogs were getting closer. Any moment now, they would be caught. They needed to run or—

"Miss Verity? What are you doing?" said Olive's distant voice. "Blast, there are roots everywhere. I might have fallen, had you not stopped."

Verve's eyes opened.

Olive was no longer lying wounded on the ground. She was standing a few yards ahead, staring at Verve with relief written across her face. The relief, however, soon turned to fear when the dogs continued to howl. "Run."

There was no time to wonder how or why she had seen a potential future just then. Verve shook off the vision she had experienced and caught up with Olive, both picking their way more carefully across the lumpy ground.

PART TWO

CHAPTER TEN

It had been five days since Verve left Fenn in Letorheas. At least, that was her estimation. Her hours were filled with trekking through forests with the unshakeable feeling she was being watched. There had been no hawthorn sightings. No humans crossed their path, and the apples they had gathered were long since gone.

Olive faded with each passing mile. Her initial complaints of hunger and fatigue all but stopped. She was quiet. So was Verve, lost for words as to how she might encourage her.

So much for being the Fire Queen. Raw power won't make edible food or potable water. "Why don't we stop for the night," she said after Olive had stumbled for the fifteenth time that day.

The crone did not argue nor make a suggestion, but collapsed in what Verve took to be either relief or despair. She stared into the dim woods, her expression blank. "I let terror get the better of me."

Verve set her burden of books down and sat across from her. "I know." They had been over this a dozen times.

That did not stop Olive from croaking out her regrets. "I should have just made another gateway with that hawthorn, traceable or not."

"It's all right."

Olive ignored her. "I've made an enemy out of the trees. Now we shall die as mortals." She looked at Verve, her eyes glassy. "Well, *I* shall die. *You* will go on." Her tone was bitter and she curled up in a ball on the ground.

As she did every time Olive grew morose, Verve drew upon her store of magic and conjured a floating ball of blue fire, which hovered in the air between them. It let off a great deal of warmth and usually was mesmerizing enough to keep the crone distracted. Today was no different, it would seem. Olive's mouth closed and she stared at the orb as though it might bring her salvation.

There was nothing to say to Olive to comfort her, so once Verve was certain the woman wasn't going to wander off or accidentally harm herself, she got to her feet and set up a protective wall of magic around them. It had taken her two days to sort out the magic, but the more frustrated she grew with each passing hour, the easier the power came to her fingertips and did what she bid it to do. *Protect us from harm*, she thought as she shoved her agitation and magic together in a wide arc surrounding them. A barrier rose up around them, encasing them in a dome of light.

Satisfied with her work, Verve left the safety she had created and began to forage. Mushrooms were out of the question, as she had never learned to discern between what was benign and what was poisonous. Instead she looked for root vegetables and edible weeds. Earlier, she had found an underground spring, and they had drunk eagerly from it and filled several canteens Verve had magicked from blades of grass, so drink was not a current concern at the moment.

Verve rubbed the back of her neck, feeling again like she was being observed. As always, she used through-sight to locate whoever might be watching her, but there was no one there. No one for miles and miles. She closed her eyes, returning her vision to normal, and went back to scrounging about in the dirt.

You're on the wrong path.

The words had been a soft sigh borne on a breeze, and Verve dismissed them at once as a hallucination. She was weary and hungry. Of course she wanted to hear Fenn's voice, for that was what it had sounded like to her.

Tears gathered in the corners of her eyes and she continued to labor, but she brushed them aside and stood. Perhaps the next clearing would yield something edible. Verve stumbled around the base of a maple, wishing desperately it had been a seed-bearing oak. "I could roast acorns," she murmured.

Firstblood, use your magic.

Verve scoffed. Her mind was cruel, playing tricks on her like this. "Quiet," she said. The next clearing yielded nothing, as did the trees surrounding. She pressed on.

Take the old woman and head west. You are going the wrong way.

A shiver worked its way down Verve's spine. The voice had been louder, clearer just then. "Am I dying? Is this what starving to death looks like?" Belatedly she amended, "*Sounds* like?"

There was no answer. Not that Verve had been expecting one; hallucinations rarely co-operated, she imagined.

Now the sun was on its way down, the land was growing dimmer by the minute; she had traveled ever so many miles, and there was nothing to show for it. Frustration gnawed at her mind almost as much as hunger pangs gnawed at her stomach.

Oh, for pity's sake. Can you not hear me?

Verve shook her head, turned, and ran back in the direction she had come. Full speed was not an option; she would need the remainder of her stores of energy to keep Olive warm that night, and running would deplete them. Soon she slowed to a stroll.

West. Head west.

"Leave me alone," said Verve.

There was a sigh. *Do you need a sign to know I am not of your imagining?*

Verve slowed further still. "I have been accused of insanity before. Perhaps my family was right. Perhaps I am just—"

A flash of near-blinding light streaked across the sky. Something, miles and miles away, struck the earth with a *thud* and a *hiss*, and then all was still.

Have I got your attention now?

Verve blinked. Again there was an overpowering sense of being watched. She looked about her, raising a protective shield around herself. But as always, no one was there.

Who knew the Fire Queen would be so woolly headed? The voice was bored, the tone droll. It reminded Verve very much of Dacre, but for the fact that it had the same tenor as Fenn's.

"What do you want?"

Ah, she can *listen.* Another sigh. *Return to your camp, gather your servant and belongings, and head west. You are a day's journey from the city of—*

Verve started running. The voice had gained more clarity, as though someone were perched in the tree branches above, looking down on her and shouting out directions.

Slow down, slow down. You're hard to reach when you're running.

She did not slow down, though her energy was flagging and her legs protested. When she arrived back at camp, the orb she had made still glowed brightly, and Olive had fallen asleep. "Olive," Verve said, stepping through the bubble of protection. "We've been found."

The crone groaned and sat up, blinking and rubbing her eyes. "You found food?"

"No." She dropped the magic powering the orb and lifted the sack of books. "I said someone's out there in the...woods." Verve frowned. All had grown silent. The only noises she heard were Olive's heart and breathing, plus her own. No living human soul was around for miles. "Odd." She waited for the voice to speak to her again, and when it did not, she set the books down and scanned the woods surrounding them. It didn't take through-sight for her to know her ears were right.

Olive scowled at Verve. "You woke me up and extinguished the fire for what reason? To stare stupidly into the distance?"

Verve's temper flared and it took barely half a thought to create another fire orb. "Someone spoke to me out there."

"I'm sure they did." Olive shivered and drew closer to the orb, flopped back down, and curled up in a ball once more. A moment later, she surprised Verve by saying, "You heard someone out there?"

"Yes. That's what I've been telling you."

Now Olive sat up once more, her eyes widening in horror. "We've been found?" Joints creaking audibly, she pulled herself to her feet and looked about. "That must mean there's a hawthorn nearby…." One look at Verve silenced her.

"There's no one out there." Above them, somewhere way up there, someone was watching. She could feel them. When Verve spoke again, her tone was measured, fearful Olive would think her mad. "I think it was some sort of vision."

Olive blinked. "You saw something?"

"No, but a voice told me to go west, that we were headed in the wrong direction." Verve hoisted the book sack over her shoulder, one foot pointed toward the fire orb, the other toward the west where the sun was setting. "What if we *are* going the wrong way?"

Olive sighed. "It wouldn't hurt us to change direction. We've been wandering south-east for quite a few days now."

Verve smoothed a shaking hand through her hair. "So you think the voice I heard was real?" It was almost too much to hope for.

The woman paused. "Well," said she, "whether it was real is irrelevant, I think. What really matters is if it was benign or malevolent." She scanned the wood surrounding them and turned in a slow, deliberate circle. "And you say you don't hear anyone out there?" Olive did not wait for Verve to repeat herself before lifting her allotment of three canteens from the ground and slinging them over her shoulders.

"There isn't anyone else out there," Verve said, her voice gaining more assurance as she mulled over events. "It must have truly been a vision. But can it be trusted?"

"Trusted or not, we can't keep going on blindly like this. Sometimes, you have to do something before you can discern the director's intent."

Verve nodded. "We'll go west, then, and keep vigilant."

With renewed purpose powering their steps, the pair picked up their camp and moved onward, setting their sights on the sun.

★ ★ ★

They traveled until darkness overcame them and then made camp several miles west of where they had been. Verve kept watch through the night in hopes she would hear the strange voice speak to her again. The hope was in vain. All was quiet.

The next morning, they packed up their meager supplies and began their slow trek westward. Their canteens were now bone-dry, and Verve knew they would have to find a way to replenish them. It was impossible to create drinkable water or edible food from nothing, though Verve knew Fenn could produce water without having any on hand. When she mentioned this to Olive, she had shrugged and said he must wring it out of the air. It made sense, as Fenn had the ability to manipulate water. Verve, on the other hand, wasn't certain if that was one of her gifts or not.

"If you created a spile, perhaps we could drink the sap of trees," Olive said after some time. Her breaths clouded the air in front of them, and her joints creaked like breaking sticks.

Verve took pity on the woman and slowed. "There are maples around here. I suppose they would be acceptable."

Olive licked her chapped lips as if in anticipation. "I'm not going to last much longer, Miss Verity. We need to stop now." She set down the one canteen she was carrying and collapsed with a groan.

"I'll make a spile," said Verve, wondering if she knew enough of the object's structure to do so. Besides, sap flowed slowly from trees; they might just get a few drops, nothing to satisfy. Still, Olive was right when she said they wouldn't make it much farther without satiating their thirst. Verve plucked a blade of grass from the earth, closed her eyes, and tried to picture the spiles she had seen during sugaring season back home. Once the image entered her mind, Verve fed her magic, feelings, and intentions into the grass and produced a hollow pick that broadened to a spout on the other end.

"Are you done?" Olive sat up with the first flicker of excitement in her hollow eyes Verve had seen in days.

"Almost." Verve approached a maple and placed her hand against the bark, which pulsed cold beneath her touch. Like one burned,

Verve pulled away with a yelp and studied the tree in bewilderment.

Olive was on her feet. "Is it a hawthorn?"

"No. It – it's cold."

Olive pushed past Verve and placed her hand on the maple. The ensuing look she gave Verve was one of disgust. "It's just a normal tree. Lack of food and water is feeding your imagination."

Verve clenched her jaw and shoved the spile into the trunk with more force than perhaps was needed. As expected, nothing happened besides a few beads of moisture forming. With a shout of frustration, Verve struck the tree with her fist. At the contact, the tree shuddered, and water gushed forth, soaking Verve's front. Somewhere overhead, Verve thought she heard someone laughing. "Well, that answers my question."

"What?" Olive snapped.

Verve turned to face her, and stared down at her own front with a gaping mouth. "I *can* control water."

Olive wasted no time in reaching the tree, which now only dripped light drops of sap. She rapped her knuckles on the trunk and nodded. "You've tapped this one dry. Try another."

"Right." Verve yanked the spile from the maple and moved to another. She thrust the tool into the new tree and struck the bark with her fist again. As she did, Verve became aware of a twisting sensation in the pit of her stomach, one she recognized from before but had thought to be a hunger pang.

Olive drank greedily from the spile as watery sap rushed out. She did not stop until she was satisfied apparently, and Verve let her, though she was parched herself.

In all, they tapped out two trees, one to quench their thirsts, the other to fill their canteens. Verve slung the straps over her shoulder, picked up her books, and they were on their way once more.

Soon the sun shone brightly overhead, filtering down through the tree cover and making Olive look at the canteens they carried with covetous eyes. The woods began to thin suddenly, and in front of them sat a dusty road.

Verve froze and put out a hand for Olive to stop. She could hear carriage wheels rattling and rolling in the distance, men calling out, and women bickering and bartering.

"Miss Verity?"

"We're close to civilization." At once she ran a hand down her face and pushed her magic down so she wouldn't be conspicuous. One look at her trousers, however, reminded her they were in Etterhea and she would stand out like a sore thumb, magic or not. Women didn't go around wearing men's attire. They just didn't. But she wasn't sure she had the ability to make clothes that fit without help, as Fenn had aided her in the construction of what she wore now.

Olive tamped down her magic as well, her hands shaking. "Where in the world do you reckon we are?"

"Your guess is as good as mine. We're going to stand out, Olive."

Olive shrugged. "Better than us starving to death in the woods. Do you have any coin?"

Verve gave her a look. "You know I don't."

"Hmm. Do you think you could make some?" She reached down and plucked a yellow flower from the ground. "Just turn it into gold and don't worry about making it into a coin."

"Very well." Verve took the flower, closed her eyes, and fed feelings of desperation and hunger into the blossoms as she forced her magic to work. When she opened her eyes, she was holding a lump of silver.

Olive sighed. "Let me see." She snatched the newly made metal from Verve and studied it, nodded, and passed it back to Verve. "That should pass. We will at least be able to purchase food and perhaps a room at an inn."

"Will I be overly conspicuous, though?" Verve placed the lump of silver into her sack of books, which she then swung over her left shoulder.

"Do you mean the fact that you're carrying several heavy canteens or that you look like you've been traveling in the woods for many days?"

Verve paused. "Those are problems bigger than trousers."

"I would say so."

In the end, they abandoned two canteens and cleaned up as best they could with the water from them. Again Verve checked her magic before they emerged from the woods and onto the road.

At first they saw no one close by. The nearest travelers were several miles ahead of them. Focusing her eyes, Verve could make out the town in the distance and the sentries that stood atop the wall surrounding it.

You'll want to find the Library of Aslillian, said the voice from above, startling Verve.

She looked at Olive, but the woman showed no signs of having heard. "Aslillian?" she repeated.

Now Olive gave her a strange look. "Aslillian? We're headed for the Village of Lost Souls, are we? There's a Mortal Gate not twenty miles from here." She swore and spat. "There will be other fae in the city, no doubt. We'll have to keep our heads down. I'm certain there is a prize for bringing you to the Starsides."

"There are more Starsides besides Dacre?"

Olive scowled. "Of course there are. They're scattered far and wide. Don't worry too much about it; none of them are as powerful as his lordship. I imagine you wouldn't have much trouble defeating any that came after you, but we want to avoid causing a scene and attracting more attention to ourselves than we no doubt will."

There was no disagreeing with that. Again Verve slowed her steps to better match the crone's. "We'll purchase food first and then see about finding accommodations." She adjusted the sack she carried.

No. You need to get to the library before it is known you are in the city.

Verve shook her head. The voice was louder than it had been earlier, and it hurt her ears.

"Miss Verity?" Olive frowned in apparent concern.

"You really can't hear that voice?"

Olive squinted at the trees on their left. "Is someone out there, you think?" Her steps slowed as she unstoppered her canteen and pulled deeply from it.

Never mind if the halfling can hear me or not. There are many fae in this town, and your description will be in the minds of some of them.

"What?" said Verve sharply, causing her traveling companion to slosh water down her own front.

Keep your head down and stay out of the market area. You need information about the Lands of the Dead.

"I have a book on the Lands of the Dead."

Olive looked around them, her expression darkening. "Shade and shadow. Are you speaking with a specter or some sprite?"

Verve ignored the woman as the voice was talking again.

That book of yours has been tampered with. You'll see what you are meant to see in it and nothing more.

"How do I know I can trust you, whoever you are?"

A soft gust of wind kicked up dust on the road ahead of them. *You are simply going to have to take a chance, Firstblood. Get the information you need on how to find the Gate of the Dead and leave the city at once.*

This was far from ideal, trusting a disembodied voice only she could hear. Verve shook her head and turned to Olive. "He's telling us to get to the library, gather what information we need on the Lands of the Dead, and then leave." She looked at Olive expectantly, hoping she would have some insight into the matter.

"After we've found food. We're not going to make it very far until we've broken this extended fast." They walked in silence for a few paces as the road sloped upward. Once they had crested the hill, the city came into clearer view, and Olive took another pull from her canteen. "And we'll want to refill these. I can't say sap is my preferred beverage."

"He says to avoid the marketplace."

Olive blinked at Verve. "He wants us to starve, then?"

"Perhaps—"

"No. We are replenishing our wares. If there's a place to do that other than the market, this mysterious voice of yours can provide a better solution."

Verve waited, thinking the voice might offer an answer. When it remained silent, Verve said, "We'll avoid large crowds and wait for a break in the market traffic. Once we have enough food for the next few days, we leave immediately. Does that sound like a good plan?"

Olive stumbled and Verve caught her. "You'll need gloves if you don't want to hurt anyone," said Olive. "I would make a pair quickly, before we reach the gate." She nodded to the looming city wall.

The energy it took to magick gloves on an empty stomach made Verve's head spin, but a quick swig of water helped. They had reached a point in the road where two other paths, one from the right and one from the left, joined together and the way widened considerably. There wasn't much traffic, just a cart up ahead and a few travelers on foot to the right.

At the center of the wall, which stretched north to south for several miles, was a gateway wide enough to admit two horse-drawn wagons side by side. Atop the entryway there was an iron gate, ready to be lowered at a moment's notice, apparently, by a guard sitting on the wall next to a lever.

"Try not to look so much like someone eyeing the exits," whispered Olive.

There are two ways out of this city, said the voice. *This is the easiest way. The other gate is on the opposite side of the city, and it is heavily guarded, as it faces the Mortal Gate.*

"I'll avoid it, then."

That is the quickest route. Travel that way or you will lose a day going around the city. Besides, there are bandits on the roads, and creatures coming to and from Letorheas.

Olive jabbed Verve in the side. "Stop looking at the sky so much. And don't speak to the voice; others will think you are mad."

"Perhaps I am."

The wagon in front of them finally was cleared by a sentry wearing chain mail, and they rolled and rattled through the gate. "Next," said the sentry.

Verve stepped forward with Olive at her side. The man was holding out his hand, and Verve was uncertain for what, until he sighed impatiently and said, "All weapons need to be declared and examined before you are permitted to pass."

"I have no weapons," said Verve, her hold on the pack on her back tightening. "Nor does my companion."

That made the man's eyebrows rise. "Well, that is rather foolish of you both. Do you have any traveling papers or form of identification?"

Verve shot Olive a look, but the woman didn't seem to understand what the man was saying. "We don't have any papers. I didn't know we would need any."

The man shook his head. "No weapons. No papers. You'll simply have to check in with the registrar so his underlings can assess your threat level." He passed Verve two red cloth patches the shape of a half moon. "Until such a time as you reach the registrar, keep these on your persons at all times. They identify you as guests of the city that have yet to be approved. If you lose one, the penalty is a two-hundred-mark fine and two days' imprisonment. Head straight for the registrar and make no stops elsewhere. Next."

"But where is the registrar?" Verve asked, much to the sentry's apparent annoyance.

"Two blocks from here, just this side of the marketplace. Large black building. You can't miss it. Next!"

Verve grabbed Olive by the elbow and pulled her through the gate. A large queue had grown behind them, and there were many impatient mutterings and dirty glances being thrown their way. "Here, take it and don't lose it." She passed Olive one of the half moons and clutched the remaining one in her right fist. "We need to make for the registrar's office." The crone had slowed, and it took all of Verve's patience not to drag her.

"We need to register to enter the city?" Her tone was incredulous, her expression dark. "I've never heard of such a thing in my part of Etterhea." Nonetheless, the old woman tucked the fabric in her fist and leaned heavily on Verve. "Let's hope this registrar isn't a great distance."

"Indeed."

After a matter of steps, they were swallowed up in a crowd of people, though most seemed to have an innate sense to give Verve plenty of room. Twice she nearly became separated from Olive and feared the old woman would be trampled, so she tucked an arm through hers and pulled her closer.

The air stank of sweat and waste, and Verve caught herself before she could retch. A few people gave her strange looks and then headed off in the opposite direction, making signs to ward off evil. But for the most part, no one seemed to pay much mind to the pair, other than to avoid touching them.

"Do you know where we're going?" Olive asked, her nails digging into Verve's arm.

Verve held her back as a cart and horse came screaming from a crossroad, nearly clipping an unwary boy who had stepped off the corner. "The sentry said it should be this side of the marketplace."

"And that is where, exactly?"

"Two blocks," said Verve, her voice taut. She'd always hated crowds, and this hatred was now compounded by the fear that she might accidentally touch one of them and send them into a fit or worse.

Thankfully, the tall, black building came into view soon enough. "Papers! Have your papers ready," shouted a sentry to Verve's left.

Verve pulled Olive along a little more quickly, which unfortunately drew the man's attention.

"Oi, stop there."

For a moment, Verve wondered if she should pretend she hadn't heard. But soon enough, the sentry was there and had grabbed her sleeve, forcing her to stop.

"Did you not hear me?"

Verve looked to Olive. "I—"

"Do you have any identification on your persons?"

Swallowing hard, Verve held out her gloved hand and revealed the red half moon. "No. But I was told—"

"Did he not tell you to head straight for the registrar's office?" The sentry looked at her more closely then, and his eyes widened considerably.

"That's where we are going, sir," said Verve.

The man scowled and snatched the half moon from Verve's palm. "I don't want any trouble in my city."

Verve nodded and made what she hoped was a sympathetic face. "Of course."

He studied Verve a moment more, and then pocketed the half moon with a sneer. "No good can come of your being here. Leave as quickly as you are able, scum."

Olive's grip tightened on Verve's arm, as though she were afraid Verve would do something rash. "What did he say?"

"Hey," said Verve as the sentry stalked away. "Hey! I need that badge."

But the man was swallowed up in the crowd, leaving Verve cursing in his wake. "Blast. I needed that badge or face a huge fine and prison." She turned to Olive, who not so discreetly moved her own badge behind her back.

"Sorry. I've had my share of prison, thanks."

Verve gripped the woman firmly by the elbow and steered her into an alley, away from the ebb and flow of the crowd. "Let me try to copy it." She looked around for grass or straw, something insubstantial she could use for transformation. It was all dirt and stone.

"That's not going to work so well," said Olive, nodding at the pebble Verve had scooped into her palm.

"Keep watch. I can't be seen doing this."

Olive grumbled something about 'starving' and 'nosy onlookers', but turned to face the mouth of the alley so Verve could get to work. "Pebbles and rocks have too much weight to them. You won't be able to do more than change its colors, I'd wager."

"You're not helping." Verve closed her eyes and fed magic into the rock, which grew warm in the palm of her hand. When she looked again, the rock had shrunk and done nothing else. With a curse she tossed the pebble onto the ground and then nudged Olive back into the open. She could try to make one from nothing, but that wasn't a reliable method. "We'll just have to be careful to avoid scrutiny until I find something I can transform."

"It might not be duplicable."

Verve looked up sharply from the road. "How do you mean?"

"It feels very...coarse and – my, I think there might be some Glamour in it. Glamour is very specific to its creator and not possible to copy." Her grip on the badge tightened. "Should we leave the city at once?"

"Watch where you're standing," said a man wearing a turban. He took one look at Verve and his face paled. "Sorry." And he hurried away.

Verve weighed Olive's words and frowned. "Why would someone running the city have badges with Glamour in them? This place is full of mortals."

Olive shrugged. "We're so close to a Mortal Gate, no doubt there are some fae in leadership here. Perhaps it would be wise of us to avoid the registrar and any city officials, for that matter." It was her turn to tug Verve out of the way of passersby. She looked at Verve expectantly. "The library?"

"The library. Then we leave."

★ ★ ★

They allowed themselves to be swallowed up in the crowd again, not wishing to stand out to the officials or any busybody who might turn them in. Verve instructed Olive to make certain she didn't walk into anyone, wishing to use through-sight to locate the building they were looking for. That did not go well. There were so many sights, so many sounds, all of them whirling around Verve, that her senses at once became overwhelmed and she had to return her sight to normal.

"Any help would be appreciated," Verve said, her eyes on the sky. If the voice was able to understand her over the din, she wasn't sure. As it was, she heard nothing in response.

After they walked for half an hour in the hottest part of the day, the crowds began to thin a little. Olive moaned. "We need to head to the market to get food. My senses are not so strong, and I can still hear your stomach rumbling." The tug she gave Verve was weak, and Verve was able to resist it.

"Not an hour ago you asked if we should leave the city for fear of being caught."

Olive shook her head and straightened. "If we can't go to the marketplace, then.... There, he has bread." Her pace quickened as Verve noted whom she was pursuing: a lanky man with a long loaf of bread tucked under his arm. "I'll keep watch and you convince him to hand it over."

"It's too dangerous. I can't use you-know-what in the open like this." But Verve found herself matching Olive's strides and did not stop her when she tapped the man on the shoulder. When he turned, he did not seem particularly disturbed to see the pair, though he wore a slight frown.

"What do you want?" he asked.

Verve swallowed. "Would you mind very much giving us a hunk of your bread? We haven't had a meal in a while."

His eyes narrowed. "Then go to the market and buy something. I'm busy." The man started to leave, and Olive gestured wildly at Verve.

After a moment's hesitation, Verve ran after the man. "Please, sir. We'll pay you for the loaf."

The man waved her away as though she were some pesky fly. "Do I need to summon the town guard?"

She took his sleeve and stopped him. "Please. We're desperate."

"Unhand me, you filthy rat." His hand flew out and struck Verve across the face. At the contact, he fell over, writhing on the ground.

Olive snatched the loaf from him and ran as a few passersby came to a stop to stare at the spectacle of the man foaming at the mouth. This left Verve no choice but to run after her, leaving the poor soul to his fate.

Verve did not stop running, her eyes fixed on Olive, who had just dived into another alley. When she was certain no one had pursued them, Verve folded her arms across her chest and glared. "Well, this is a mess."

Olive looked over her shoulder at Verve and growled. "You didn't need to go drawing everyone's attention." She met Verve's stern gaze and took a step back.

"Let's hope no one got a good look at either of us." Verve held out a hand and Olive tore the loaf in two with apparent reluctance and passed over one half.

The pair devoured the bread in uncomfortable silence until Olive said, "A woman was staring at you rather intently. I tried blocking you from her view, but it seemed she recognized you."

"Blast," said Verve after swallowing the remains of her loaf half. Her stomach twisted. "Why didn't you say something?" They moved farther into the alley when loud voices drew near.

Olive pulled her down another alley to the left and they kept moving. "Can you shape-change?" she asked abruptly.

"I don't know. I've never tried."

That seemed to frustrate Olive, but her tone remained patient. "His lordship can change forms. It stands to reason he passed the ability on to you." They made a quick turn and then another, soon spilling out onto a back road with few occupants.

There were several men who stared at them with open curiosity and perhaps a touch of suspicion but quickly returned to their business and didn't give the pair another glance. Thankfully, there were no lawmen in sight.

Someone sighed. *The library is on the west side of the city, near the other exit. You'll need to make haste if you wish to reach it before closing,* said the voice.

"We need to move more quickly," Verve murmured to Olive, taking her arm in her own again.

"The voice?"

Verve gave her a curt nod. "Why he didn't speak sooner is beyond me."

I've been preoccupied with some business. I can't stand watch all the time, you know.

"No need to get snippy," said Verve, her tone snippy as well. "I don't even know who you are and if I can really tr—"

Patrolmen. Go into that shop.

Verve pulled Olive into the store on the right, bumping up against a display of ceramic pots. "Sorry," she said to the shopkeeper, who gave them a concerned look.

After a moment, the man swore. "Two *feeën* in my shop? And one a mighty? Bless the Gate, I never thought I'd live to see this."

"Is there a back way out of here?" asked Verve, looking around desperately as she heard voices outside spouting her description.

The shopkeeper, a squat little man with brown hair and a scraggly beard, practically beamed at them. "Careful where you go, *Vuur Koningin*. Bad men are everywhere." He bowed deeply and motioned to a table. "Care for tea? Chao-Scholz is the best of tea merchants in the western seas. You will drink only the finest here. Please, sit." He pulled out a chair and waited as Olive tugged on Verve's arm.

Verve's blood had run cold and she stared at the man in stunned silence for a long moment. "He just called me… *Vuur Koningin.*"

When she said the words, the man's smile widened. "I know the name in seven languages." He pulled down the neck of his shirt and showed a tattoo on his collarbone: a single flaming teardrop. "Given to me by my da; it's the mark of the Expectant Enlightened. You care for tea, my queen?" He lifted a silver teapot from the table in front of him and gestured to it.

Verve shook the confusion out of her head and stepped forward. "Is there a back exit?"

The man set the pot down and motioned for them to follow

him. "No back exit, but there is a back room. Are you in trouble? Saints, but you must be careful here, Majesty." A line had formed between his eyes and his smile faltered. There were voices outside the shop's door, and the shopkeeper motioned for Verve and Olive to follow him.

"Why does he think you're the Fire Queen?" Olive demanded in a whisper as she and Verve hastened after the man. "I speak his language, you know."

"Sorry, Your Majesty and friend. 'Tis a small room, but you'll be safe in here." He opened the door to the back room, a broom cupboard, and all but shoved them inside and closed the door in their faces.

They had hidden not a moment too soon. Verve heard the front door open to admit two people, both with mortal heartbeats.

"Welcome, friends," said the shopkeeper. "Would you like tea? Chao-Scholz is the best of tea merchants in the western seas. You will drink only the finest here."

Verve used through-sight to observe what was happening in the shop. Two men dressed in red tunics and black trousers stood in the entryway, their expressions stern and alert.

The taller one, a balding man perhaps in his fifties, said to the shopkeeper, "We're looking for a woman who's just been sighted in the city today." He held up a piece of paper. "She was seen fleeing in this general direction not twenty minutes ago."

The shopkeeper took the paper from the other man and held it up to the light. "Oh. Criminal?"

The second man shifted his weight, his hand resting on the pommel of the sword at his side. "Something like that. Have you seen her?"

"I might have done." He lowered his voice, and Verve stiffened. "Chao-Scholz was smoking out front before you came. Saw someone like that and an old woman run past."

Both men looked at each other. "Her description has been circulating for a month now. Surely you were going to report this incident to the Trusted."

It was Olive's turn to go rigid.

"Oh, yes. But Chao-Scholz cannot leave the shop unattended for long and was going to file the report after closing." He handed the paper back to the balding man.

"What direction did they go?"

The shopkeeper moved toward the door and opened it. "That way." He pointed in the direction from which Verve and Olive had come.

"You're certain?"

"Yes, Chao is certain. The old one was limping so you shouldn't have trouble catching them." He stepped back and waited as the two men looked at each other.

"Should we summon him, do you think?" asked the smaller of the men.

The one with a balding head made a face. "Not until we've apprehended her or have her cornered by enough Trusted." His shoulders heaved and he turned to Chao-Scholz. "If you see or hear anything more, contact us immediately."

"Oh, yes. Chao will. Thank you."

"This woman is wanted for killing some foreign dignitary. It's of the utmost importance she is brought in alive for questioning. Are you certain she went east?"

Chao-Scholz nodded. "We are certain."

The shorter man turned. "*We*?"

Olive closed her eyes, her hand gripping Verve's arm tightly.

"Chao and his sister," said the shopkeeper, a slight quaver to his voice. "Laine's out of the city now. Should be home any day now with fresh teas for customers. Chao's other sister is the one who saw the pair. Keye just ran home. But I can fetch her, should you need confirmation."

Verve did not like the look that passed between the two men. If she didn't know better, she would say Olive was praying silently next to her.

"Perhaps we should risk a bit of our acquisition to explore the building," said the balding man.

"Why?" said the other. "I don't smell any residual bursts. Using acquired magic here will alert fae for several blocks."

Chao-Schulz gestured to the door. "Shop is for paying customers only. Either customers place orders or leave. Please, come or go. You are letting in flies."

There was another moment's hesitation on the men's part, but they at once sprang into action when there was a shout outside the door and an almighty crash. They both ran from the shop, knocking the shopkeeper over in the process.

"Filthy so-called 'Trusted'." Chao-Schulz pulled himself to his feet, spat at the men's departing backs, and shut and locked the door behind them. His heart was racing and he stood in silence for another minute before saying, "You can come out, but no using magic. Chao can't promise your safety if you do."

Olive was first in getting to her feet, using Verve to help herself rise. She hesitated a moment, opened the closet door, and looked around the locked and shuttered shop. "It's safe, miss." With a nod, she stepped out of Verve's way and prowled toward the door.

"We can't leave yet," said Verve wearily. She closed her eyes, and her sight returned to normal. "There are two men watching this shop right now, and I imagine it's not because of the tea served here. No offense...?"

"Chao," he said happily. "And no offense taken."

Verve glowered at Olive. "What are the 'Trusted'? And how did those humans know about residual bursts?"

"Careful," said Olive from the corner of her mouth. She nodded at Chao, who was smiling again.

"He knows what we are, Olive." Verve scrutinized Chao, who flashed his teeth even as he blushed. "And he didn't turn us over to those men."

"The Trusted," said Chao. "Those men were from the Trusted."

Olive sighed and sat down with some force in one of the nearest chairs. "I need a drink."

"Chao gets you tea!" Before Olive or Verve could stop him, the apparently unflappable man disappeared into the kitchen and could be heard striking a match and clattering pots and pans in his wake.

"Well?" Verve demanded.

Olive rested her head in her hands, propped her elbows on the table. "His lordsh— *Dacre* always talked about forming his own army of middlings, should things go awry with his plans."

Verve jumped when Chao popped his head through the kitchen doorway and said, "Who wants honey cakes?" When neither woman responded, he disappeared again and knocked what sounded like a whole stack of iron pans onto the floor.

"Middlings have been going missing in Etterhea." Verve sat across from Olive, her heart sinking. "Fenn was right. This is all connected."

"You should have told me about the middlings," Olive said. "This makes things even more urgent."

Temper flaring, Verve tucked her hands under her bottom so she wouldn't shoot sparks at the crone. "This isn't the time to deal out blame. Why is Dacre building an army and why with middlings?"

The look Olive gave her was incredulous. "Middlings are the only mortals who have a one hundred per cent success rate traveling through gateways. And besides." She leaned back in her chair and met Verve's stare with her own. "They're the only mortals upon whom power can be bestowed."

Fear stirred in Verve's stomach, making her want to vomit. "So he's been transforming other middlings?" The room spun as Verve remembered the horrible sensation of water and Dacre's magical blood filling her lungs. He had held her under, had tried the procedure several times before Fenn had saved her.

"No. Not a full transformation." Olive looked at Verve with pity in her eyes. "Just what you did for me: a single drop of magical blood down their throat. It would give them some of his magic, which he would still be able to control." She sat forward and clasped her hands in front of her on the table. "He's going to use them to come for you or ferret you out. It was his contingency plan." After making that dreadful statement, she leapt to her feet in a startled declaration as Chao burst out of the kitchen with a plate of scrumptious-looking frosted cakes.

"Water is heating for tea," said Chao, obviously oblivious to the tension in the room. He set the plate between them and stepped back and frowned. "You need more sustenance? Yes? Chao will return soon with more food."

Neither woman said anything as the strange man disappeared back into the kitchen. When they were alone once more, Olive sat and Verve lowered her voice to a whisper as her stomach began to clench.

"How do you know this? Olive, have you really been in that prison all this time?" She thought of reaching out, of trying to discern the woman's motives with whatever extra sense she had, but she stopped herself. Any active use of magic could lead someone right to them, if some of the Trusted truly had the ability to smell residual bursts.

Olive frowned. "Of course I have. But this was decided upon long before you were dragged from your realm."

Verve sat forward, waiting. When Olive hesitated, Verve slammed her hand down on the table, causing her to flinch. "We don't have time for this. You need to tell me everything you've been holding back, and don't say you haven't been hiding things, because—" she gestured toward the door the Trusted had come in, "—that makes it obvious you have."

Chao chose that moment to enter the room once more and set down a veritable feast in front of them: cold chicken and tongue, bread rolls, carrots mixed with snow peas and tossed in something that smelled like vinegar, and some unidentifiable dish that was clear and also gelatinous. After he filled the table to near overflowing, he gestured at the feast and bellowed, "Eat. Tea needs longer."

"Thank you, but we can't pay for this," said Verve.

But the man bowed away from the table and returned to the kitchen without another word.

Verve turned back to Olive. "Well?"

Trembling with some barely suppressed emotion, the crone nodded and stared at a spot over Verve's shoulder. "Do you really think you were the first Lord Dacre Starside believed to be the Fire

Queen?" Her words were bitter, venomous, and it was Verve's turn to recoil slightly.

"I know I wasn't. There were two or three other attempts—"

Olive's hiss silenced Verve. "Oh, you were the first attempt, but before you, there were two other young women from Etterhea his lordship believed fulfilled the conditions of the prophecies. One died shortly after arriving in Letorheas. The other...well, I think you can guess who the other middling was." She held up a hand to waylay Verve's words. "He said he loved me and was going to make me his forever. Young, foolish, and in love myself, I thought he knew what was best and was going to go along with whatever he wanted. Until I overheard him being advised to end me, that I was not the one prophesied." Olive sniffed angrily. "So, I ran away. He hunted me for days, all the way to the nearest Mortal Gate. By the time he found me, I was half-dead. Pity took over and he fed to me a drop of his power, reviving me and binding me to him." She shrugged and stared at the food, her eyes glassy. "He looked after me for a while, kept me close and allowed me to think I was still special, and I tried to be grateful. But when I started getting old and gray, his attention turned elsewhere and it became harder and harder not to grow bitter." Olive sighed. "From the time he started forgetting about me to the time your arrival seemed imminent, sixty years had passed."

Verve processed this information quietly, cringing every time Chao made an excited exclamation to himself in the kitchen. At length, she broke the silence. "But if you were forgotten, how did you know about the Trusted and his plans for them?"

"You must understand, Miss Verity, that forgotten people are invisible people." She smiled ruefully. "I could go almost anywhere on the estate, do almost anything – except leave – without so much as a batting of anyone's eye. It was forgotten by those important to Dacre that I might have conflicting interests, and they spoke openly in places I could hear. It would seem the idea of my escaping or communicating with a soul outside of the household didn't occur to those arrogant fools. I didn't know about the Trusted until a glimpse of the Cunning Blade had been sighted. Some mortals stumbled into Letorheas, found the blade, and ran off with it. Anyway, I overheard Dacre's advisors discussing his plans to bring a mortal to Letorheas, one that supposedly had information about the blade's whereabouts. That might have been the intent, or it might have been a ruse, but one thing quickly became clear: he had studied the prophecies and knew he would need more than his own might to control you."

The kitchen door swung open and Chao strode out, a cup on a saucer in each hand. When he looked at the table, his smile faded. "Queen and her company should eat." He set a cup in front of each of them and pulled up a chair and sat sideways on it.

Verve blinked away her confusion and stared at the sliver of light leaking beneath the shop's door. Perhaps it was her imagination, but it seemed to have dimmed considerably from when they had first hurried inside. "What time is it?" She nodded to Olive, hoping she could convey to the woman that they would discuss her history and knowledge more once they were alone again.

"It is past the midday hour. Chao wonders why it is so dark." Chao got to his feet and moved toward the shop's one window, which had been shuttered the entire time Verve and Olive had been there. Before either could warn him, the man pulled back an inch of the fabric and peered out. "Ah. Storm is coming." To Verve's relief, he covered the window once more. "Strange. Bad weather not in Chao's forecast."

"You predict the weather here?" Olive asked incredulously.

"Oh, yes. Chao is an excellent forecaster." He returned to the table and gestured once more at the food. "An excellent forecaster who will be very sad if you let good food go to waste, yes?"

To placate the man and her now-growling stomach, Verve picked up a chunk of dark chicken meat with her bare hands – as there was no serving utensil – and tore into it. "Aren't you afraid of being hanged? Burned at the stake? Disemboweled?" Perhaps she oughtn't be so forceful and blunt, but she couldn't bring herself to mince words just then.

Chao laughed heartily but stopped once he saw she wasn't joking. "It is science. Nothing is wrong with science. Or magic," he added. He smiled when Olive picked up a roll and bit into it. "Good, yes?"

Lost in thought, Verve didn't answer but continued eating. She paused as she reached for a roll and her heart took off at a sprint. "How accurate would you say your weather forecasts are, Chao?"

A line formed between the man's eyes but soon smoothed out as he grinned. "Chao's forecasts? Oh, Chao predicted the Storm of Fish ten years ago. You see, great swirling winds drew fish from the canal and – BAM!" He slammed his fist on the table, causing both she-fae to jump. "Fish raining from the heavens. It was an amazing sight, and Chao predicted it. Well, not the fish, but the strength of the storm." He turned a quizzical eye on Verve.

"Olive, can weather-makers control weather in Etterhea?"

The old woman did not seem pleased by Verve's use of fae words in front of the mortal shopkeeper but did not comment on it. Instead, she said, "The very powerful ones can, yes. But, goodness, you don't think someone would be trying to control the weather over the city?"

Verve stood, wiping her hands on her torn and already-soiled trousers. "I don't know."

"What purpose would it serve?"

Thunder rattled the shop and violet-colored lightning flickered beyond the dark curtains. The small hairs on Verve's arms stood on end, and a reflexive growl tore itself from her throat. "It's a signal," she said without knowing how she knew. Her stomach twisted and her palms grew slick. "Dacre's being summoned."

CHAPTER ELEVEN

Rain and wind battered against the windows as the sky darkened further still. The air smelled of cinnamon and ozone. A chill filled the room, and Chao shivered.

"Chao better light more lamps. Soon it will be too dark to see hands in front of faces." He leapt to his feet just as one of the candles near the window guttered out from a draft.

"Wait a moment," said Olive. "Darkness would make a good cover. Miss Verity?"

Verve's breaths were short and shallow, and she was having trouble getting enough air. "We have to get out of here. He's coming, Olive." At the words, she convulsed and the room went black for a moment. When she returned to her senses, there were gray spots on the outskirts of her vision and she was on the floor with a worried Chao standing over her.

"My queen, you must lie down," said the shopkeeper.

"She's lying down now," snapped Olive, pushing the man aside. "And she's done enough of it. Collect yourself, Miss Verity, and think. Just because there's a Mortal Gate nearby, it doesn't mean his lordship is minutes away. Why, he could be in any part of Letorheas or Etterhea. Don't let fear cloud your thoughts."

Verve gave her a terse nod and pushed herself to a kneeling position. Everything spun around her and her breaths were still ragged, but she fought the rising hysteria and said, "If we're going to make a move for the library, we should do so soon. Dacre might know where we're headed, and once he gets here, your magic isn't strong enough to fight him, and mine doesn't work against him." Using the table and chair for support, she got the rest of the way to her feet.

"Oh, the Library of Aslillian?" Chao asked. His smile had vanished since Verve's collapse. "That closes during storms." When Verve gave him a questioning look, he shrugged and said, "Texts don't like getting wet."

"We could break in," Verve mused. "I know how to pick a lock."

Olive nodded, her eyes distant as though the problem were a speck on the wall. "And, worse comes to worst, you could use magic to get us in."

Now Chao seemed agitated, pacing and shaking his head as he murmured to himself. "Dangerous. Too dangerous." He stopped and held up a hand as if the two she-fae were about to rush out of his shop that moment.

"We need to get into the library, Mr. Chao-What's-Your-Name, and your tiny mortal self isn't going to waylay us," said Olive.

The funny man laughed once, a nervous sound, and his grin returned. "The library is guarded not just by regular guards. There are many high fae who take protecting knowledge very serious. Very serious indeed. And you will be recognized, *Vuur Koningin*. Your description? All over the city." He gestured around them widely to emphasize his point.

That did not bode well. Verve knew she was powerful, but could she successfully fight off several high fae attacks? She could best Fenn when she wasn't worrying about hurting him, but if Dacre joined the fight, Verve wasn't as sure as to what the outcome might be. "We need that information. I need to reach the Lands of the Dead."

Chao whistled. "That does not sound like a nice place."

Olive's brow furrowed and she folded her arms across her chest. "You could try shape-shifting." She sounded doubtful.

"If I use magic and someone smells the residual burst...."

"What other options do we have? If your voice guide is correct, the information you need is there."

Verve threw up her hands in frustration, and her fingertips flickered with fire, filling the room with the odor of burned sugar. Hastily she put the blaze out and looked at Olive, eyes wide.

"Well, now we certainly have to leave." Olive turned to Chao and gestured to the food. "Do you have anything we might pack the rest of this in? Goodness knows when we'll next be able to get another decent meal."

Verve was already moving toward the door with her bag of books. "There's no time. If anyone caught a whiff of my magic, they'll be here any minute now." Again lightning flickered behind the curtain, and the thunder answered in a resounding boom.

"You said men were watching the shop," Olive reminded her and then turned to Chao. "Is there a window in the kitchen we could climb through?"

Chao smiled. "Not in the kitchen, no. But there is the smugglers' tunnel." He ran into the kitchen and came out a minute later with a length of oilskin. "Chao just pack up food for you and then show you the tunnel."

Practically vibrating with anxiety, Verve helped him wrap up the remainder of their meal – what would travel well – and then stuffed it on top of the books in her bag. "Why didn't you mention the tunnel earlier?" It was hard to keep the irritation out of her voice so she didn't even try.

"Oh, that is easy. Chao was sworn on penalty of death never to tell the fae about it," he said cheerfully. "Follow and I will show you, yes?"

Olive shook her head. "Fool," she said, but she sounded mildly impressed.

They followed Chao through the kitchen, skirting around the odd pot or pan that had fallen in their path, and to a closed door, for which Chao produced a key. The shopkeeper fit the key in the door's lock and turned it once left, then right, then left again. He grinned sheepishly. "Guess I left it unlocked."

Verve stepped after Chao into what appeared to be a small accounting room. There was a desk against the left wall, piled high with books and stacks of paper. The air was musty, rife with the odor of mildew. A wave of nausea swept over her as she spied the black mold growing on the ceiling.

"Please, we must be careful," said Chao, reaching past the women to close the door. "You need map for underground, yes? Chao will get you one. Just – burn when you're done. Or if you get caught." He moved toward the stacks of paper and made a gesture to his ear, to Verve, and then to the door, indicating she should listen for trouble.

She nodded and moved to the door, throwing the door's bolt. "And the underground leads to the library?"

"Oh, yes. Every public and government building has tunnel access. Ah, hold these," said Chao to Olive.

Olive accepted a stack of boxes with a grunt. "You say these are smugglers' tunnels." She frowned at the man. "What exactly might you be smuggling?"

Chao was rapping his knuckles on different places on the back wall, whence he had moved the boxes now in Olive's arms. He paused in his work, nodded, and turned to face the fae. "To smuggle ourselves, of course. Now, can one of you move the desk?"

"Smuggle yourselves?" asked Olive, handing the boxes to Verve. "Who exactly might you need hiding from?" After rolling up her sleeves, the crone gave the desk a shove and managed to push it back up against the far wall.

"The fae," said Chao. "You can set those boxes down in front of the door. Oh, and stand back, yes?" With that said, he went back to tapping on the wall.

Verve frowned as she set the boxes in front of the door. The storm without was still raging, and she could hear the rain beating against the walls and the thunder rumbling in the near distance. She tried to shut the noises out as she turned to Chao and asked, "Why would you need to escape the fae?"

The look Chao gave her was serious. "Middle children each have access to this tunnel and pass down the maps and instructions to their middle children. Enough of us have been taken over the years through the Mortal Gate. None of us have come back." He shrugged. "Let Chao try one more thing…."

It was as though a cold hand had grasped Verve's heart. "So – fae taking middlings isn't anything new?" She turned to Olive for confirmation.

"Most fae think humans are barely living, sentient beings. Their views have improved over the years, but yes, there are no laws against snatching the occasional middling from Etterhea." Olive nodded to Chao, who had continued his series of taps on the wall.

With a soft click, the room vibrated and a large square trapdoor opened in the floor. "Aha!" Chao rubbed his hands together, approached his desk, and pushed one of the decorative flowers that had been carved into its front. The flower disappeared farther into the desk, and a panel shot out partially from a leg.

Olive swore. "What in the world...?"

Chao grinned as he removed the panel and pulled out a rolled piece of paper, which he handed to Verve. "Magic." He winked. "And there is your map."

The paper looked like new, as if it had only been made yesterday. Verve frowned as she unfurled it. "When was this made?" *And how accurate can it be?*

"Chao redraws it every year to better keep it in memory. No one is supposed to keep a physical copy of the map, so if it were to fall into the wrong hands...." He drew a line across his throat with his finger as his face contorted in mock agony.

Verve studied the map, committing its details to memory. Once she was certain she had taken in every detail, she rolled it up and returned it to Chao. "If we can't risk magic, we'll need a light source." She shifted her weight to her right foot as Chao reached for the metal kerosene lamp on a side table. They really were asking a lot of this man.

"Last Chao was in the tunnels, there were still spun lights."

"Spun lights?" Olive prompted.

The shopkeeper's eyebrows rose. "Eternal lights. Spun from fairy magic, you know. Well, not ones humans made, obviously. Some of us – a long time ago, mind, so don't be angry with Chao

– stole eternal lights from the fae outpost guarding the entrance to Faerie." He pulled a cigarette lighter from the side table's drawer and went to work trimming the lamp's wick, checking the amount of kerosene the base held. Next he lit it and replaced the vented glass lid.

"The entrance to Letorheas is guarded," Verve groaned, resting her head in her hand. "That complicates things."

Olive accepted the lamp from Chao and held out her hand until he passed her the lighter as well. "Of course the entrance is guarded. That's why we'll need to find a hawthorn instead." She nodded at the trapdoor. "I'll go first and make certain the way is clear." And then she was climbing down, clutching the lantern in one hand and holding on to thin, metal rungs with the other as she went.

Verve licked her lips, which were suddenly dry. "And the tunnel doesn't lead to Letor— I mean, it doesn't lead to Faerie?" Though she knew from the map that it didn't, the slow shake of Chao's head still made her spirits sink into the floor.

"And you'll want to leave the library the same way you came in. And if Chao may suggest? Wait for daylight and then emerge through Dinao's Bakery on the north side of town. Tell Din that Chao vouches for you, and all should be well, yes?"

"I don't know how I can thank you enough, Chao."

The shopkeeper blushed. "Chao's pleasure. Please, don't mention it." He gestured to the hole in the floor, whence came the sounds of sloshing water and Olive's mutterings. Chao reached out a hand to help Verve, who accepted.

"I hope you stay safe." And with that said, she adjusted the sack on her back and began her descent into the network of tunnels below. The light down here was dimmer and an unnatural blue. When she reached the bottom, the water came up to her knees, and before she could wave at the shopkeeper, the trapdoor shut, sealing them down there. Verve took a few deep breaths, trying to compose herself.

"This is an awful mess," said Olive. To illustrate her point, she kicked up a spray of water, which struck Verve in the face.

The water was ice-cold and stank of human waste. Verve glared at Olive and moved toward her. "We should get going." *Before the tunnels flood.* She cringed at the thought and gestured for the lamp, which Olive handed over with apparent reluctance. "Can you carry the books?"

Olive shook her head. "You know I'm not strong enough. But if you were to give me more power...." She left the thought unfinished, and Verve hesitated.

After a moment she sighed and moved around Olive so she, Verve, was leading the way down the narrow, pipelike stretch of tunnel going west. Though she trusted Olive for the most part, giving her more power than she already had did not sound like a wise idea at the moment.

They waded through the water as quickly as Olive was able, which might have been considered a brisk walk for a human but was like a crawl to Verve. Twice the crone stumbled and grabbed on to Verve to stop herself from falling, nearly dragging Verve down with her in the process.

"Hold on to the wall," said Verve.

"It'll be a wonder if we don't come out of here with some disease or other. Goodness, the *smell.*"

Verve was trying not to think about the smell, breathing mostly through her mouth.

After walking for a mile, they came upon a juncture where the tunnel split into three different parts. Down the middle one, the one they needed to take, the way was dark, the fae lighting either having failed or not been installed there in the first place. Verve stretched out the lantern in front of her, took a fortifying breath, and continued on ahead.

The going did not get easier, and the water was slowly rising. Olive walked with one hand on the left wall to support herself, Verve noted as she looked over her shoulder for a moment. Water dripped from the ceiling of the tunnels, fizzing and hissing as it made contact with the lantern's glass encasement. The light stuttered and went out entirely. "Blast." They had been plunged into complete darkness.

Olive grabbed on to Verve's shoulder and gasped. "We must relight the lamp." There was the sound of her fumbling for the lighter and then a distinct *ploink* as it fell into the water, which was now up past their knees.

Not willing to risk any magic just yet, Verve handed the lantern back to Olive and said, "We'll have to use our other senses to get us out of here. Hold on to that; we might be able to find a way to relight it at the library."

The crone whimpered. "As you say."

"Keep your hand on my shoulder so we don't become separated." Verve focused her eyes and used through-sight, hoping to catch a glimpse of a light source ahead. Unfortunately, the lights had all died within the next mile going straight. At the next crossroads, one that broke into two paths, the lights were lit on the path to the right. But the path to the left, the one they needed to take, was dim for a-ways. Cursing, Verve closed her eyes and returned her sight to normal. She relayed what she had learned to Olive.

"Let's keep moving," said Olive. "I don't want to be down here when this place is filled to the brim."

Verve gritted her teeth and felt her way with her free hand as she continued to walk.

They went on like this for twenty minutes, stopping briefly every so often to let Olive rest. Finally, the water now to their thighs, they reached the next crossroads and took the path they needed to, thankful for the all-too-brief encounter with light. The next juncture, Verve noted after using through-sight, was perhaps a mile off. And soon enough, her eyes could pick up dim light in the distance, and she quickened her steps.

"There sure aren't many branches," said Olive, her teeth chattering audibly.

Verve nodded, though she knew the woman couldn't see it.

"That's probably because there are only so many entrances. Too many and you risk being discovered."

Olive coughed. "And we just so happened to come across one of the few?" Her tone was dark with suggestion.

"The voice did tell me to go into that shop. Perhaps he knew it was a safe place?"

"About the voice," said Olive. "What do you think it is? And, more importantly, why does it want us to find the Lands of the Dead?"

Though it had been troubling her as well, Verve simply kept walking and said, "Maybe it just wants to keep me safe."

"Safe for what, though? No one helps another without having some purpose in mind for them."

Verve left that statement alone, and they moved forward in silence. At long last, pinpricks of light shone in the near distance, and Verve's steps quickened, earning a groan from Olive. "We take a right here," said Verve after a moment of recollection. "There then should be another crossroads in less than half a mile, from where we should soon come to the entrance to the library." *And I don't think it'll be a moment too soon.* Indeed, the water was up to her hips, and she knew the storm aboveground was still raging on.

There was a great gurgling noise, and Olive yelped. "There's something alive down here."

"Then let's put more haste in our steps," said Verve, who had already spied multiple bloated rat bodies floating around.

Again there was a great burbling sound, followed by a distant groan, like rusty hinges opening, followed by a *ploink.* Verve put her finger to her lips as Olive opened her mouth to say something else. "Someone else is down here," Verve whispered. Indeed, she now heard the distant splashing of water and two, thankfully human, heartbeats and breaths. That didn't mean they weren't among Dacre's Trusted, however. "Set the lantern going down the left path. Maybe whoever's down here will think we've gone that direction instead. Quickly!"

Olive did as Verve asked and they pushed on as quickly and as silently as they could through the water.

Their pursuers were not trying to be quiet now as they splashed through the tunnels. Verve tried not to let panic get the better of her. Whoever was behind them might be smuggling something or running an errand. *In these conditions? That's not very likely.* The thought nearly took Verve's breath away, and she had to remind herself she was not powerless any longer, that she had a great deal of magic she could wield if she were in danger. That calmed her somewhat, but the fingers of her hand not holding the book sack sparked, filling the tunnels with the aroma of burned sugar.

"Control yourself," Olive murmured and squeezed Verve's shoulder, though not in an affectionate or reassuring manner. Verve could smell and see the crone's terror, though in her current state, it was not appetizing. If anything, it made her feel nauseated.

They reached the next juncture, took a left, and were met with a wall and a rusted metal ladder. Verve paused and listened, and was relieved to hear only one heartbeat following them now. One pursuer would be easier to deal with in case of a fight.

"What are you waiting for? Climb the ruddy ladder or get out of the way so I can."

Verve held up her hand, listening for sounds above them, though she wanted nothing more than to claw her way out of that hellhole there and then; the water was waist-high at the moment, and still rising. Hearing nothing overhead, she nodded and hurried up the rungs. On the ceiling of the tunnel, she found the outline of a square hole roughly the size of the one back at Chao's shop. Verve squinted in the dimness but still couldn't find a lever or knob that would open the door, so she began doing what Chao had: knocking on random parts of the tunnel wall.

Below her, Olive was growing more and more upset by the second. "You're making far too much noise. You're going to bring whoever's down here right to us in a moment."

"Is there a lever or something out of the ordinary down there?" Verve asked through her teeth. No matter where she rapped, nothing happened to the trapdoor.

Olive began running her hands over the walls, water lapping up against her waist. Their pursuer had grown silent, but for the quick beating of their heart. "There's nothing here," she said.

"Did you check the ground?"

"How am I supposed to see anything on the ground? It's as dark as sin down there. I—"

There was a shrill whirring sound as a stream of red shot toward them, striking the wall by Olive's head. The air smelled of bitter coffee, and Verve knew the Trusted had found them. There was a moment's reprieve before another blast of magic flew at them, heading straight for Olive, who threw a shield up just in time.

The next bolt of fire nipped at Verve's heels, scorching through her shoe right down to her skin. Exasperated but unhurt, she released her hold on the ladder and let herself plummet briefly, and then pulled up so she was hovering with just her feet in the water.

Another blast flew at them and another, ricocheting off Olive's shield, which was losing vibrancy. "Stop him!" Olive cried. "What are you waiting for?"

Verve looked at the man in the shadows, hesitated a split second and threw up a more powerful shield between him and them. "I don't want to hurt you," she said. "I know you've been taken from your home, most likely against your will. Can we just talk for a minute?"

Olive groaned. "Miss Verity, the water's rising still. End this."

Their assailant's head cocked to the side and he made eye contact with Verve. And that was when she knew there was no saving him. She thought of lifting her shield, but that would expose Olive to danger, so it remained. The man charged at them with hands raised out in front of him as he rained blast after blast of magic at them. He hit the shield and a look of surprise registered on his face as he disintegrated.

Bile rose in Verve's throat but she managed to choke it down. She let the shield drop. "Well, they know we're here. There's no sense in not using magic now."

"He was being controlled," said Olive softly. "His eyes just –

weren't right."

Verve cringed. The fact that the man was being controlled made what she had done ten times worse. Trembling, she placed her hand on the door. The magic she fed into it was too much, and the square of metal flew off its hidden hinges with a resounding boom.

"Well, so much for arriving unnoticed."

The library was quiet, though. No one took up the alarm, no one came running. In fact, the nearest heartbeats Verve could hear were muted by the walls of the library. "We're in here alone," she said, rising through the door. Confident what she had said was true, Verve got to her knees and held a hand out for Olive.

"What exactly are we looking for?" Olive demanded. She emerged into the library, dripping stinking water everywhere just as Verve was.

Verve lifted the door she had blown off and forced it back in place as best she could. "We need books on the Lands of the Dead."

Olive stared at her incredulously. "And how do you propose we find them?"

They both looked around them at the vast collection of books. Olive was right: there were hundreds of shelves. How would they find anything without knowing where to look? Verve shook her head. "Is there any magical way to find them?"

"Not that anyone ever taught me," Olive said with a huff. "We need to leave the city before his lordship arrives. I don't think I need to tell you what he'll do when he finds us."

Verve suppressed a shudder. "I'm well aware, thank you."

"Might've thought more about it before you led us here." She moved toward the nearest shelf, which she began to scan. "The voice you're hearing didn't tell you anything else?"

"No." Verve took another shelf, and at once her curse extended to some of the texts, the print on their spines vanishing. "Blast."

"I can't read any of this nonsense. Can you?"

Verve hugged herself. "I can't."

Thunder shook the building, and a few lamps on the walls blew out in the unnatural breeze that followed. "Miss Verity, we need to leave."

Frantic now, Verve started grabbing texts at random, whether or not she could read the spines or if the book was conveyable. The conveyable ones caused the base of her skull to itch, but she ignored the uncomfortable sensation, taking no care in where she let the books land.

Olive was at her elbow. "This was a fool's errand."

Verve's speed increased, no doubt making her into all but a blur of color and movement to Olive. "The answer has to be here somewhere."

"You're going to get yourself captured and me killed. Life debts or no, I'm not staying another moment."

Verve laughed without humor. "You've already left me to fend for myself twice now. I don't think...." She paused. There were a great many heartbeats now, all converging on the library. Verve inhaled. The air smelled of coffee, chocolate, and hot metal. "He's sent an army after me. Olive, we need to—" But when Verve looked around, the crone was nowhere to be found, nor was the sack containing the food from Chao and the books she had stolen from Dacre's estate. Verve cursed Olive and ran back to the tunnel entrance. Water was pushing up through the cracks outlining the trapdoor. *Trapped.*

Her breaths were quick and ragged as she ran for the nearest exit, having counted only four. How had Olive managed to escape? There was no time to puzzle over that. The din surrounding the library made Verve's ears ring, and she forced herself at top speed through the back door, only to run headfirst into a magical shield.

With a yelp, she fell backward, her clothing singed. The contact had stung, but Verve knew she would be all right, though it might have killed a mortal.

Gloved hands reached for Verve, even as bolts of azure fire came screaming toward her face. Instead of engulfing her in flame, the magic formed a barrier of wind behind her, forcing her toward the assailants. All of their eyes were dead, their faces expressionless, and

Verve knew they were being controlled.

Still the mob reached forward and attempted to subdue her, even as she bucked one after the other off. Among the Trusted, Verve heard several fae heartbeats. They were pushing through the throng.

Three of the Trusted surprised Verve from behind and quickly wound a thick metal chain around her waist while several others attempted to pin her arms to her side. "Gently, gently," said a woman's voice. "We're to delay or subdue her, not harm her."

Verve recognized that voice, knew it to belong to one of Dacre's allies. Instinct took over. She pried her right arm from the mob's grasp and touched the chain the others were trying to bind her with. At the contact, Verve pushed feelings of fury and desperation into the metal links, and magic burst forth from her fingertips. The chain exploded, and the twenty nearest Trusted surrounding her collapsed onto the ground screaming and writhing in apparent agony as red welts formed on their skin.

"Stay where you are," said Verve, raising her hands in front of her.

But the Trusted did not heed her warning and those remaining swarmed forward. It was suspicious that none of the fae in the crowd aided those being controlled. They remained hidden among the mob, which seemed to be growing by the minute. Perhaps they were afraid and were sending the humans to weaken and tire her before they swooped in and finished the job they had been sent to do.

Verve needed to end this before Dacre arrived or one of the fae intervened. But knowing the mortals were being used as pawns made her sick to her stomach, and she hesitated to use force against the rest.

As one, those who were still on their feet cast a web of magical netting at Verve, ensnaring her. "Hold it steady," cried one of the fae from a distance.

Verve howled in rage. Her vision blurred as magic poured forth from her body, much like it had done the day she had killed Helena. Wave after wave of pure power swept over the horde in flashes of blinding white, and thuds louder than thunder echoed all around her. The air smelled strongly of caramel and blood, and when Verve finally managed to regain control of herself, bodies littered the street around her. Those nearest to her had disintegrated, leaving piles of ash amid the puddles of water.

The storm had ceased, and now the air was eerily still. Horror at what she had done overcame Verve and she shrank back toward the library behind her. But where there ought to have been a solid building, she now found a partially collapsed heap, the roof having caved in and the western wall pushing inward.

A gust of wind tore Verve's hair out of its tangled knot. Sobs wracked her body and her vision blurred once more.

There was a low moan, which snapped Verve to attention. She pushed off from the ruins of the library and stumbled around corpses, looking for the source of the sound. As she walked, Verve forced herself to look at each body. "I'm sorry," she said, her voice cracking as she spied a young girl among the crowd. She looked not much older than Dav, her eyes wide open in horror even in death.

Again someone moaned, and Verve tore her eyes from the sight and searched for whoever had made the noise. There were at least a hundred bodies here, and though she listened, she could only detect two heartbeats among them, one human and the other fae.

Verve found the human first. He was a young man, not much older than Verve, it would seem. His eyes were no longer blank as one being controlled, but wide and alert with terror.

When Verve knelt next to him, the man attempted to crawl away, whimpering like a frightened animal as his eyes rolled around in his head. "Please. Don't kill me. I didn't – I didn't mean to…I don't know what happened."

"It's all right," said Verve hoarsely. "I know, and I'm not going to harm you."

That did not seem to bring the man any relief. He shuddered mightily and crawled over a neighboring corpse. "P-please. Leave me. You're so bright it hurts." He flinched as Verve magicked on a pair of gloves and produced a clean piece of linen and tried dabbing at the blood on his forehead.

"It's going to be all right. I'm going to get you home to your family. You have my word. No harm will come to y—"

The man began convulsing and coughing as though having a fit. There was a mighty cracking sound, followed by the stench of burned chocolate as he at last lay still.

Stunned, Verve gently shook the body. He didn't move.

Strong arms grabbed Verve from behind and attempted to subdue her, but they were no match for her. She easily managed to free herself from her attacker's grip, and caught them by their upper arm.

The she-fae blanched as Verve accidentally crushed her bones. "You need to come with me," the creature said, her voice thick with pain. "You don't know what you're doing." Her eyes were clear, telling Verve she was not being controlled.

"What does he want with me?" Verve demanded. When the she-fae did not answer, Verve shook her by the shoulder.

"He is the true king. His time is coming, and none will delay him."

Verve bared her teeth. "What does Dacre *want*?"

Of all things, the she-fae smiled. "You, my queen."

As one burned, Verve dropped the creature. She surveyed the carnage surrounding them, her breaths coming in sharp, terrified gasps. This was not the time to have one of her attacks, she knew, but she couldn't stop her vision from blurring and darkening as she swayed on the spot, consciousness threatening to leave her.

The she-fae took advantage of Verve's state and attempted to lift her, but Verve pulled off her right glove and grasped the creature by the throat. The skin-to-skin contact caused the she-fae to scream in agony and collapse. And as she lay on the ground, trembling, Verve picked a path through the bodies and ran away as quickly as her unsteady legs would carry her.

No one attempted to stop her at first, not that they could even if they tried. There were shouts in the distance, people gathering to the scene of destruction Verve had created. The thought of the amount of carnage she had caused made Verve falter on the outskirts of town. She allowed herself a moment to pause and breathe deeply in a back alley, and then rested her head against the cool bricks of the northmost building.

Keep moving, said the voice. *You need to reach Nefalla before Lord Starside does.*

Verve closed her eyes and tried to slow her breathing. "What is Nefalla?"

There was a pause. *A place in the Lands of the Dead. It will give you what you are looking for.*

"How am I to reach it now? I have no idea where I'm going. Do you?" She ignored the commotion in the city, voices calling for a witch hunt, and rested her head in her hands.

Imalkis knows where the land of the living touches that of the dead. He is in hiding because Lord Starside is hunting him. When she did not respond or react to the voice's information, the man, wherever and whoever he was, let out an impatient huff. *You're going to get yourself caught and burned at the stake if you sit there much longer.*

Verve shrugged. "Maybe I deserve it." Her voice was hysterical and raw, and she couldn't stop shaking. "Besides, I don't know who you are or why you are helping me."

I am helping you, foolish woman, because you are the Fire Queen and I will one day require your help in return. Now, stop wallowing in self-pity. There are men who saw you come this way, and they are but two blocks behind you. He was silent, though his irritation with her was palpable.

With reluctance, Verve nodded. "All right. Where am I going?"

Head north as though your life depends on it. When you reach the wall, do not stop for the guards. Push through the gate or find a way over.

She wiped the tears from her eyes so she could see better and staggered through knee-high refuse and all but fell into the open road. Upon emerging, however, she regained her balance and took off at a run. Her pace was far from supernatural, but enough to outrun all but those who were competitive runners.

They've set up road barriers and the gate is closing.

She did not pick up her pace. The attack she'd experienced had been short, but it had taken its toll on her body and mind, as had the events from earlier. "Where is Imalkis? Or do you not know?"

The being sighed. *Don't worry yourself with the potion-maker yet. Focus on the road in front of you and how you'll escape the city.*

Verve shook her head, leaping over a wagon that had been set in the path in front of her. The startled looks of the soldiers patrolling might have made her laugh, had she not just murdered so many people. "You don't know where he is. Why else would you send me to the library for information?"

I sent you there first because it would have been easier to get the book than face Imalkis. He is crafty and you will have difficulty getting a straight answer out of him.

Verve dodged an arrow she sensed flying her way, then another. At last she was forced to increase her speed as armed men and women came into view, all standing guard at the closed gate.

The voice swore. *You'll have to find a way around.*

She ignored that and kept running at the soldiers. More arrows screamed through the air, all coming shy of their mark, as she dove and danced around them. Soon, however, the air was peppered with them, and Verve was forced to take more evasive maneuvers. She feinted to the east then banked to the west, her speed increasing as she approached the wall as close as she dared.

Soldiers came at her, swords raised in a seemingly impenetrable wave. How word had gotten to them so quickly, Verve couldn't say, but it mattered not now. They charged at her, fear alive in their eyes. Some were too quick to be human, but they did not possess the power she did.

Unwilling to harm one more soul, Verve used her momentum to soar high into the air and urged herself over the men and thence over the wall. She dared not land even after she had cleared the men atop the bulwark, since there were soldiers standing in lines on the ground. With a deafening grinding sound, the gate was raised. Horses whinnied and hooves pounded the dirt road far behind Verve, so she increased her speed and veered to the northwest, leaving them far behind and unable to follow in a matter of seconds. The line she cut was over a pathless forest of trees; no horse could easily make its way here.

Soon Verve was satisfied that a good five miles lay between her and the soldiers and, not wishing to be sighted by the watchers she knew stood near the Mortal Gate in the distance, she landed. Her energy might not yet have been spent, but her mind was awash with conflicting thoughts and feelings. Bleary eyes made for difficult navigation, and her fingers kept pulsing with barely contained fire, so she allowed herself a moment to rest and regain control of herself.

You don't have that much of an advantage, child. You'll need to make a gateway before the day is through.

Verve scowled at the heavens whence the voice came. Its owner's presence had felt stronger the moment she left the city, and she could not help but wonder where exactly he was. "For pity's sake, give me a moment. I just killed—"

You just took care of yourself in a less than fair fight. There was a short pause and then an impressed and yet annoyed, *I did not know you could fly. Is there anything else the Fire Queen can do that I ought to know of?*

She did not respond but closed her eyes and counted backward from twenty. The fire in her clenched fists dimmed. Shaking still, Verve took a calming breath and pushed forward. As much as she hated to admit it, it remained likely that someone had spotted where she had landed and could be on her trail within minutes. "Where is Imalkis? Or should I just make a gateway to this Nefalla you mentioned?"

You cannot portal directly to Nefalla. There are no hawthorns there, he said impatiently.

That made Verve frown. "Then how am I to get there eventually, if that is the goal?"

The man sighed. *It is within the Lands of the Dead. And before you ask, you cannot open a gateway to the Lands using any old tree. It has to be a very specific hawthorn, one whose whereabouts Imalkis alone knows of.*

"Right. That's why Dacre's after him." *But what does Dacre want in the Lands of the Dead? And why does he seem to want me there too?* The thought made her feel ill. Whatever Dacre had in mind could not be pleasant. And Olive…was she all right? If so, would Verve see her again? Perhaps the old woman would betray Verve in exchange for peace.

He's after you as well, said the voice. *The Fire Queen is the only one who has the power to open Death's Maw. Make haste. Get to Githtariel before Starside does. It is vital that you are not caught.*

CHAPTER TWELVE

With the voice urging her on, Verve pushed through the woods, slowing only every now and again when she believed she had sighted a hawthorn. There were many trees with light gray bark here and even similar-looking leaves, but when she pressed her hand against them, all she was met with was silence. "Where in Letorheas is Githtariel?" she asked.

Don't say the name so loudly, woman.

Verve clenched and unclenched her fists, fire crackling through her veins. "Fine. Where is the place?"

It's a small village within a wood on the southernmost tip of Letorheas. Beyond that is the Tyrant's Sea.

"And you know Imalkis is there how exactly?"

The man, or whatever he was, huffed impatiently. *I have been tracking Imalkis's movements for some time now. That is why I've been negligent in my attentions to you and…well, your mate.*

"That explains nothing, you realize." *And makes you sound rather much like a peeper.* She cleared her throat and hastened onward. "Where are you exactly? If you're not some figment of my imagination."

There was a soft chuckle. *I am not something of your imagining, but it is rather complicated to explain right now. You still have someone following you,* he warned her. *Lose them and focus on the task at hand.*

Verve could hear them, a mile off, picking through the woods behind her, so she decided to test the limits of her speed. Soon the trees were blurs whipping past her face. Her mind tried to keep up with the rate at which scenery was flying by, but it was too disorienting and she plowed straight into a great oak, which cracked right down the middle at impact.

I said lose your follower, not draw them directly to where you stand.

Ears ringing, Verve righted herself and wiped at the silver blood leaking from her nose. Whoever was pursuing her was still a-ways off, but they had no doubt heard the noise she had made, so it would be in her best interest to find a hawthorn quickly. "Can you see any suitable trees?"

There are none within the next half mile, but adjust your course a few degrees – north by north-east – and you should come across a cluster within the next minute.

Soon enough, after changing her direction and speed, she reached several large trees that looked somewhat different from their neighbors, but she wasn't entirely certain they were hawthorns. Yet when she pressed her hand against one of them, the tree quite obviously recoiled. "I'm not going to hurt you," she whispered.

"You set the one ablaze," said the hawthorn in response. Its voice was young, small.

Verve sighed. "I put her out of the misery someone else was causing."

You must have a knife, said the guiding voice. *Make haste and end this conversation before you are found.*

"I'm sorry to have caused any pain, but I really need—"

"Where? Just tell me where and then leave me be," said the tree.

Verve could have collapsed in relief and said so softly she wondered if the tree would be able to hear, "On the outskirts near Githtariel."

At once the young tree's trunk split down the middle, its overhead branches twining to form the top of the gateway. *"Go. Go and don't hurt any more of my kind. Others are not as forgiving as I."*

Not wishing to remain a moment longer, Verve ran through the passage the tree had made and into a dimly lit wood. There were many voices in the near distance and the smells of magic having been spent. Thankfully, the residual bursts were none she recognized. Perhaps she would be safe here…as safe as she could be anywhere these days. Verve took a tentative step forward, but paused. The gateway behind her had closed, but she had the distinct feeling of someone standing not ten yards back.

Yes, there was a heartbeat, fae, and soft breathing. Whoever they were, they did not speak nor make themselves known in any other way.

Verve turned, and whoever had been watching her ran. For a moment she considered running after them, but she hesitated too long and a tree groaned. Seconds later, the wood behind her was silent, indicating the fae had created a gateway and was beyond pursuit.

Unease came over Verve and she forced herself to move forward. She hadn't drunk any water since before her escape from the city, and her throat was dry as a bone.

Don't answer me, as you will be overheard, but do as I say, said the voice. *You look positively wild right now and will frighten the villagers if you don't tone down your magic a little.*

Verve frowned and opened her mouth to make retort. She thought the better of it at once and simply rolled her eyes.

Good girl. Dampen your magic.

She ran a hand down her face, as Fenn had taught her, focusing on feelings of wariness as she pushed them and the image she wanted to convey into her skin. It burned as it always did, but the pain wasn't too much to bear, and it was over quickly enough. The air smelled of toffee.

I guess that will have to do. For future reference, however, dampening magic would mean you cut off all or most of your power from being observed.

Verve cast her gaze heavenward.

Knowing she should get this over with, Verve strode toward the village. There were a dozen or so fae on the outskirts, some on horseback and others on their hands and knees in the dirt, planting or weeding, apparently. They looked up as Verve approached. Some squinted and then recoiled as they better beheld her, while others merely turned back to their work. Among the cluster of fair folk was a child who looked no older than eight years physically, but his eyes were quite old when they made contact with Verve's. At once the woman nearest the fae child took him by the shoulder and steered him away from the path Verve was taking.

Don't bother with them, said the voice, startling Verve enough so she jumped. *Imalkis will not be among the servants.*

When the young one looked her way once more, a small smile pulled at the corner of Verve's lips before the woman with him shot a dirty glare her way. At that Verve moved more quickly.

The village gates were open and no sentry stood guard, so she walked through and tried to look as though she belonged. Men and women bustled to and fro as they laughed and drank from a marble fountain's crystal waters. One fae caught sight of Verve and stopped in his tracks and nudged the man at his side.

"Look at what the gods have brought us," he whispered.

Keep moving. You don't want to draw attention to yourself.

"I know," Verve murmured as others began to take notice of her presence.

Soon a tense silence fell over all, and the fae stopped what they were doing to openly stare at her. None stepped in her path, though none moved out of her way either. There were so many of them that she was forced to stop or risk bumping into more than one someone.

Verve flinched as one of the males reached out and waved a hand in front of her face, his expression unreadable. At the gesture, she felt her disguise slip and her power thrum dangerously close to the surface. He smiled and nodded at those surrounding him.

Some knelt, others moved toward Verve as though to touch her, but she backed away and they froze. "What are you doing?" she demanded of the two she-fae who took her by the arms, their hands close to touching her flesh.

The creatures did not answer but led her farther away from the gates, their fellows following closely in their wake. The sea of fae in front of them parted. All stared, many smiled knowingly at her, though a few seemed uneasy and went into buildings, closing the doors behind them.

Verve could have easily broken the creatures' hold on her but not without hurting them.

I don't like this, said the voice. *They know who you are, child. You might have difficulties leaving.*

"Please, I don't want to hurt you," said Verve. "I'm—"

"Cursed?" asked the she-fae holding her left arm. She grinned at Verve's bewildered expression. "This day was prophesied many centuries ago, my queen. I'm afraid we have an unfair advantage in knowing more about you than you would have ever heard of us." The creature gave her arm a reassuring squeeze. "We know who you seek and why. Don't worry, Your Majesty, we'll help you soon enough."

Though their grip was gentle, Verve couldn't help feel a bit like a prisoner being led through the streets. She pretended to stumble to see what her escorts would do, but the women merely stepped away, gave her a moment to right herself, and then made to take her in their grasp again. Verve, however, was unwilling to submit and held them off with her palms raised threateningly.

The she-fae exchanged a look. "Please, be patient with us," said the woman on Verve's right. "This is how things are done."

Verve shook her head. "I don't know if it's a fae custom, but where I am from, this is called being taken prisoner." At the words, sparks flew from her fingertips, and the crowd surrounding her backed away, all but for the two guards, who seemed unmoved and unconcerned.

Ask them where Imalkis resides.

"So, your magic is tied to your temper?" asked a man from the crowd.

From behind, someone ran their fingers through her hair. Another unseen fae placed a firm hand on her shoulder. All suddenly seemed to want to touch her, though they obviously knew the perils of doing so.

There was a flash of bright light plus the aroma of sage, and those pressing in fell back once more, and the two she-fae hurried Verve along at a greater pace. "Sorry," said the woman on her left. "I'm Elaia, by the way. Welcome to Githtariel."

"I'm—"

"Verity of the No Lands. We know."

Verve frowned. "No Lands?" The trees had been saying something similar, but she'd never paid it much mind.

Elaia seemed surprised. "You don't know yet? Well, I'll speak of that when it's safe."

"We should get her indoors quickly," said the other woman. "And we'll need a duplicate." The words had been said in a low whisper, and the one named Elaia did not respond.

Be careful. Once inside, I won't be able to see or communicate with you.

Soon they arrived at a shack with broken shutters and a battered brown door, which whined open at Elaia's prompting. They hurried Verve in ahead of them, then shut and barred the door before setting up numerous wards that smelled of roses and musk.

Wary, Verve backed away from the women as they worked and took in her surroundings. The house was larger on the inside than she had expected – much larger. While from the outside it appeared to stand a single story, from inside it stood three tall, apparently. Verve used through-sight into the rest of the rooms and was startled to find the house went on for many rooms and was long and wide enough to rival even Dacre's mansion. All was plain here, however, with the bare minimum of furnishings and what appeared to be a staff of no more than seven servants.

"You're famished and weary," said the one fae. "I'm Ardyth. I'll have someone fetch food for you." She smiled at Verve and snapped her fingers.

In response, two maids appeared out of thin air, causing Verve to gasp and clutch a hand over her heart. The air smelled of lilacs. "Don't do that."

The two women seemed amused but turned their attention to Ardyth. "Yes, miss?" they chorused.

"Food for Her Majesty, clothes, and a bath in the guest suite," said the she-fae.

Instead of vanishing into thin air, the she-fae gave Verve a curious look, curtsied, and bustled out of the room. Her hosts – or were they wardens? – gestured to a settee in front of a fire, which had leapt to life in a circular pit in the middle of the floor.

"Please, do sit. We mean you no ill," said Elaia when Verve's gaze turned to the door.

Would there be harm in sitting? She had run and walked a great ways, though she was wearier in heart and mind than in body. "Am I a prisoner here?"

That question seemed to startle the women. "No, of course not."

"Because things won't end so well for any of us if it turns out to be the case." Verve folded her arms across her chest and tried to look more menacing than she felt at that moment. She might be powerful, but the spells they had cast to protect the house were complicated, and Verve was inexperienced. They might very well be more than an equal match for her.

"You are free to leave at any time," Ardyth reassured her. "Though I would advise against it. Most here will worship you, but there are some who have dreaded this day since it was first prophesied." She gestured to the fire once more, and when Verve did not move, she and Elaia both sat in two seats next to the settee.

Verve's stomach twisted. "Worship? That's not right."

The two women shrugged. "When confronted with something greater than oneself, that is oftentimes the reflex reaction…wrong or right," said Ardyth, smoothing out her frock. "Now, how can we help you in your quest for Ithalamore?"

"We know you seek Imalkis." Elaia smirked when Verve felt her eyes widen. "That part was easily deduced from the nature of the prophecies. But don't worry too much about him. The moment a whisper of you was heard in our world, he was seized and taken to a holding cell where he is being interrogated for answers."

That did not sound good. Verve wanted answers, yes, but to have someone held against their will in order for that to happen? She shuddered. "You're not going to hurt anyone, are you?" She cleared her throat and moved toward the settee, her nerves singing as she tried to calculate her next move.

Elaia's thin eyebrows rose. "That doesn't have to happen, if you don't want it to."

Verve blanched. "Of course I don't want it to."

A new servant, male, entered with a tray of steaming-hot food and a glass of wine and placed them on the table next to the settee. He was practically vibrating with nerves as he bowed to Verve. "Is there anything else I can get you?" His emotions swirled around him in a visual, tangled mess, and Verve flinched as she felt his discomfort as her own.

"No, thank you."

Then, as quickly as he had come, the manservant left. Once he was gone, Ardyth said, "You wished to know about the No Lands part of your title."

Reluctantly, Verve perched on the edge of the settee, ready to flee if anyone so much as moved an inch too close for her liking. "I had been wondering about that," she admitted. "The trees have been using a similar term for a while with me."

Now the women seemed to have questions of their own, but they did not voice them. Instead, Elaia sat forward in her chair and began speaking in low tones. "There is part of a prophecy, one that has existed since the beginning of the age, which speaks of a woman who can traverse between realms unaided. She was said to have been of mortal beginnings, but would go on to be the most powerful creature any of the known worlds had ever beheld."

Ardyth explained, "You must break ties with your mortality. Only then can you start on the path that leads to all roads." They watched Verve closely, tension written across their brows.

Verve ran her hands over her arms. "I still don't think I understand. What are the No Lands?" Her tone held more frustration than she had meant it to, and both of the she-fae recoiled. Verve put on an apologetic smile.

"Why, the No Lands refer to the paths between realms. These you should be able to traverse once you part with your mortal ties."

"That confuses me as well, though I've heard the reasoning before," Verve admitted. "I thought I was no longer mortal." Saying as much might be foolish, but she wanted answers, and since these women seemed willing to part with information, she was willing to take the risk.

Ardyth spoke first. "You are still part mortal and thus vulnerable." She looked to the other she-fae for confirmation.

"It is true. It would be very difficult to kill or harm you – not that any of us would ever dream of trying. But you need help from the Pure Daughter of Ithalamore. Since you are cursed, the only way to separate and thus kill your mortal self without harming your immortal self will be with the help of Igraine, the late mentor of Imalkis."

Verve rose and paced. "So it comes back to potions?" When the women did not respond, she stopped and regarded them with dread. "And it really must be a potion from Igraine?"

They nodded. "You must journey to the Lands of the Dead."

"Only then can you be truly free."

That did not make Verve feel any better. "And there is no one else who could make the potion I need?" She interrupted the women before they could interject anything. "Imalkis was her pupil. Surely she passed along the knowledge to him?" Verve threaded her fingers together to keep them from pulling at her hair, something she had done as a child when distraught. It didn't seem right, traveling to such a land alive. Would she be able to leave again? The thought of Helena and Father being there crossed Verve's mind, and gave her pause. She had asked Fenn about raising the dead, and he had not come out and directly said it was impossible. Perhaps, if she could find her sister and father, there would be something she could do for them.

The she-fae had been watching her face with interest the whole time she was thinking, and their expressions had darkened considerably. "It is not with a light heart that we send you to the hereafter. If we thought Imalkis wise and trustworthy enough to produce such an elixir, then we would not have suggested you travel to Ithalamore," said Ardyth.

"Know this, the Lands of the Dead are not without their dangers."

"Or temptations."

Verve looked at them expectantly. "Such as?"

It looked as though Elaia was going to answer her directly, but instead she paused and said, "Your food grows cold. Surely you're hungry." She nodded at the table next to the settee meaningfully.

Not wishing to offend, especially when the women held answers and might potentially help her, Verve took the food and sat, tentatively sniffing for anything that smelled wrong and might be harmful. There was nothing she could detect and, being rather hungry as they had stated, she took a bite of the freshly baked bread and had to suppress a satisfied moan. "What are the temptations and pitfalls?" Verve took a sip of the sweet wine and relaxed a little, so she set the cup aside at once; she needed a clear mind for the journey ahead.

Elaia sighed. "Well, there are said to be gateways to other realms down there, easily stumbled upon and invoked by accident. I would watch my step while I was there. Don't touch anything until you are absolutely certain it is not transportive or conveyable."

Verve nodded solemnly at the warning. "That is good to know."

"Also, bringing back a spirit is highly dangerous." The way Ardyth watched Verve while she said this was not to Verve's liking, but she tried to look innocent as she took a bite of the green apple on her plate.

"How so?" Verve asked after she had swallowed.

"Without a body, a spirit can be highly volatile and hard to manage, in Letorheas even. In Etterhea or any other mortal realm, the effects would be devastating. It would be best not to talk to anyone deceased but Igraine once you are in Ithalamore."

Before Verve could protest, Elaia said, "Igraine was pure of heart and was granted a special non-body to travel back and forth through the realms of the living and the dead. You would be sacrificing everyone else's safety if you attempted to bring back another deceased soul." Her tone brooked no argument, so Verve did not ask the questions overwhelming her mind.

Instead, she finished the rest of her meal in silence as the two women talked to each other, their topics nonsensical to Verve. It was clear they were giving her time and space to digest what they had told her, though she knew from their not-so-covert glances her way that they had questions of their own. "I am ready to talk to Imalkis."

That did not seem to please the she-fae. "Once you have seen him, you will no doubt wish to be on your way, but I'm afraid that is unwise." Elaia gave Verve an apologetic look. "You don't seem as one in full possession of their faculties at the moment."

"You need rest," Ardyth cut in.

Verve set her plate aside and rose. "I don't think that's a good idea." She was so close to ending this, to being free of Dacre and his curse at last. If what she understood was true, the curse and Dacre's invulnerability to her attacks were both tied to her mortal self. He had, after all, remade her before the Cunning Blade had done its work. Since his inability to be harmed by her was because of a shared magical – and thus blood – bond, why wouldn't the curse operate in the same manner? In her bones she knew she was right. The thought did nothing to dispel her anxiety. In fact, if anything, it increased it.

"My queen," said Ardyth. "If I do not speak plainly we all will regret it. You have the air of one who has recently expended a great amount of magic."

Elaia nodded. "Death's Maw awaits, and the toll it exacts is not of the ordinary kind, if legend speaks truly. Then there is the potion, of which we know precious little."

"Even our Fire Queen is not immune to fatigue and collapse. These things might make you vulnerable to attack, and we know there are those who do not have your best interests at heart. You are strong, yes, but not unbreakable – tempered but still glass."

Verve ran a hand back through her tangled hair. They made good arguments. "And it's safe? I noticed some fae didn't seem too happy about my being here."

"As we said earlier, there are a few who have always dreaded this day. But they mean you no ill," said Ardyth. "And even if they did, all will have come to believe you've left the city." She gave Verve a smile that bordered on mischievous, piquing Verve's interest.

"How do you mean?"

Elaia grinned. "We sent out a shape-changer in your form. There are precious few of them in Letorheas, and the one who serves us has kept it a secret from the general population." The she-fae rose and moved past Verve toward the winding set of white stairs at the far end of the room. "You will have been seen by reliable busybodies by now, sneaking out of the city with two of our men trailing you at a somewhat conspicuous distance."

Verve followed the woman at a slow pace, blanching when she sensed the other following closely. "And the wards I sense?"

Not for the first time the she-fae looked at each other and then at her in surprise. "You can sense those?" asked Elaia. "They are protective wards, meant to keep visitors or anyone not working for us at bay. Don't worry, they are very effective."

"And you are the governing forces here?" Verve hesitated at the foot of the stairs, unwilling to be potentially trapped on the second floor.

"Of a peculiar sort," said Ardyth. When Verve looked at her blankly, the woman colored and shrugged. "We're of a secret sect of fae, trained from our younger years what to do when the Fire Queen arrives." She gestured at the stairs, which Verve still refused to mount, and her shoulders heaved. "We've been sworn to protect you, even from yourself, if need be."

Those words did not sit well with Verve. She took a step away from the women, and thankfully they did not make any moves toward her; Verve didn't like the thought of fighting two fae who had been trained for this very day and might have some foreknowledge she did not. "And what might that entail exactly?" Her voice was like ice, and she was satisfied when both of the she-fae flinched.

"Well," said Elaia with apparent reluctance, "some scholars of Second Age prophecy suggest you would arrive here troubled in the mind and heart." She shrugged when Verve's eyebrows rose. "We thought you might be in danger of self-harm."

It was Verve's turn to blanch. "No, I'm not."

At those words, Elaia and Ardyth relaxed visibly. The former said, "That is good to know. We weren't entirely certain."

Verve realized she had assumed too much of these women when they mentioned protecting her from forces that meant her ill. Steeling herself for a fight, she asked, "And what of Lord Dacre Starside? Would you consider him friend or foe?" She waited in tense silence as the women looked at each other, their expressions baffled.

"The dead king's pet?" Elaia snorted. She frowned as Verve cocked her head to the side. "I thought you had killed him."

Ardyth nodded. "That is what the rumors have been in our backward part of the world, anyway. But I wonder if we might have missed something." The she-fae studied Verve closely. "He's alive, is he?"

"That would explain the potency of the curse. It was he who cast it upon you, was it not?"

As quickly and with as few details as possible, Verve told them Dacre was very much alive and was in pursuit of her for unknowable reasons. The surprise and alarm on their faces assured Verve they were not on Dacre's side...or at least not in communication with him.

"Oh, dear." Elaia backed away from the stairs and went into a room adjoining the one they stood in. When the she-fae returned a minute later, she was flipping through a large text emitting the scents of sage and vanilla. "There are three prophecies about how this day will unfold, and they each contradict. One is older than the other two, so we've always given more attention to its credibility."

"What does it say?" Verve asked.

Elaia did not look up from the crimson-edged pages. "It is sparse in details, which is another reason we go by it rather than the other two. The first prophecy claims you will arrive on such a day as today, weary of body and heart. You seek counsel and knowledge of Death's Maw – the Gate of the Dead – and that you leave two days hence in the company of two Faithful."

"But that can't be now," said Ardyth, her expression darkening. When she looked at Verve she shook her head. "Because the first prophecy hinges on your greatest enemy being dead or powerless."

"The Traitor King," prompted Elaia. "We assumed you had killed him and he was no longer in play. But now that he's alive and still pursuing you and your mate, that means the first prophecy was a fraud and that we must look at the second and third. Let's hope it's not the third." With that ominous statement, the she-fae continued turning through pages until she arrived at another. "The second prophecy is but rarely studied in wider circles, yet Ardyth and I and all Faithful First Women are required to study it. It says you will be a danger to yourself and that herbs will be needed to quiet your mind. Are you sure you're well in your thoughts?" She sounded so hopeful that Verve was not, Verve began to worry even more about the third prophecy.

"I am distraught but not in that way," Verve admitted.

The two she-fae exchanged a frightened look, and Elaia closed the book. "Then that prophecy was false as well. I've one more text to consult, and then we must visit Imalkis." She hastened from the room, and the sounds of her riffling through drawers and scattering papers here and there were nigh deafening, and shattered what remaining calm Verve had.

Ardyth attempted an encouraging smile that did not quite reach her eyes. "Not all prophecies come to fruition. Some can be thwarted."

Verve didn't even pretend to be encouraged by the statement but approached the room Elaia had disappeared into. At the sight of the she-fae desperately searching, Verve's hopes sank even further. "Do you need help?" In response to the nervous look Elaia gave her, a reflexive growl escaped Verve's throat.

"It's not here."

The other she-fae moved past Verve. "What? It has to be. I consulted the beginning of the text not two days ago."

"And you don't remember what any of it said?" Verve asked, her hands balling into fists as the temperature in the room dropped with her shifting emotions. Soon the walls began to drip as though perspiring, and the two she-fae took her by the arms and led her down a corridor, around a corner, and to a locked and guarded door.

"Any word of him breaking?" asked Ardyth of the guard on the right.

The man shook his head. "No. He seems willing to suffer for the answer."

Verve's heart stuttered at the words. "I don't want anyone hurt."

They only ignored her concern. "We have a traitor," said Elaia. "Someone has taken one of the prophecies." She pointed at the door. "No one is to enter until the interview is over, do you understand?"

Both the male and female guards nodded, the latter producing a ring of keys from her belt. "How long do we have?" She twisted the key in the lock, which clicked audibly. The door swung open on its hinges, silent.

"I don't know. But see that the usual wards are doubled."

"Tripled," Ardyth amended. "And no one is to leave their post." With that said, the she-fae stepped through the doorway and began the descent down a long flight of iron stairs leading into darkness.

Elaia's left eye twitched as she motioned for Verve to go ahead of her. "Make haste," she murmured. "I do not know the third prophecy in full, but you are running out of time before something undesirable happens." Twisting her wrist, Elaia created a glowing orange orb and allowed it to bounce through the air in front of them.

Verve did not hesitate a moment longer. She raced down the stairs after Ardyth, using the side railing for support as she went. Its presence was solid and somewhat comforting beneath her touch.

"Do not look him directly in the eyes," Elaia warned. "Imalkis is talented at bewitching fae and mortal alike. They will have dosed him with something to dampen his power and loosen his tongue, but he most likely has built up immunity to such things."

Waiting at the foot of the stairs with Ardyth was a grim-faced she-fae with gloves on her large hands. She made a quick curtsy and gestured for Verve to follow her down a dimly lit hall. "We have had little luck in breaking him. Imalkis is immune to most tactics we employ, and goodness knows we've already exhausted them all." She drew a ring of keys from her belt and thrust a large bronze one into the door on their left. It must have been a bespelled key, for the aromas of burned sage filled the air, an obvious residual burst.

Verve followed the woman through the doorway, Ardyth and Elaia close behind. On her way down the stairs, she had been able to hear distant shouts and cries, all male, followed by the low, threatening tones of two females. Here, however, the volume increased tenfold and Verve had to cover her ears.

The warden, for that is what Verve assumed her to be, turned and regarded Verve with confusion. She looked to Ardyth, her expression incredulous. "She can hear through the Silencing?" The look she gave Verve was amazed, bordering on terrified.

"What are they doing to him?" Verve demanded through her teeth. Her head throbbed and her jaw ached from the tension.

"She does not wish for us to harm anyone," said Elaia to the warden. She sounded exasperated.

"Then we shall abide by Her Majesty's wishes. Not that I wish to spare the vermin that is Imalkis Dovecote, but can't you see his cries are causing her pain?" The warden shook her head and hurried down the hall.

Verve made to follow her, though the noises the man made caused her distress and discomfort, but one of the she-fae placed a staying hand on her shoulder. "What are we waiting for?" Verve asked.

"She's got to secure the site first," Ardyth explained, squeezing Verve's shoulder in what she must have thought was a reassuring manner.

All Verve could think was that she was being restrained. She shrugged the woman off and continued forward. If they had as little time as they claimed, every moment was precious and she would not wait for the area to be secured.

"Be cautious, Your Majesty. The Silencing isn't working on you, so he might very well be able to charm you through verbal means."

That gave Verve pause. She turned and looked at Ardyth and Elaia, who both seemed relieved that she was listening. "Would he be able to control me?"

Elaia drew a sharp breath, but Ardyth answered, "No, but he might be able to influence you if you're not on your guard." When Verve moved forward again, the she-fae took her by the shoulder once more. "Please, be very careful."

Verve growled at Ardyth, who hastily removed her hand and backed away. Then, unable to stand there doing nothing for a moment longer, Verve took off in the direction the warden had gone moments earlier, and followed her ears around a corner where the hall ended in a door pulsing with magic. She reached out toward the handle, hesitating as the magic reared up from the door and tickled the palm of her hand. Having seemed to sense she was friend and not foe, the magic relaxed, and the door opened inward.

The room Verve stepped into was round and covered in mirrors. Bright light shone from five different orbs scattered throughout the small space, and Verve had to squint.

"Well, well," said a man's voice from across the room.

Verve's head snapped up at the sound. The lights dimmed at her approach, and she could now better make out the three figures on the far side of the room.

A bloody, filthy male fae in rags sat bound to a chair. On either side of him stood a fae guard, swords at their sides and a constant stream of white light flowing from their hands and into the chains binding the prisoner.

"Imalkis?" Verve asked. She looked him briefly in his deep blue eyes before remembering she ought not and then fixed her gaze at a point over his right shoulder.

The man laughed, a pleasant sound. "Majesty. Forgive me if I do not bow, but I seem to have been mistaken for some criminal and placed in this arrested position." He quirked a smile, and the air filled with the scent of smoke.

Both fae guarding him grunted and threw out their other hand with more magic to counter whatever he was attempting. "Behave, Dovecote," Elaia warned.

Verve jumped, having not noticed both the she-fae slipping in behind her. In an attempt to get her nerves under control, she drew a deep breath through her nose and then addressed Imalkis. "Let's not play games. You have information I want—"

"I have information you *need*," he corrected her. "Sorry to so rudely interrupt, Your Majesty, but I believe we should be clear where everyone stands here. No secrets."

Her eyebrows shot up; she could see herself reflected clearly in the mirror behind him. "Very well. What do you want in exchange for information?" She waited.

Imalkis's shoulders rose and then dropped, Verve noted from the corner of her eye. There was a faint aroma of smoke, and light flickered in her eyes, forcing her to look away from the mirror and accidentally glimpsing the eyes of the man she was supposed to be interrogating. The man winked at her. There was another residual burst as he attempted to mesmerize her.

Something tugged at Verve's sympathetic feelings, making her want to blast the guards to pieces and free this poor, innocent man. After all, what had he done wrong? Verve blinked and the sympathy passed. No one else seemed to have noticed what Imalkis had attempted. "Please answer my question." Was it her imagining, or did the man seem surprised?

"I would oblige, Majesty, but I'm afraid that knowledge is not meant to fall into the hands of the living."

"And yet you possess it," she rejoined.

Again Imalkis attempted to draw her attention to his face, his residual burst as faint as it had been the time before. When she did not look him in the eye, he shifted in his seat, and his guard quickly followed his movements, whacking him upside the head with a wooden club when he strained against his bonds.

"That's enough," said Verve.

The woman who had struck Imalkis blinked, her hands still raised with the club, and murmured an apology as she replaced the weapon at her side. "With respect, Your Majesty, he's not going to tell us anything through polite conversation."

"Beatings haven't yielded anything either, I trust." Verve glared at the woman, daring her to disagree.

It would seem the guard was unwilling to agree or disagree. She simply went back to standing at attention, her hand still feeding light into the prisoner.

Verve watched the steady stream of magic as one entranced, something tugging at the back of her mind. "What are you currently doing to him?" she found herself asking. She flexed her dominant hand instinctively, magic pulsing hard in her veins, wanting to escape.

The guard who had not done the beating responded. "It's to keep him from blowing this room to bits." She nodded at Imalkis. "He's a combustible."

"Dovecote could bring the whole house down around our ears while he makes his escape," said Ardyth. "It would kill our elves and half-fae, which he cares little about."

Imalkis made a tutting noise. "I never said any such thing, dear, and I think you know it."

Another wave of his magic assailed Verve, breaking the memory she had begun to recall and severing the magic itching at her fingertips. This time, it nudged at her thoughts, tempting her to release him from the magical bonds and the streams of light controlling him. Surely he wouldn't actually blow anything up? His wardens must be lying. Imalkis seemed a genial enough man, one who did not deserve to be in these circumstances.

Someone took Verve by the chin and steered her head so she was looking in a different direction. On instinct she slapped the woman's gloved hand away, drawing a cry of pain, before she realized she had been staring Imalkis directly in the eye without having even realized it.

"You need to be careful," whispered Elaia through her teeth. "He is very good at what he does."

"Sorry," Verve said. She looked up at the ceiling. "Mr. Dovecote—"

He chuckled. "Just Imalkis, Majesty. I do not like these formalities, and I sense they annoy you as well."

That made Verve roll her eyes. "Fine. Imalkis, if it were just the two of us, would you tell me how to reach the Land of the Dead? I swear I won't tell another soul."

She felt his eyes sweep over her but held steady. "You and I alone? That sounds pleasant."

"Watch your words and eyes, Dovecote," said the warden from behind Verve, surprising them all apparently. All eyes briefly traveled to her tall frame and then returned to the man in chains.

Imalkis cleared his throat. "My apologies for appreciating the female form." He shrugged. "And what would you do with this knowledge of the land beyond? No doubt locate Death's Maw and then enter Ithalamore. You are, after all, currently the only one who can open the gate, and you need what's within. Why wouldn't you attempt it?" The man paused for effect. "But we all know there is more to this land than potions and ancient spells. There is power. So much power. What's to stop you once you've tasted what the dead lands have to offer the living?" A wave of less subtle magic drifted toward Verve, and she swatted it away.

"I just want this stupid curse lifted, and they tell me you are unable to replicate Igraine's potion." Her voice was smaller than she would have liked, and she made the mistake once more of looking Imalkis in the eyes.

He took advantage of that moment and held her gaze, his magic latching on to her mind with such intensity, her head felt as though it was being pricked with dozens of white-hot needles.

No one moved, and the air was filled with the aroma of smoke once more. The streams of magic being fed into the prisoner had frozen, and Verve realized with a start that no one would be able to save her from this creature.

He smiled apologetically. "Yes, I've temporarily stepped out of time with you. Let's see what's in that mind of yours…."

Verve was rooted to the spot, forced to continue staring into his eyes as the burning pain continued. She fought him as she felt him riffling through her thoughts. Unbidden memories leapt up to meet her as he sorted through them, and she was untrained in how to prevent this sort of attack, so all she could do was relive them with him.

She was a child again, stuck at the bottom of a well. Father had found her days after she had disappeared, but not before she'd developed a life-threatening case of pneumonia and a crushing fear of being trapped.

Imalkis studied this memory twice, forcing Verve to relive it again. He moved on to her captivity at Dacre's estate. Most of her days there he regarded with little interest until he alighted upon the moment Dacre transformed her into a half-fae. Three times he reviewed this memory and then moved on to her first meeting Fenn. "You've had some interesting times, I see."

Verve clenched her teeth as the world turned black. "Get out of my head."

Imalkis took pity on her and released her, his expression thoughtful. "Your husband ought to teach you how to block mind reading, though you've successfully blocked full control."

Time restarted with a visible shake and the smell of smoke, but the others in the room did not seem to notice anything had happened.

Except for the warden, who said, "He's done something. I can smell his residual burst."

Imalkis grunted as the one guard hit him once more with the club. "You may mean it now, Your Majesty, that you don't want more, but you will crave power. If you think the Cunning Blade gave you plenty, you are mistaken. There is so much more to be had, and you will try to take it all. The Fire Queen is not exempt from greed." But he sounded less certain than he had moments earlier, and Verve decided to press him further.

"I killed my own sister with this power, Imalkis. Why would I want more when I can barely control what I have? Please, I would only break the curse and then leave. That's all I want."

The prisoner shook his head. "But what is to stop you from bringing a bodyguard with you on this perilous journey? Or telling a lover? What's the harm in just one other person knowing?" He laughed bitterly. "The word spreads, and the Traitor King gets what he wants, access to the otherworld. Do not be deceived, Your Majesty. You are being played like a fiddle."

"You are wasting your words," said the warden to Verve. "The only language this sort of creature understands is pain."

But Verve held up her hand. Was Imalkis right? Perhaps she was being selfish, risking whatever lay in Ithalamore all for a cure that might not even exist. She was about to turn and leave the room, but her thoughts strayed to Helena. At once she hardened her heart and approached the prisoner, who leaned back in his chair. "I'm not going to hurt you, but you are going to tell me where to find Death's Maw and how to safely pass through to Ithalamore."

Something akin to fear and admiration flashed in the man's eyes, but it was gone as quickly as it had appeared. "I have been tortured for your benefit this past hour and have revealed nothing. How are you going to persuade me to part with my knowledge short of reading my mind?" He leveled a challenging look at her, but Verve did not take the bait; she could not read minds – or, at least, she couldn't yet – and they both knew it.

It took her a moment to recall precisely how she had managed to control Fenn, but when she did, golden light poured out of her fingers and struck Imalkis in the chest. "Tell me what I need to know." Her eyes closed as she fed a continuous stream into the man, though now she could see the whole room as a third-party observer.

"Death's Maw is hidden in the mortal realm," he said, his voice tight as he tried in vain to fight Verve's magic. "To reach it, you must create a gateway to the island of Lovelourn. The hawthorn itself is a deep black and stands the height of twenty men. You'll find it by following the coast all the way north." He was glaring at Verve now, and his face was red with rage. A vein pulsed in his forehead and spittle flew from his mouth as he continued. "There, on the brink of the forest just off the tip of the northernmost shore, you will find the tree you seek."

"How does it open?" asked one of the she-fae surrounding them. Verve didn't observe who, for her attention had homed in on Imalkis's face once more, trying to discern if he was truly under her control.

The stream of light intensified as Verve pushed more of her magic at him. "Tell me, Imalkis. How do you open Death's Maw?"

Now the fae was panting, his eyes rolling around desperately. "As all of the Great Gateways do, with a complete blood offering."

Verve frowned. "Complete?"

He shuddered and closed his eyes. "All of one fae's blood, spilled by your hand. But this is just for the first time; after that, you will be free to use Death's Maw as you would a normal hawthorn."

With a revolted gasp, Verve let the magic drop and backed away. It was hopeless, then. The curse would always be with her, and she had caused others so much pain and loss for nothing.

Imalkis eyed her thoughtfully, his face pale and his body trembling. "You have bested me, it would seem."

Shame ate at her, though she tried her best to keep her feelings from her face. Still, she knew from the knowing look Imalkis gave her that he was fully aware of what was going through her mind.

"You must share this information with no one," he said. "And I would advise you to kill everyone in this room to prevent it from spreading."

Verve shook her head. "No."

Imalkis sighed. "Then you are foolish and weak." He licked his lips and attempted once more to look her in the eye; Verve did not, could not. "Please, you have to—"

"Stop tormenting her," said the warden. "Come, let us leave this place." The she-fae reached to take Verve by the arm, but she pulled away.

Dazed, she followed Elaia and Ardyth through the door as Imalkis shouted warnings after her. It was when she had rounded the corner and started up the stairs that Verve felt another's magic tingling against her skin, and she smelled the faintest aroma of chocolate.

CHAPTER THIRTEEN

At once Verve's muscles tensed and magic rose within her, ready and threatening to spill forth. As she hastened up the stairs, encouraging the she-fae in front of her to hasten as well, the smell intensified and was accompanied by burned coffee notes as well.

"What is wrong?" asked Elaia, walking more quickly.

"He's here," was all Verve could gasp out. Fire tickled the tips of her fingers and it took all her self-control not to light the place ablaze. Any fear she felt she managed to push aside…mostly. She focused on her rage, how she had felt when she accidentally murdered the Trusted who had come for her. That had been the wrong memory to latch on to. Her power stuttered as she emerged at the top of the stairs and stumbled upon carnage.

Bodies of what must have been half-fae or elves were strewn about here and there, their eyes wide in death. Each of their throats had been slit, suggesting their attacker had come at them from behind and silently…unless magic had been involved. And judging by how the air reeked of it, it had been.

A cry came from Elaia as she finally seemed to understand the scene. She collapsed next to one of the bodies, a male in black livery. Touching his face, she ignored Ardyth and Verve, who both drew more power into their hands.

"We will help you to the border. If you wish to travel in search of Death's Maw, we have time to put together a small party." Ardyth spoke barely above a whisper as she motioned for Verve to follow her into another room. There were fewer bodies here. All was silent and still; the only heartbeats Verve could make out were her own and those who had come up from the prison with her.

Verve froze when she caught a glint of metal on the floor next to a lone corpse. She bent down to look at it, her mind racing as she tried to process why the woman's fingers appeared to have been holding the bloody knife that had so clearly slit her own throat.

"We don't have time," said the warden. "We must away from this place."

Dazed, Verve noted the strongest odors of chocolate and coffee came from the corpse with the knife. Verve frowned and moved to the next room, fast on Ardyth's heels.

"Shouldn't you be at your post?" Ardyth rasped at the warden as she pushed open a secret panel in the wall.

The warden laughed without humor. "Be thankful I'm here. Whoever did this can't be far away, and having one more fae who can fight will be beneficial to you." She took Verve by one elbow and Ardyth took the other, and pulled her through the panel and out into a back alley, where stood a lone dappled gelding. The creature regarded them passively as it chewed on a mouthful of grass.

"He is well-trained," said Ardyth, noting the look on Verve's face. "You don't need to be afraid."

But that wasn't what had Verve concerned. Something wasn't right about the murder scene they had walked through. Besides not disturbing her as much as it once would have, she had noted a pattern. The residual burst smelled of chocolate and coffee – *old* chocolate and coffee, like the magic had been done ages ago. That couldn't be; they hadn't been down in the prison for more than half an hour. Did bursts even linger that long? Then there was the murder weapon, lying by the one body. "Did something seem strange to you?" she asked as she was all but dragged toward the horse. Verve dug in her heels and brought them to a halt.

"You said he was here," said the warden, sounding terrified. "Doesn't that mean we should be going?"

Ardyth put up a hand. "You're staying here." When the warden opened her mouth to protest, Ardyth said, "That was always the plan.

Don't think it's changed now just because the third prophecy seems to be the correct one."

"B-but we don't even know all that is in that prophecy!" the other woman wailed.

"The murder weapon was just lying there." Verve pulled her arm out of the warden's grasp. "Either Dacre was scared away after he finished killing the household or—"

"He is still in the house, trying to get to you," said Ardyth.

Verve shook her head. "I heard no other heartbeats."

"Maybe he can silence his heartbeat?" The warden looked doubtful as she twisted her gloved hands together nervously.

Dacre was so able, but it made no sense. He would have heard Verve and come right for her, once the threats had been removed abovestairs. Ardyth and the warden would be a threat, certainly, but that wouldn't have stopped him. Verve was missing some vital bit of information, and yet instinct told her the danger was not inside the house any longer. "What if the killer was being controlled remotely?"

That made the warden's eyebrows rise. "What do you mean?"

Verve shook her head. "What if he or she were bewitched to kill everyone?"

"That doesn't seem—" the warden began.

"Where's Elaia?" asked Verve.

"We don't have time for this," said Ardyth. "You are still in great peril." She moved toward Verve, who backed away a step. "What's wrong?"

Could her instincts be right? Verve moved toward the horse, only to be blocked by the warden. "Move."

The warden shook her head. "In a moment. Dacre Starside is a shape-changer, is he not?" Her gaze hardened and landed on Ardyth, who frowned.

"What are you saying?"

Unmoved and unblinking, the warden nodded at the woman. "You heard me." She looked at Verve. "Do you trust that this creature here is who she says she is?"

Verve swallowed and backed farther away. "Don't come near me."

Ardyth shook her head. "I am exactly who I say I am, my queen. Please, I know you must be careful whom you trust, but—"

"She's been attempting to get you to leave with her this whole time," the warden practically spat. "And your instinct is telling you to go inside, isn't it? That it's safer in there. After all, there are others in the prison who would fight for you. What exactly is 'Ardyth' leading you away to?"

Now Ardyth's face had grown pale. "I can only think of one reason for you to suggest such a thing."

The warden cocked her head to the side. "And that would be what?"

As soon as Ardyth opened her mouth to answer, Verve dropped to her knees, screaming in pain. It felt as though her head were being cleaved in two, right down the middle, and the world grew far too bright.

The air smelled potently of coffee, and strong arms grabbed her. There was a resounding boom, a flash of even brighter light, and Verve was unceremoniously thrown across the back of the gelding.

Someone jumped up behind her, binding her hands with invisible magic, as a woman in the near distance moaned. "Easy there, love," said the warden's voice into Verve's left ear. She shifted shapes into Ardyth, even as the real one convulsed on the ground.

Verve desperately reached for her magic, but it had retreated deep within herself, like a frightened, scolded child. She was positioned upright on the horse, which took off at a gallop with a kick from its rider. It occurred to Verve to throw herself off the horse, but her captor anticipated this and snagged an arm around her waist and pulled her more tightly against their body.

Dacre – for she was certain it must be him – rode at a terrifying speed through the streets, scattering fae in his wake. None sought to stop them even if they recognized Verve, no doubt thinking she was safe with 'Ardyth'.

Screaming for help was of no use; Dacre made certain to silence her with a spell. She struggled and attempted to break whatever arrest he had put on her abilities, but it was to no avail. All too soon they were on the outer rim of the village, and the gates remained wide open for them to race through. And then they were not alone.

Several horses charged from the sparse woods surrounding, and for a moment Verve thought she was being saved. However, Dacre slowed his steed to a walk and nodded in greeting to the men and women on horseback, whose numbers increased as they rode. "Relax, Verve, no one's going to harm you," he said into her ear, having rid himself of Ardyth's form. "I'm sure you have many questions, and I'll try to answer them soon enough. But first we must get you to safety." Of all things, the man had the nerve to kiss her softly on the cheek.

Verve jerked her head away and leaned suddenly to the right, hoping to unseat herself. She was not so lucky.

Dacre merely clamped his hand down harder on her waist and said conversationally, "I could render you unconscious if you're going to be difficult." He laughed when she attempted to turn and spit at him. "I see you have lost none of your fire. Good." They veered to the right slightly, aligning with a path that led into the woods up ahead. Dacre was surrounded by the other riders now. Five rode before them, and many more rode behind, while there were perhaps six on either side. As they reached the woods, the horses and their riders were forced to travel single file.

Though she sought to catch the attention of the horsemen around her, few would look at her openly, and those that did were…strange. Their eyes were unfocused, hazy, and they reeked of Dacre's magic. Horror filled Verve as she realized Dacre must be controlling them like he had the Trusted she had killed in Aslillian.

As if on some silent cue, the riders on their mounts came to a halt. Then, after looking to Dacre, who nodded, the men and women dismounted.

"Do we have a location, my king?" asked a she-fae with clear eyes.

King? Verve shook her head and tried reaching for her magic once more.

Dacre dismounted as well and pulled Verve down after him, staying her before she could escape. "Lovelourn of Etterhea. Tell the others to be wary. I sense our source has not been entirely...open with us about what lies in store."

"Very good, sire." With that said, the she-fae pushed through the crowd, which parted, making a path for Dacre to follow.

"Easy, Verve. You need to calm down." Dacre handed his horse's reins to a man whose eyes were glazed.

Calm down? That was not going to happen. Verve twisted and writhed as Dacre attempted to reel her in, and she tugged in vain against the magic bonds securing her wrists. What had he done to her that she could hardly sense her magic any longer? It was disorienting, to say the least, going from feeling ready to explode with power to weak and unable to fight him off. She was a clawless kitten, and Dacre easily subdued her with a mere wave of his hand. Her muscles went rigid, and she was unable to move a finger.

Obviously satisfied that she was no longer a threat, Dacre scooped her up into his arms and carried her toward where his followers had gathered. "I can see that you're upset, and I understand. But you and I have merely had a misunderstanding."

Verve's eyes rolled around in her head as she tried to think of a way out of this situation. She couldn't fight or run. *I can't even scream for help.*

The she-fae Dacre had spoken to moments ago had drawn a knife and was slitting her own hand before stabbing the hawthorn's bark. At once the tree began begging for mercy. To this the she-fae said, "Grant all the fae and horses and middlings in this company safe passage to Lovelourn and you will be spared."

The tree moaned and shook its branches. *"Surely you must not go there. Please, anywhere else—"*

"Lovelourn or I burn you to the ground. I'm certain one of your siblings here would be more than happy to oblige me." The she-fae wrenched the knife from the bark only to stab the tree again, this time with more force.

Screams filled Verve's mind, though no one around her seemed to bat an eye. Then, with a whimper, the hawthorn's form changed. The trunk split in two and the branches furled together to form the top of the gateway.

Through the portal lay a land wreathed in shadow. Rain fell in heavy sheets from the heavens, so Dacre conjured an umbrella, which hovered over him and Verve in preparation. "Send a few of the expendables through first," he said to the woman before him. "We must make certain there are no traps or tricks."

At his command, the she-fae gestured to a group of men and women, who then moved forward in unison toward the gateway. They walked single file before spreading out and were not five steps through when there was a loud shriek.

The group tensed, and Verve strained even more against the magic holding her still. How had Dacre been able to do this? The bond between them should have been broken when she became Fenn's wife, preventing Dacre from controlling her. Unless this was some magic she hadn't heard of, they had been terribly wrong.

For a moment, there was no sound, and then a wail was taken up in the distance. The landscape through the gateway sprang to life, the trees beyond attacking the middlings that had been sent through.

Dacre rushed forward but did not intervene, simply focusing his attention on what was happening. Whatever spell he had the human middlings under broke, and the terrified men and women scrambled back toward safety, only to be snatched up by branches and borne skyward, raised out of sight, and thrown to the ground with such force, the impact was louder than their cries as they plummeted. All was silent once more, but for the steady rush of wind and rain.

"Stay close and keep your shields up," said Dacre, setting Verve on her feet. He took her hand in his and moved forward with her in tow, her movements entirely out of her control. After first putting up a magical shield around him and Verve, he stepped through the gateway.

Overhead, branches moaned and snapped, bending close to the shield and shying away at the last minute. Every tree they passed under was like this.

"Your new power suits you." Dacre laughed when Verve's eyes widened, startled; at least she had some control over part of her body. He guided her around some raised roots, taking care that she remained in the bubble of protection he had generated and beneath the umbrella. "It's a pity it had to come to this. I had been hoping we could work together to find Death's Maw, but it would seem that is too much to hope for right now."

Verve envisioned herself ripping her hand from his and throwing a fireball at his head. As if in response to the thought, the magic buried deep inside her churned, fighting to rise to the surface, and her hand grew hot.

Of course Dacre noticed and quickly pushed down her magic with his own, giving her a knowing look. "I'll give you back some control once I know you're not going to do anything foolish." He squeezed her hand and turned his attention to the way before them.

Soon enough, they entered a clearing, bringing them relief from the trees' relentless attacks. Dacre did not relax, however, nor did the men and women in his company.

"We need to head west," said the woman who had created the gateway.

Dacre's head snapped back toward the she-fae, who had flanked him and Verve on the right. With a growl, he moved Verve behind his back, shielding her. "You sense no magic from that direction either, I gather."

The fae simply dipped her head in acknowledgement.

"The coast lies that way," Dacre said, looking west. "We're not three miles off. Do we know of any sea monsters in this region?"

"Here in Etterhea? Unlikely."

Dacre shrugged. "Just because we can't sense magic it doesn't mean there aren't any mortal traps. Remain vigilant."

"If I may, sire," said a male voice behind them. "Might we send a few of the middlings before us to clear the way?"

The screams of the now deceased 'expendables' still echoed in Verve's ears. These men and women before Dacre now presumably had little to no magic to defend themselves from whatever horrors might lie ahead, and they were human; they would tire and injure easily. Verve thought she might be sick when Dacre nodded.

"Send only a few. We don't want to use them all at once." Dacre pulled Verve in his wake, keeping himself between her and the other fae. His shield's glow intensified, and the smell of burned coffee filled Verve's nostrils.

As she watched, three middling humans were trotted out before them, one taking the far-left part of the brush, one the middle, one the far-right. Nothing happened, so Dacre motioned for his company to follow after the trail-makers.

"You look like you could murder someone," he said conversationally. His thumb stroked the back of her hand and he slowed his pace somewhat. "Speaking of murder, I bet you're surprised to see me alive." His voice was soft, pleasant even, though Verve could hear an edge to his words, as though there were some wound he was nursing. He was silent for a time as he led her through the overgrowth.

Though Verve now had more endurance than a mere human, she'd barely had a moment's respite since fleeing Aslillian. She stumbled, despite Dacre being in charge of her movements. Fatigue sank into her bones, dug its fingers into her thoughts, making them murky.

After steadying Verve, Dacre stopped his company once more and called for a horse. The gelding they had ridden on earlier was brought forth, and Dacre set Verve atop the creature, extending his magical shield so it covered her as well. Then, manipulating her once more, Dacre made it so her hands were grasping the pommel and her feet were in the stirrups. Once they started moving again, he surprised her by saying, "I don't blame you for trying to kill me. You were, after all, new to your power, and I can only imagine what that might do to someone's mind and emotions." He looked at her sideways and afforded her a rueful grin. "And I know you don't quite see things as I do. Thank the stars for mastership magic, or else you'd probably try something rather dramatic."

Verve's head began to spin. Mastership magic? Fenn had been meaning to use it on her. A great shiver rippled down her spine.

"You're probably wondering where I got the idea for that particularly difficult and hard-to-come by magic," Dacre said, his expression smug. "Next time I see Fenn, I'll have to thank him for leaving dangerous conveyable texts lying around. You shouldn't do that, you know. Anyone might snatch them up."

The muscles around Verve's mouth twitched, though she was unable to force them into the puzzled scowl she wished to wear. Dacre hadn't been on the estate; Fenn's family estate's wards wouldn't have allowed it. That could only mean.... *Tilda.* Curse her. Olive and Fenn really had been right not to trust the she-fae.

He gave her a knowing glance and looked ahead once more, leading the horse by the reins. "My second-in-command is around here somewhere," he said. "She must be avoiding us. I daresay she is rather frightened of you." Dacre chuckled.

They walked on without event for the next half hour, covering the span of a mile. The going was difficult for the mortals, and a way had to be cleared several times for Verve's horse to get through. Each delay brought hope to Verve that she would be able to find the means to overcome the magic controlling her and fight her way back to somewhere, anywhere else. But the hope, it would seem, was futile. Dacre's hold on her magic was a tight fist, and the weariness that sat on her made her eyelids droop.

A scream just before them rent the peace in two. Verve's horse hoofed at the ground, an unhappy snort fogging the air before his muzzle.

Dacre steadied Verve's mount, soothing the creature below his breath as the path parted and showed the source of the scream. Several yards away in a clearing, one of the unfortunate middlings had sunk waist-deep in quicksand and was being sucked farther in with every thrashing movement he made.

Verve tried to shout for him to hold still, to wait to be rescued. Of course she could do no such thing: Dacre had not given her back her voice. Instead, she watched, helpless to do anything, as the company simply moved around the man as he sank farther still.

Perhaps sensing her feelings, Dacre peered up at Verve once more. "We can't expend so much magic or energy before we reach Death's Maw," he said, his tone patient. "We don't know what waits for us in Ithalamore. We need our wits about us and as much strength as we have at our disposal."

If anything, that doubled the heat of Verve's hatred for Dacre, and she sat atop the horse seething as she was led past the poor wretch. Soon his cries were silenced, and Verve closed her eyes.

The next two miles were passed mostly in silence, the fae tense with anticipation or dread, Verve couldn't be certain which. Every once in a while, Dacre would send a mortal scout ahead farther and wider than he had before. Nothing more befell the humans, so the fae company moved through the hanging boughs and over the heavy undergrowth, emerging on a beach covered in blood-red sand.

As before, Dacre sent out a few mortals to scout the area. He reached into the horse's saddlebag and produced a canteen, which he made Verve drink from, before taking a few gulps himself. "I've seen plenty of hawthorns since arriving here. Any one of them might've served as an entrance gateway, and that would have saved us at least some travel." He replaced the canteen and shook his head. "Can you see how far there is 'til we reach our destination?"

Unwittingly, Verve's magic uncoiled. Her eyes unfocused for a brief moment before switching to through-sight, and she was able to seek out the path that lay before them. Death's Maw was close. It sat inland a-ways, but close enough to the beach that they would no doubt be able to hear the sea's roar. Then, having ascertained that it was just another three miles away, Verve's eyes blinked closed and opened once more, her sight returned to normal, and her magic was cut off.

"You have powerful through-sight," said Dacre before turning to address his men and women. "We're close. If the middlings find the beach clear, we should reach our destination within the next twenty minutes. But do not let your shields drop even then. We do not know what we will encounter." He patted the flank of Verve's horse almost absently.

Now Verve's heart raced. Whatever Dacre wanted in Ithalamore, she couldn't let him have it. Again she tried reaching her magic. For a moment, she thought she might have brought some power to the surface, as heat licked at her fingertips, but her captor must have sensed it too, for he pushed back with his own magic. Verve's vision clouded and her head pounded with a headache. She struggled against him until the pain became nigh unbearable.

"Verve," said Dacre sharply. "You're just hurting yourself. Stop it."

With an involuntary whimper, Verve released her magic. She slumped forward in the saddle and clutched more tightly to the pommel, though not by choice.

Now Dacre leapt up behind her without warning, startling her in the process. "You're exhausted." He pulled her back against him and she felt her magic being manipulated once more. "Sleep."

And, unable to resist, she did.

* * *

Even in her unconscious state, Verve was aware of the horse riding across the beach, of fae men and women gaining confidence as they traversed the terrain. She fought the sleeping spell she was under, but it was her own magic being used against her, and it was potent. At last she succumbed entirely and was lost in a strange dream. It involved a walking shadow that Verve instinctively knew was meant to be Olive, wading through murky waters as she raced to reach an unknown destination.

"Get there in time, repay it somehow, and leave," thought Olive the shadow. Her emotions were mixed, fear and desperation

roiling just below the surface and barely controlled. Verve could see it clearly.

Verve's dream shifted to Githtariel. Dead halflings were being carted away by their fellows as weary fae looked on. The air reeked of blood and sweat, of tears and dread. There was little hope here.

"The third prophecy," said one she-fae to another in the dream. "Did we ever find it?"

Her companion shook her head. "How did he even infiltrate our ranks? Githtariel was supposed to be a safe haven for our queen, and instead we practically handed her over to the Traitor King." She moaned. "Is this how the world ends?"

Once again Verve's sleeping mind bore her elsewhere. This time, it was she who stood in a space without light. She sensed there was something up ahead that she wanted so desperately, she would do anything for it. Fleetingly, she caught a glimpse of light and moved forward, thinking perhaps her moment had come. There was a cruel laugh and someone pushed her from behind. Verve had the sensation of falling forward and jerked awake.

She was lying on her side, her hands and ankles restrained in the dimness. Grit was on her face and head, which was propped up on a pillow, and her dry mouth tasted of the sea. Though her magic still lay dormant – Verve reached for it several times before the pain became too much – she could now move her body of her own volition. Waves pounded rocks in the near distance. Over all was the strong aroma of coffee, mixed with chocolate and spices. A groan escaped her lips before she could stop it. Blessedly, no one seemed to have heard her.

Verve blinked, trying to make sense of where she was. The ground beneath her was sand, and light flickered across it as did creeping shadows. A fire's warmth radiated toward her, making her sweat and wish even more for a glass of water. With some difficulty she maneuvered herself so that she was looking up at the sky…or, rather, where the sky should have been. Overhead stretched a dome of red fabric, shielding her from the rain that beat against it in relentless sheets. Outside the tent sat the fire, which was shielded from the water and winds with magic. There were voices nearby. They sounded excited, impatient.

"Is she awake yet?" asked a woman's voice, one that Verve recognized but couldn't quite place in her groggy state. "I thought I heard someone groaning a moment ago."

A sigh was given in response, and a moment later, Dacre spoke. "I'll check on her soon." He sounded exhausted.

The woman agreed with Verve's assessment, it would seem. "You should sleep. Mastership magic can be draining when it's used on someone like her."

"I'm quite aware of that," he said, his tone a warning that she should pursue that line of discussion no further. "You keep the shields running for a while. It's about time you pulled some more of your weight here."

Footsteps approached Verve's enclosure, so she closed her eyes and attempted to feign sleep, hoping to buy herself some time to think or at least delay what might be the inevitable. "Hello, Verve," Dacre all but whispered. "Are you awake yet?"

A gentle hand brushed away the strand of hair that had fallen across her face when she had moved onto her back. She willed her muscles not to tense and betray her. If only she hadn't made a sound! That would have given her time to attempt to free herself from her bonds. Then, perhaps, she would have been able to crawl through the gap at the bottom of the tent and—

"Verve?" Dacre laid a hand on her right shoulder and shook it with care. When she did not respond, he tapped her face gently with the palm of his hand. Eventually he stopped and sighed. "Do you wish to do things the difficult way, then?"

She had no time to think what he could mean by that before a small bolt of electricity flowed into her left temple. It stung and startled her, and against her will her eyes opened.

His grinning face was inches from hers. "Welcome back. I trust that you slept well."

Verve pushed against him with her bound hands, sending him sprawling. She sat up and wiggled her way toward the edge of the tent, only to be seized by the ankles and dragged back. "Let go of me," she said, her voice raw and rough.

"Easy there." He flipped Verve onto her back and loomed over her.

She struck out with her bound feet, but it was of no use: easily he dodged her attack and scooped her up into his arms, where she thrashed and swore at him with words that would have made a soldier blush.

The rain was still coming down as he carried her out of the tent, though there was a break in the clouds on the horizon. Ice-cold droplets stung against her skin before Dacre magicked an umbrella overhead.

Fae men and women emerged from identical tents surrounding Verve's, and others rose from the sand on the beach, all eyes on her. "Do you need help?" asked a voice that made Verve struggle even more.

"Stay where you are, Tilda," said Dacre through his teeth as he nearly lost his grip on Verve. "I'm sorry to do this, love, but...."

As they had before, Verve's muscles froze and she was unable to move. All she could do was glare at Dacre as he bore her into the woods along the beach.

"We should leave some men to guard the entrance," said Tilda. Her voice was near the left and slightly behind Dacre's shoulder. This sounded to Verve like an old argument.

Dacre shook his head. "Once we're through and the gateway is closed, no one will be able to follow us. Besides, I'll need everyone to keep an eye on the dead while I'm vulnerable."

Tilda snorted. "But we could still be ambushed once we emerge. Fenn is still out there and he's not stupid. He could—"

"I'll have enough power from the pools that any attack won't matter when we emerge. Relax, Tilda. I have things under control."

The pools? Verve's mind raced as she tried to remember everything she had studied about the Lands of the Dead. She didn't recall having heard anything about power-giving pools, but that didn't mean none existed. After all, she hadn't read the entire book she'd stolen from Dacre's house, and the voice that had been helping her mentioned its having been tampered with. Where was that voice now, she wondered. Help would be more than welcome, especially as a large black tree came into view.

"I'm sorry about this, Verve," Dacre murmured as he set Verve on her feet. To Tilda he said, "Bring me the prisoner."

There was a wail in the near distance and the smell of ginger filled the air. Several creatures hauled a male fae in chains into Verve's line of sight and rested him against the tree trunk. "Please," he said, looking at her with desperation in his eyes, "don't kill me. I have a family."

Dacre slid a hand down Verve's collarbone, and her magic rose within her. The initial thrill of thinking her power might return under her control faded, and terror filled its place as Dacre manipulated her, reaching for her ability to kill an immortal being.

"Don't do this," Verve managed to say, before Dacre magically silenced her.

The look he gave her was pitying, but there was resolve in his eyes as, using his control, he raised her right hand. "It must be done." And with that said, he channeled his power through her, forcing killing magic up through her veins and out through her outstretched hand.

With an almighty ripping sound, the prisoner's body cracked open down the middle, spilling his silver blood and ending his life. The air stank of vanilla, coffee, and something metallic.

Dacre wasted no time. He kicked the body aside and pulled Verve toward the tree, placing her hand against its bark.

This strange hawthorn did not speak at first, instead it growled, causing the other fae to back away. *"You have found me, Firstblood of No Land. For better or for worse, you have gained access to the wonders and terrors of Ithalamore."* It was a deep and ancient woman's voice that spoke.

Don't open. Please don't open, thought Verve.

The tree cackled. *"It is too late, my dear. You cannot stop what has been put into motion, cannot un-spill the blood that has been let. Would you if you could? I wonder."* The ground trembled. Black lightning flashed across the sky and struck the tree, which evaporated into a mist.

Verve's ears were still ringing when the haze cleared, revealing a monstrous gateway outlined in black thorns. The land beyond was dark, indiscernible.

After placing a protective arm around Verve, Dacre conjured several balls of light and sent them on ahead into the Lands of the Dead. All was silent and still. "Send in a few middlings and warriors; the Fire Queen and I will follow close behind."

His orders were followed swiftly and without comment. Too soon Verve was led through the gateway, and the remaining fae followed on her heels. With an ominous rumble, the opening closed, and they were plummeted into near darkness.

More fae formed balls of a magical light, filling the cool air with different hues and smells, mostly metal and spice. "We're looking for the archway, right?" said Tilda. She pushed through the crowd, her eyes on Dacre.

Dacre nodded. "This is the antechamber." He studied Verve. "If we barricade the entryway behind us, that will keep her safe 'til I return."

Tilda huffed. "We should get moving." She started toward the tunnel that stretched out on their right, only to stop when Dacre raised a hand. "Majesty?"

"Send the others ahead to clear the way, and then return to me for further instruction." Without waiting for a response, Dacre forced Verve to follow him to a stone pillar that reached higher than she could see. He maneuvered her into a sitting position on the ground with her back pressed against the pillar and then caused glowing bands of light to snake around her body and wrists, effectively binding her in place. "Let's see if these hold." With that said, he released his control over Verve's movements and crouched next to her.

Verve screamed bloody murder at him when her voice returned, and she thrashed and struggled against her trusses to no effect. "Let me go, you fiend!"

He studied his handiwork as she continued to rail against him, tightening the glowing ropes just to the point of being uncomfortable but causing no pain. "I know you're upset with me, but this will be over soon enough and you will realize I did this for you as well." Dacre brushed away a few furious tears that ran down her face.

"You murdered a man for *me*?" She spat at him and then broke into hysterical sobs. "You killed him. You used me to kill him."

Dacre sighed as he wiped the spittle from his brow. "So I did. But he's not the first you or I have killed, and he won't be the last."

"I hate you."

His responding grin was positively predatory. "We'll work on that, my queen."

She strained and tried to pull away as he leaned in and pressed his lips against hers. The kiss was possessive and demanding; it frightened and disgusted Verve, and she redoubled her attempts to free herself.

Finally, he pulled away. The outer room had emptied of all but Tilda, who stood watching Verve with apparent dislike. Dacre, however, did not seem to notice. "You'll stay here and make certain our Fire Queen doesn't do anything tricky."

A tremor ran through Verve's body. What would happen if she was left alone with the she-fae? Nothing good would come of it, she reckoned. At the very least she wouldn't be able to find a way to escape, at the worst.... "You can't leave me with her," she blurted.

Dacre looked down at her, his brow furrowed. "She's not going to hurt you, Verve."

Verve glared at him, her thoughts racing as she tried to come up with a good reason for Dacre to mistrust Tilda. "She's Fenn's cousin and she betrayed him."

"Yes, I realize that."

Tilda rolled her eyes. "I don't wish to remain with her either. You'll need me to fight off any guardians you might encounter."

But Dacre shook his head. "You're the only one I trust who isn't under my control. Keep a close watch over her and don't let her talk too much. She can be rather convincing, once cornered."

When he turned and started to walk away, Verve became even more desperate. "She tried to kill me."

That made Dacre pause. Ever so slowly he pivoted back to face her, his expression darkening. "That's quite a serious lie."

Verve felt an attack coming on, only instead of trying to stop it, she let her breaths come in desperate gasps and welcomed the shaking that sometimes accompanied them. "You can't – trust her. She blew up Fenn's estate. I only just escaped." *Please believe me.*

A crease formed on Dacre's brow and his eyes narrowed. "*You* blew up the estate?" he asked Tilda, his voice cold. "You said the overeager weather-makers were responsible."

Tilda took a half step back. "I-I can explain."

"I thought I told you to not do anything that would put her in danger." He stalked toward the she-fae, and for a moment, Verve thought he might strike.

"I didn't detonate the explosive package until she was safely away. You have to believe me."

He seemed to turn over her words for a moment before saying softly, "Why should I believe you?"

The she-fae's throat bobbed as she swallowed. "She's trying to come between you and me. You said it yourself: Verity can be persuasive once cornered."

"That's 'Her Majesty' to you." His head tilted to the side as he studied Verve, whose vision began to blur.

To her surprise, she felt Dacre's fingers against the pulse on her neck, felt lethal magic rising from deep within her. She tried to say something to dissuade him, for though she hated Tilda, she did not wish to kill her, but all that came out was a weak whimper.

There was the sound of fast retreating footsteps and the darkness exploded with light as Dacre used Verve's magic to slay the she-fae. Then, as though nothing had happened, Dacre stroked her cheek and rose. "You'll be all right. Killing gets easier the more you have to do it."

Verve choked on bile. "Like you killed my father?" she managed to gasp out.

Dacre sighed. "That was truly an accident, one for which I am deeply sorry, Verve. But come, that is in the past now. Surely you'll forgive me for the slip soon enough."

"Never." She blinked her eyes furiously, willing herself to calm down from the attack.

He laughed, and she could just make out the image of him shaking his head. "Time will prove you wrong." With a parting grin, he turned once more and walked away. "I'll see you shortly. You'll be safe enough without me, but just to be certain…." He threw up a hand, and the outer room filled with the scent of chocolate as he cast a protective ward. And then he was gone.

Though she howled and wriggled and writhed, he did not return and the bonds did not give. *Trapped.* Spots filled the corners of her vision and her shaking grew worse. Nausea tore at her empty stomach and sweat rolled down the back of her neck as she slumped forward at last, knowing herself defeated.

It was in the ensuing silence that Verve heard it, the soft beating of a second heart in the outer chamber. She thought little of it, wondering absently if it were some specter come to torment her, and began to cry in earnest.

"Shh, you'll draw him back," someone whispered.

Verve's chest heaved as she attempted to quiet her breathing. "Hello?" she whispered back. Though she tried, she could not make out any person near her, though she heard their soft footsteps treading toward her from directly ahead. The closer they got, the louder their heart beat, and Verve's pulse began to race. "Who's there?" Was it some trick of the mind? Perhaps her agitated state caused her to imagine that someone had come to her rescue.

There was a great sigh. "Well, that went not entirely to plan." A moment went by, and then there was a soft popping sound accompanied by a weak whiff of vanilla, and in front of her stood Olive. The elderly woman winked at Verve, taking in her startled appearance.

A million questions flooded Verve's mind as Olive bent over her and studied the magical ropes binding her in place. All that came out was, "How did you get in?"

Olive grinned and produced a wicked glowing blade from her side and took to slicing through the bindings. "I'll tell you all about it, but keep your voice lowered. Surely you can hear the Traitor King on the other side of this wall." She jerked her head toward the wall on Verve's right, and sure enough, there were shouts and the sounds of weapons striking, although it was so faint, she wondered if Olive might be mistaken about the distance.

"How?" Verve asked, trying to hold still as Olive sawed.

"Well, after I...left you at the Library of Aslillian, I tried making my way to the Mortal Gate, only something would not let me." She took a break from her work and looked away from Verve, ashamed apparently. "Well, some*one* would not let me is more like. When one gives their magic to another, it binds them. You were lucky to escape Dacre when you did all those months ago, what with his magic in your veins. Probably something to do with the fact that you were taken instead of running away yourself. Then you were smart to bind yourself to someone else through marriage." She took in a deep breath and returned to her work. One cord gave way and another, but there were many still left to free Verve from.

Verve tried to remain still, but with each cord that was cut, she became more and more restless. The glowing blade nicked her arm at one point, and she began to bleed profusely.

Olive swore below her breath and hastened her work. "Keep still. I could have cut something vital, and in your state.... It won't kill you, obviously, but it won't do you any favors either. Ah, almost there."

Not knowing enough of how her own power worked, Verve asked, "My magic compelled you to follow me?"

Olive's eyebrows rose at that. "To say the least. Trying to run away was pain, pure and awful pain – not that I didn't have it comin'.

Anyway, I followed your trail from Aslillian, and was just going to make myself known in Githtariel, but I saw that one woman grab you and attack another she-fae, and I knew it must be Lord Starside in disguise, so I made myself invisible and followed you on a horse I stole. A riderless horse chomping at the bit gets odd looks, let me tell you that. There we are." She cut Verve free from the final strand of rope and then put pressure on the wound she had inflicted.

"Thank you." Unsteady, Verve managed to get to her feet. But she was lightheaded from blood loss and had to lean against the pillar for support.

"Let me see if I can heal that," said Olive. She rolled up her sleeves and pressed her right palm against the cut, which hissed and sizzled as the skin knitted itself back together.

The process burned, but Verve didn't mind; she was too glad to be free to care much about pain. In the next chamber over, the otherworldly screams and cries came to a climax, and then all was still.

Olive looked toward the lone black hawthorn, from which the gateway had formed. "We need to leave here quickly. I don't know what Lord Starside is about, but it can't be anything you'll benefit from."

As tempting as that was, now that she was in the Lands of the Dead, Verve knew she had to at least *try* breaking the curse Dacre had put on her. She took a steadying breath and used through-sight – he'd left her access to that much, at least. The chamber next to theirs was littered with the bodies of middlings. Verve looked beyond that cavern and into the next, hoping to catch a glimpse of what Dacre and his remaining soldiers were doing, but they had disappeared from view. "We need to find Igraine," Verve whispered. When Olive did not respond, she continued. "She alone knows how to brew any potion that might help me."

For a time Olive simply looked at her, her expression unfathomable. Then she shook her head. "That is how Lord Starside lured you here."

"But the books said—"

"You said yourself that those books had been enchanted, and I think we both know his lordship did the enchanting. There's nothing here, Miss Verity. You're going to have to accept the fact that your curse isn't going to be lifted anytime soon." Her expression was pitying but anxious and she moved toward the hawthorn. "I'm sorry. I truly am."

Verve shook her head. "But the voice said I would find the means of breaking the curse here."

"And you think you can trust any disembodied specter that whispers honeyed words into your ears? Face it, dear, you've been lied to."

That was almost too much to bear. Had she really abandoned her soul's mate and risked so much only to come away emptyhanded? No, worse, with a list of deaths to her name. Verve expected to fall to pieces then and there. Instead, she drew in a deep breath and steadied herself. "You may go back, Olive, but I'm not leaving this place until I'm cured."

Olive snorted. "You still have hope? Hope is for foolish mortals who don't know when they've been truly beaten."

Verve pushed away from the pillar and staggered toward a tunnel on the wall opposite the archway Dacre had passed through. There was no way of knowing if it would lead her to Igraine, but it was better than remaining here, waiting for Dacre to return. "I'll send you back to Letorheas or Etterhea, if you wish, Olive. Foolish or not, I'm staying."

Olive gave the tree, which stood in the middle of the cavernous room, a look of longing before drawing in a deep breath. "I don't know if your magic will let me go. I still owe you one debt yet, and until that is paid...well, I guess I'm at your service." She gestured to the tunnel and steadied Verve, who had stumbled forward. "Easy there, miss. Watch for the body."

Tilda's body lay on the cold stone, her eyes wide and clouded in death. Verve looked away and took Olive's arm for support.

"That magic he used to arrest your powers...."

"Mastership magic," said Verve. "What of it?"

Olive hesitated. "It's made you more vulnerable here, I believe. You won't be able to fight off any spirits, should they attack. And if you are wounded, it appears you aren't healing as you ought."

Verve forced a smile. "Then I'm glad I have you to protect me."

Olive gave her a sideways grin. "'Twas a good thing you gave me some of your power, then. I'll have my debt repaid in no time."

CHAPTER FOURTEEN

Onward they walked in semidarkness, the way ahead of them lit by only one orb of light that Olive produced. The protective shield Dacre had erected only stretched so far, and when they'd reached the end of it, there was an audible *pop* and the air grew colder. That had been half an hour ago. Now they moved forward with less certainty. There was a presence in the air, not malevolent exactly but neither was it benign. A few times Verve caught sight of a glowing human form a-ways ahead. But before they could get closer to ask for help or direction, the image dissolved, leaving them to wonder at what they had seen.

They had to stop after an hour of walking, as Olive was tiring. Thankfully, she had a canteen with her. She took a few small sips and then passed it on to Verve, who tried not to drink too greedily; if they became lost down here, it might be the only water they would have for days. The look the two women shared was bleak, and Olive snatched the water vessel back once it had been stoppered. "You don't remember anything that might help us? Anything from your books or that your mate told you?" She let out a great *oomph* as she sat on a boulder.

Verve sat next to her. "Most of what he told me was in verse, and none of it applied to anything to do with the underworld. Well, other than the fact that only two fae would ever be able to open Death's Maw."

Olive bit her lower lip at that and her eyes grew distant. "They were wrong about that, weren't they? The prophets were, I mean. You alone were able to open it."

Verve licked her lips, the water but a memory. "Dacre mentioned pools and something about getting more power. Maybe he'll gain that ability too. Do you know anything about it?"

"Some children's stories say there are pools down here, meant to give the worthy terrible powers, but I never thought.... You must believe me, Miss Verity, that I would never have been on his lordship's side had I known he was after that sort of magic, or that it actually existed." She nodded toward the darkness they had left behind them as her orb of light bobbed closer.

A shiver went down Verve's spine at the woman's tone and she drew her arms about herself. "What is that sort of magic and why is it bad?"

"Magic is neither good nor bad, it's all in how one uses it," said Olive. "But to answer your question, you know there are many realms, yes?"

Verve nodded. "Etterhea and Letorheas, yes."

That made the crone laugh. "Aye, but there are many more than those, ones that are not so easily traveled to or known of, but all have one thing in common, where their dead come before they go to their final rest."

Verve blinked. "Ithalamore."

"In legend, or in rumor at least, every realm has its own chamber to hold the spirits of those waiting. Before they are, shall we say 'processed' and allowed to move forward, they are stripped of their magic, which is cast into its own pool." She looked at Verve like a teacher waiting for a pupil to come to her own conclusion on a particularly trying lesson.

"Dacre can gain the powers from every realm if he bathes in each pool."

Olive sniffed. "More like drown himself in each." She gave Verve a knowing look. "You remember how it felt. It will greatly weaken him at first. He will be as close to death as any immortal can be. Perhaps we were unwise to pursue your cure over his demise."

That made Verve shudder mightily. "I don't want to kill anyone."

"And yet you have. Accidents count as well, Miss Verity. Your hands are quite bloody."

The words sat between them for a few moments, and Verve turned them over in her mind. At long last she spoke. "I regret the lives I took, though few, if any, I've taken were on purpose. How does one move on from such things and continue to live?"

The look Olive gave her was sharp and wary. "You don't live *despite* the deaths you caused, Miss Verity. You live *because* of them. Honor those who died by doing what they cannot, and try to make your peace."

"That's easy for you to say."

Olive rose. "Is it? I killed two elves out of pure spite. You killed over one hundred people to save yourself. Which is the more evil of the two of us? I could not say."

As if in response to her words, the orb of light flickered and died, plunging them into complete darkness. A soft breeze began to blow. Verve sensed that Olive had got to her feet, hands raised in front of her. "Miss Verity," she said, her words deliberate, "something's interfering with my magic."

There was a howl in the distance, followed by a brief silence before several dozen other creatures joined in.

"Run!" Olive shouted. She took Verve by the arm and started to lead her away, but something unseen came between them and threw the two women asunder.

Verve was tossed several paces and struck the cavern wall, emptying her lungs in one loud gasp. Spots filled her vision as she tried to draw breath, but something cold had clasped her by the throat and pinned her against the slick rock at her back. She clawed and batted at the invisible hand holding her, but her flesh passed right through.

"What do you seek and where do you make?" The woman's voice was soft and rhythmic, a clear taunt as Verve struggled. An icy finger trailed down her cheek, catching beads of sweat as it went. "She has power – great power, even – but cannot reach it." The woman tutted. "What a waste. What a shame."

Nearby, Olive was fighting against her own attacker, swearing and thrashing as the air filled with her residual bursts. She managed to form another ball of light, and it floated between them, illuminating the ghost that had Verve pinned.

The woman holding Verve was a small creature, somewhat see-through, wearing a blackened robe made of a gauzy fabric. Her grasp on Verve tightened until the latter's eyes bulged. "She cannot die. 'Tis true and 'tis a pity. But oh, what fun I shall have in making the murderess suffer."

A bolt of red light struck the ghost in the shoulder, passed through, and hit the wall next to Verve's face. There was no accompanying residual burst. "That's enough," said a soft yet authoritative voice from behind the ghost.

The being growled but dropped Verve, who fell to the ground, coughing and massaging her throat. "Must you deny me every bit of joy which comes my way?" asked the ghost. "Honestly, if I didn't know any better, I'd say your sense of humor died when your body did."

For that she was rewarded with another bolt of magic, this one catching her in the chest and not passing through. "There is a protocol, specter, a way of doing and being in Ithalamore. Perhaps it is time you moved on." The newcomer sounded bored.

Verve blinked, trying to take in the scene in front of her, but Olive's light had dimmed, though it sounded as though she was still fighting. Verve tried her voice, hoping to ask the new creature for help, but instead she retched on the ground and broke into another fit of gasping. It still felt as though that icy hand was around her throat, though she knew it was gone. *I'll be rather bruised here soon.*

The first creature wailed. "No, no. I can't move on. I won't move on. It's too good here, too familiar. You can't make me, Mother."

"Go prove yourself useful, if you wish for more time. Help the other middling and bring her hither. And child? No more choking."

When Verve managed to sit up, she flinched. The second creature, the one the other had called 'Mother', towered over her, a faintly glowing sword clutched in her left hand. Where her eyes should have been were two coals of red fire. Her hair was so black it was blue and it stood on end in places, as though she had just risen from bed or had been given a shock. And, unlike the first creature, this woman seemed entirely solid and not a bit see-through. Verve's hairs rose on end, and she tried to crawl away, but found there was nowhere for her to go.

"So, you are the one who has been foretold." The woman stretched her sword out toward Verve, catching her gently under the chin and forcing Verve to look up at her. She frowned. "You have not come into your full power yet, I see, which is a pity. I would have liked to see it all." The woman sighed, pulling the sword away, its tip slicing Verve on the jaw.

Silver blood trickled down Verve's neck and dripped down her front, but she made no move to stanch the flow. Words failed her as fear took hold.

The woman sheathed her sword and studied Verve, a frown forming on her pale face. "You still have mortal blood, I see. And a curse has been placed on you."

Olive screamed and swore as she was led by the scruff of the neck toward the swordswoman. Then, with a great grunt, she was tossed onto the ground next to Verve. At the sight of the new threat, Olive cowered and seemed suddenly lost for words.

"Here, Mother," said the specter who had subdued Olive. "I hear others making a nuisance of themselves. Mightn't I investigate?"

'Mother' studied Verve's face, her expression unreadable. Whatever she saw, Verve couldn't be certain, but the woman did not look away as she said, "No. Gather your sisters and stand watch. Sound the alarm, should they move this way."

The specter snapped a smart, if not sincere, salute and glided away into the darkness whence Verve and Olive had come.

Now they were alone with the woman, whose hand rested on her sword's pommel. Her glowing eyes turned to the crone briefly before once more coming to rest on Verve. "I believe you have a favor to ask me, Your Majesty."

Verve gulped. When she spoke, her voice was hoarse and barely above a whisper. "I'm looking for Igraine the potion-maker. She is said to have been the only known fae capable of brewing the potion that will...."

The swordswoman raised her hand. "Forgive me, but I will save you some time and trouble."

"Now see here," said Olive, her courage rising apparently. "We've come a long way and have braved many perils for this information. And you would deny us when we have come this close? Typical of the dead." She spat onto the ground in front of them.

"Careful, mortal," the swordswoman said. "You do your mistress no favors by wagging your tongue at the one person who can help her."

Verve frowned and rubbed her throat once more. "But I thought you said you can't help us."

The woman huffed and shook her dark hair from her face. "I said no such thing."

"Implied it, then," said Olive, before adding a forcedly polite, "ma'am."

That seemed to do little to placate the swordswoman, who narrowed her eyes at the crone and continued speaking to Verve, her voice taut. "I am the Guardian of Secrets, Watcher of the Pool of Ith-Letor, Mother of the Dead, and Grand Traverser of the Underworlds. It is within my power to help or hinder you, children, so I would choose my words with more care and caution." Her chest heaved and the light in her eye sockets flared.

Verve could not tear her gaze from that terrible face. She needed to be the one to address the woman, as it would seem Olive had already started them off at a disadvantage. But Verve knew her temper was worse than Olive's; she would have to keep herself in check. Thinking back to the book of manners and polite society Mother had read to Ainsley, Helena, Dav, and her when they were little, Verve took a deep breath and spoke. "Milady, please forgive our intrusion into your...realm."

The swordswoman's eyebrows rose at the words. "You may call me either Mother or Igraine. As far as intruding, you are not sorry.

No one who enters here does so by accident or with reluctance in their heart. Enough of your pretty words with false meanings. You wish to break the curse put on you, and I am the one whose help you need."

"Will you?" Verve asked, forgetting her manners. "Will you help me?"

Igraine smiled, and Verve didn't know if she should be encouraged or terrified. There was something there that was not quite fae or elf and not quite human. Verve knew the woman must truly be dead and yet not, and that was most terrible of all: a creature passing between. "I will help you, Verity of the No Lands, if you make an oath."

What could this creature possibly want from Verve? She almost said as much but held the words back. "I'm listening." Her legs were beginning to cramp so she pulled herself to her feet, though she still was lightheaded and weak.

"There was once a line of fae and elves that did my family sorely wrong. One in particular was quite evil." Igraine held out a hand for Olive, but the stubborn woman stumbled to her feet on her own. "The thief took from my mother her foresight, though men can rarely wield it well and he proved no different. He took my father's gifting ability, which I think was the most unfair of all, for I know the thief would never use it to aid another. My aunts, uncles, cousins, and brothers all lost their most precious abilities to this cad ere he was banished. You must swear to me you will find this man in his exile and take from him what he took from my family, and if they can be found, you must return the gifts to each." She studied Verve closely, her eyes brightening as the moments ticked by.

"Where would I find him?"

"Oh, you will find him easily enough, I daresay. It has been Seen."

Verve nodded. "Very well. But what is his name and how will I know him?"

At that Igraine's lips twisted up into a grin. "Vow to me first that you will strike when you have the opportunity. That you will be ruthless and kill him, should you fail to retrieve the gifts." When

Verve made to protest, the woman held up a hand, "He is not worth any tears or regrets and would as soon take all from you as you would blink at him. Think of your future. Do you really want to go around, unable to touch others without hurting or murdering them?"

That made Verve wince. "But killing this person…that would be only as a last resort, yes?"

The woman inclined her head. "As you say."

Olive spoke up. "What choice do you have, Miss Verity? You're powerful enough to take from this fellow whatever he's stolen. Don't worry about having to kill anyone." She gave Igraine a pointed look. "This specter here only wants to make certain you are serious in your oath."

"Oh, this isn't any common oath," said Igraine. "You must vow it in blood."

Verve drew back, thinking the woman meant to draw her sword. "I've lost enough blood today."

"No excessive bloodletting is necessary. Just prick your finger, take my hand, and repeat the words of the vow."

"But I'm cursed, you'll be—"

"I'll be fine because I'm dead. Your curse does not extend to the likes of me, as I thought you would have noticed after my subject attempted to strangle you." She nodded in the direction of said subject, though Verve could not make her out in the darkness extending beyond them.

It was a tempting offer, but was it right? Thoughts of being able to embrace Mother and her sisters again entered her thoughts, and she clenched her fists, the desire making her ache. On the other hand, what if she truly failed and had to kill this man? Verve's hands trembled as unbidden images of Helena and Father filled her mind. Dead, cold, still for eternity. That was another question for Igraine, and another boon to bargain for.

"You have another desire, do you?" said the woman.

Verve drew in a deep breath. "I want to see my sister and father again." She thought Igraine would deny her outright and warn her of the dangers of summoning the dead. Instead, the terrible being nodded slowly.

"Another time. You now have eternal access to Ithalamore, since you offered blood at Death's Maw."

Does she really expect me to leave and hope to come back someday? That would not do. There was no guarantee she would return here, should she even escape it to begin with. "Why can't I see them now?" Verve sounded like a petulant child but she didn't care. She was so close to having her curse removed and retrieving her sister and father, it would be foolish not to do everything within her power to see that things went her way.

The creature made a distasteful face, and the fire in her eyes flashed. "Your sister and father have passed on to the next life."

A sob escaped Verve's lips, and her tears started anew. "You said I could see them."

"It will take time and much power to create a way for you to meet with them," said Igraine with a hint of impatience in her voice. "These things take weeks, not hours, neither of which you have at the moment. I will grant you access to your sister and father in six weeks' time, but you must return for that to happen." From her belt she drew a dagger and extended it to Verve, who hesitated. "This is the only way."

"And if I fail to keep up my end of the bargain?"

A wicked grin rose on Igraine's face, and Verve found herself taking a step backward. "I get to pick a life to take into my eternal servitude. But failing is nigh impossible, with the two options I gave you: take or kill. It's really quite simple."

Steeling herself, Verve nodded and accepted the blade. Then she drew a deep breath before she could change her mind and pricked her finger on its tip. She hardly felt the pain and watched in detachment as silver blood dripped from where she had cut.

Igraine snatched the blade back and pricked her own finger, black droplets of blood beading there. "Take my hand and repeat what I say."

Verve grasped Igraine's right hand with her own and winced when a jolt of electricity shot up her arm. If the woman felt it as well, Verve couldn't say.

"I, Verity Springer, vow to return to Ithalamore, and from there seek out the rogue whose name shall be given me. This vow and bargain will be considered fulfilled once I have retrieved the gifts stolen and returned them to their rightful owners. If that should fail, I vow to avenge the wronged by killing the aforementioned rogue. I shall upkeep the spirit of the bargain and not seek to take advantage of the one who benefits me."

Lead dropped into Verve's stomach as she repeated the words verbatim. While she spoke, it felt as though the place where she had cut herself was being invaded, dug into with a penknife. It burned terribly, and on the last words of the oath, it grew nigh unbearable. She stumbled over the remainder, gasping as her hand shone red for a moment before returning to normal.

"Good. Now that that's out of the way...." Igraine flicked her left hand and a clear vial full of black liquid materialized in the palm of her right hand. She held it out for Verve to take, but then drew it back. "Some instruction first, I think."

Verve huffed impatiently. "All right," she said, and then waited. *This woman has a flair for the dramatic.*

The she-fae winked at her and shook her mane of dark locks. "This is called the Soul's Divorce." She shook the vial and its contents began to swirl, slowly at first, changing colors from pitch-black to gray, to white, and then all the colors Verve had ever seen. At once it stopped and the contents turned clear. "As a remade being, you carry within you your mortal self and your fae self. But, since you were remade yet again, there is a third part to this puzzle.

"It is your mortal self to which the curse is bound, the only part Lord Dacre Starside could truly hold any sway over. The fae and the Fire Queen must destroy the mortal. It's that simple, and that difficult."

These words made Verve frown. "I don't think I understand."

"That makes two of us," said Olive with a snort.

Igraine gave Olive an annoyed look and turned her attention back to Verve. "There will be a fight, two victors, one loser. Make certain the mortal piece dies." When Verve started to ask for more information, the she-fae shook her head and passed the vial over to her. "That is all I am able to tell you. You will know what to do when the time comes."

Verve made to unstopper the vial, her hands trembling, when Igraine cleared her throat. "What now?" Verve snapped.

"The name of the man you seek to avenge me is Larknott."

Her words had barely registered with Verve before the vial exploded.

CHAPTER FIFTEEN

A dull roaring filled Verve's ears while glass as fine as dust swirled in a cloud of blue in front of her. It took her a moment to recognize the name 'Larknott' but when she did, she felt the blood rush from her face. "You wretch!" she cried.

The she-fae merely quirked an eyebrow as Verve tried to step toward her. "Brace yourself. You need to step inside the vortex before all the potion evaporates." She and Olive stepped back as the intensity of the wind increased.

"Think, Miss Verity," said Olive above the wind. "There are more with the name Larknott besides your husband. Focus on the task at hand and worry about your bargain later."

Verve glared at Igraine a moment longer, drew in a deep breath, and stepped into the middle of the whirlwind. At once she was plunged into impenetrable darkness and a great howling sound filled her ears, rattled her skull, and tore at her clothing. Then there was the sensation of something pawing at her mouth, forcing her lips to part against her will. The potion once more became liquid as it hovered in the air in front of her and shot into her mouth.

It tasted of laudanum and peaches on her tongue and it burned as it slid down her throat. Verve gasped and clawed at the air, but it was too late to save herself: the air rushed out of her lungs and her heart slowed to a sluggish pace. The last thing she saw before she hit the ground in a dead faint was the face of Igraine watching her with interest.

★ ★ ★

There was darkness and water. Verve floated in a vast body of liquid the color of ink. *I can't swim.* The memory of being transformed caused her to jerk about in her suspended state, but she needn't have worried: her foot skimmed solid ground and it would appear that the water was only a foot or two deep.

"Hello?" Verve's voice echoed around her three times and stopped. *Odd.* She got to her feet and spun around. Olive and Igraine were still there, though they stood far back from her and their forms were insubstantial and hazy, almost like images from a dream. "It didn't work. Nothing happened." She waited for the women to react, but it was as though they couldn't hear or see her. Frowning, Verve looked to where their eyes were trained and screamed. There on the ground where she had stood moments earlier was a body floating in the inky waters. "No. That can't be." A great tremor ran through Verve as she examined the figure more closely. The body was tall and ethereal, glowing a soft silver. It was also very familiar.

A red version of herself sat up from the body, looked at her hands, felt her face, and glanced back at the shell she had left behind. "Blast!" said Red Verve, crawling away from the scene. The creature staggered to her feet and looked around wildly. Her eyes alighted on Verve.

On instinct, Verve knew what the creature was thinking. It was wondering if she was the version of herself she was meant to kill. Perhaps she knew because she was thinking the same thing.

"You're silver," said Red Verve, screwing up her face as if offended.

"What of it? You're red," Verve countered.

Neither of them moved for a moment as they sized the other up. It was while they were staring at each other, trying to figure out what was going on, that a third being rose from the body on the ground. This one was a blue copy of Verve.

Blue Verve dusted herself off and looked around her. "Now what am I supposed to do?" she asked Igraine.

"She can't hear you," Verve said. "And I think we know what needs to be done: two of us have got to kill one of us and then we return to the body."

"Before Dacre can come back for me," Red Verve added. "Then we leave for Letorheas."

The blue version of her nodded and backed away a few steps. "Right. But we need to make certain we're killing the correct one." She worried her lower lip and looked down at her hands.

Verve knew she was wondering if she dared kill part of herself, as she had done more than enough killing already. Verve exchanged a look with Red Verve. "Which of us are you, mortal, fae, or Fire Queen?"

"I might ask you the same question," said both Red and Blue Verve.

That made Verve pause before saying, "I'm myself. I know who I am. I must be fae."

"No, that can't be right," said Red Verve. "*I* must be fae. I know who I am as well, and I am not what needs killing." Desperately she looked between the silver and blue creatures on either side of her.

"I am not quite fae."

Verve and Red snapped their heads to look at Blue at the same moment. "Then you're the one we kill," said the latter.

"You're awfully eager to commit murder," Verve murmured, though she knew this part of herself did not relish the idea, even as the being said, "Better I kill her than she kills me."

The blue one among them held up her hands. "I am the Fire Queen. You tell me, who is fae and who is mortal?"

Verve scoffed. "You're just saying that because you're afraid to die." Even as she said the words, she knew them to be false. The part of her that stood over there did not fear for herself but for what might happen to the world, should the Fire Queen be destroyed. And yet, there was a part of both of them that wondered if she truly was the Fire Queen.

There was a flash of light as Red Verve threw bolts of magic at the other two versions of herself. The blue woman caught the magic and threw it to the side, while Verve dodged it altogether.

"What did you do that for?" Verve asked, throwing a bolt of her own. Or, rather, she tried to. She could feel the magic prickling at the base of her skull, sensed it rising up within her, but she could not reach it.

Some silent agreement seemed to pass between the other two Verves. "You can't do magic. You must be the mortal," said Red Verve.

Verve took a step backward. "But I'm me. I feel it. I'm the essence of what I am. Kill me and you kill everything Verve Springer is." Her words were desperate and muddled, though she knew them to be true. Verve backed away from the others, raising her hands, pleading to her magic to return.

Red struck first, lobbing a ball of fire at her. "You know it's for the good of us," she shouted as Verve began to run.

Water splashed against her thighs as she raced into the darkness, but soon light faded and she was forced to slow. She could not see in utter darkness; no one could, not even the Fire Queen or the fae, she knew for certain. Quieting her breaths, Verve felt around for something to hide behind.

"Come out, Silver. We both know how this has to end."

Light flared in the blackness, illuminating Red Verve not ten paces off. Another ball of fire was thrown, this one coming perilously close to Verve's face.

She held in a scream as she took off running once more. But it was no good.

A blue tendril of light snatched her around the wrists and drew her back toward her pursuers. Verve fell face-first into the water as she was dragged, though she tried to surface and catch a breath. A nonlethal bolt of magic hit her in the side, and she lost the remainder of air in her lungs.

Verve was drawn out of the water and held up over the Blue creature. The Fire Queen had produced a sword made purely of killing magic, and she looked at Verve pityingly.

"Wait!" Verve cried as the woman looked ready to strike. "Think. If you kill me, we won't be the same. We'll – you'll be Fire Queen and fae."

"What of it?" the red one asked. "This is the way it has to be."

"But that's not who you are," said Verve, addressing her words to the Fire Queen part of herself. "That's not who Fenn fell in love with."

The red, fae part of herself scoffed. "Who cares for Fenn and what he wants? This is about Letorheas, Etterhea, every realm – they're all at stake. We can't keep you, Verity. You must go."

Verve cringed, and the light binding her tightened. "But Fenn. I – we *love* him."

Both the Fire Queen and the fae cocked their heads. "Do we?" asked the fae, scornfully at first, before her expression changed to confused.

"Please, we *need* Fenn."

The fae's eyes flashed. "We need no one." She drew a fistful of magic into her hand and then threw it at Verve, who writhed and screamed. "Weak. Humans are weak. You and I? We are more." She was talking to the Fire Queen, whose expression was unreadable. "Come, you're not going to humor this part? It's she the curse is attached to. She's the one who must die."

"Then kill the curse, not me," said Verve. "Please."

"Perhaps *you are* the curse," said the Fire Queen, though Verve knew she wasn't convinced. She was, after all, part of herself, the whole.

Once more the bindings tightened, bringing Verve to her knees with a sob. "Please. For Fenn."

The Fire Queen frowned. "I see the curse. It's a stain on you." Slowly she circled, her sword outstretched toward Verve. "But you are right: you are our heart, and without you, we have no soul."

"Igraine warned us the mortal would have a cunning tongue," said Red Verve. "Think of what you're doing."

Verve whimpered as the blade traced down her neck, nicked her collarbone, and then came to rest with its point at her heart. "The soul or not, that does not mean all three of us can live."

"Then kill the fae," Verve blurted out. "Please, you have enough power without that part of us."

The expression on the Fire Queen's face hardened. Without looking over her shoulder, she said to her fae self, "Come here and hold her still, but I shall strike the blow." Her eyes never left Verve's, and for the first time since emerging from the body, Verve didn't know what this part of herself was truly thinking.

"Very well," said the fae. She came along beside the Fire Queen and placed a staying hand on Verve's right side.

"No," Verve begged, trembling. This was not how it was supposed to go, whatever Igraine had said be hanged. "Please. Don't do this."

Before the fae could react, the Fire Queen pushed the fae forward into Verve, knocking them both over. Then, in one fell thrust, the blade went through the fae's back and plunged into Verve's mortal front. Both hearts had been pierced, the fae's all the way through, and Verve's but by harmless magic and then drawn into the other creature's breast. There had been no pain in the exchange, surprisingly, only relief.

The mortal, silver version of herself faded and fell into the water, sinking below the black surface as three conscious minds became two. To her surprise, Verve found herself very much intact, but now inside the red fae's body.

"I-I don't understand," she said to the Fire Queen, who smiled cunningly. They both looked at her front, which had healed and encased the mortal heart entirely. Not a spot or stain of curse had been left.

"You were right when you said you were the heart. You were wrong, in part, when you said you didn't need to die. We are now not three parts in one whole, but one and two halves."

"But are we more than one person?" Verve asked, the question that had been bothering her.

The responding laugh made Verve scowl.

"Yes and no. Everyone has their different sides they show to the world. These are simply ours."

Pain filled Verve's breast and the water began to ripple. The Fire Queen seemed to feel something was wrong as well, as she began breathing heavily.

"Come on, we've stayed here long enough." The Fire Queen ran back whence they had come, and the other part of her, the part that was her heart and fae magic, followed.

When they returned to the cavern, Igraine had vanished, and Olive was on the ground, her throat slit open. No breath could be seen moving her breast, and her heart was silent.

"No," said Verve as the Fire Queen took her by the shoulders.

Dacre knelt by Verve's body, trying to pump life back into her with his hands and mouth. "Come on, Verve. Wake up." His movements were jerky and weak, and it was with some alarm Verve noticed a great cloud of power hovering over him.

"We have to go back," said the Fire Queen. "Verve, look at me. Once we return, we must be merciless. Dacre is weakened from taking in so much power so quickly, just like what happened to you when you were first remade by him all those months ago. This is our only chance to get away from him."

"But Olive—"

"There's nothing we can do for her. I know you see that." Her expression was rueful but determined. "We know what must be done."

Verve bit her lower lip but nodded. "All right."

The Fire Queen took her hand and together, they stepped back into the body.

★ ★ ★

It was not a pleasant sensation, returning to her physical form. The pain she had felt in the spirit-like state was nothing compared to what she felt when she drew her first breath in what very well might have been an hour. She gasped and cried out, and Dacre ceased pushing on her chest.

Orbs of light that he must have created flickered over the scene. He sat back on his heels for a moment, catching his breath apparently before saying, "I thought I'd lost you." His cold hand swept hair out of her face, and he smiled at her weakly. "What happened? I didn't think she'd be able to hurt you." Dacre nodded back at Olive's body.

Though she felt like death itself, Verve knew she needed to act fast. She reached deep within for the rage that always lay beneath the surface and pushed magic out through her hands, which she thrust at Dacre's chest.

That caught him by surprise, as he landed several yards away with a great *oomph*. He swore as she scrambled to her feet and tripped her way toward the next cavern over, praying she was headed in the right direction.

The air filled with the smell of chocolate, and a wall of his magic flew up in front of Verve, knocking her back. "Why do you have to make things so difficult?" Dacre asked, his breaths coming in gasps.

Verve formed a wall of magic of her own between her and Dacre, forcing him to stop in his tracks. Then, willing the barrier to hold, she went to work on dismantling the one he had created.

"You can't run from me, Verve. We're fated to be."

She tried to shut out his words, putting her full concentration into breaking the magic in front of her. It took her a moment of toil but then she was able to push through, just as Dacre managed to destroy the wall she had made.

He leered at Verve as she struck out with power and missed her mark. "You need training, Verve. I can help you." Dacre held out a hand, his eyes pleading. "Come, don't make me hurt you."

Temper flaring, Verve lashed out again, this time nearly striking him in the chest before he threw out a weak shield. The magic rebounded off what he had created, and Verve had to duck as it flew at her. In the distance, she could hear the magic hit a wall, and rocks rumbled as they cascaded downward.

"This is pointless."

Don't engage with him. Put your mind to work on escaping. Once she was free of Ithalamore, Verve very much doubted Dacre would be able to follow her…at least, not right away. The thought propelled her onward, until magic nipped painfully at her heels.

Dacre was doubled over from the effort it had taken to attack. He had about him a sickly pallor, and perspiration beaded on his brow. But Verve felt little better than how he looked. "The others will catch you, even if I am not so lucky," said Dacre.

At that she snorted. There wasn't a heartbeat besides her own and Dacre's close enough to be perceived. All of the other fae must have perished or fled beyond Verve's hearing.

He took advantage of her pause to catch his breath, casting a lasso around her waist and attempting to draw her near. "Last chance to come with me willingly."

But Verve's hands were free and she cast them heavenward. *To the casual onlooker, it might look like surrender,* Verve thought, almost amused, drawing power into her hands. With a flick of her fingers, the stone beneath Dacre's feet turned to quicksand, and he at once sank to his chest, his arms pinned to his side.

Unable to use gestures to enhance his abilities, it would seem he was now at least somewhat harmless. Still, Verve did not mean to tarry. "Verve," Dacre pled as his magic faltered and the lasso disintegrated. "You can't mean to leave me like this."

It occurred to her that she might use killing magic on him, but as soon as the thought was born she crushed it. Though Dacre would surely never stop hounding and pursuing her, she had been weakened terribly and did not have the strength to cast any such spell. Verve knew she barely had enough to return to Etterhea.

Verve limped away into the darkness, whispering to herself that she'd done the right thing. It took her half an hour to return to the main cavern where sat Death's Maw. She risked only a little magic in the form of a tiny orb of light to see the way.

Weak and exhausted, Verve hobbled as quickly as she could to the tree and fed a trickle of her power into its bark. The black hawthorn responded by opening a portal back to Lovelourn, and Verve stumbled through, grateful to leave the underworld behind. As the gateway began to seal, she could hear Dacre's renewed cries, which were mercifully cut short when the tree once more stood whole and tall, no gateway in sight.

Verve shuddered and collapsed against the trunk. She might have lain there for hours trying to process what had happened to her and to grow used to her new state of being. Her throat was still raw from the potion, and her chest throbbing from the powerful blows Dacre had landed in his misguided attempts to revive her. But even if she were able to move, she had nowhere to go. Should she seek out Fenn? *Not if I'm supposed to rob or kill him.*

As soon as the thought occurred to her, she hugged her knees to her chest and rested her head in her hands. *I'm so foolish.* In response to her feelings, a heavy mist rose from the ground, snaked around the tree and nearly buried her.

He was soft in his approach, so soft she did not hear him until it was too late. The glowing being lifted her as though she were nothing but a twig, tightening his hold when she began to thrash. "Shh," he soothed. "Don't strain yourself. It's all right; I have you now."

She stilled at the sound of Fenn's voice, though wariness and doubt quickly crept in. Verve bucked once, twice, then twisted, but the creature held fast. "Don't try to deceive me. I don't want to go back." Great sobs wracked her body, and he pressed her more closely to him. "No. Please, no."

He kissed the crown of her head. "You severed ties with your mortality, I see. Did anyone warn you about the process's effects?" His voice was tender as he carried her away from Death's Maw and toward a normal hawthorn. When she once more picked up her struggle, the man stopped walking and lowered himself and her to the ground. Whether Fenn or a shape-changer, Verve couldn't make up her mind. The way he held her spoke of familiarity, but he seemed so sad and weary, she couldn't help but wish it was not Fenn at all but some stranger she had so obviously hurt. Verve tried pushing away from him, but the creature pressed his hand over her heart, and she stilled. "I know you feel trapped, Verve, but I can't release you just yet. Let me get you out of harm's way and you will be truly free." His lips brushed her brow and he sat with her in silence for a while, stroking her hair and holding her still. When he seemed satisfied she wasn't going to give him more trouble, the creature rose with her and created a gateway to a land drenched in moonlight.

There was a small cottage in the near distance surrounded by wards so powerful, Verve could taste them. They passed through without being harmed, though she could hear and smell new ones being added that would make her leaving more difficult.

The front door opened for them and then was bolted with more magic. Another ward went up, but Fenn did not slow as he carried her through the little house and into a bedchamber, where he shut and locked the door and cast more magical wards. His muscles, which had been tensed the whole time, relaxed at last, and he set her on the mattress.

Verve couldn't bring herself to look at him fully, though she felt his watchful eyes on her.

"I've been following your trail for some time. I lost it at the ruins, but the Faithful of Githtariel reached out to me and – dearest, please look at me." His voice was kind – *too* kind.

Something deep inside Verve shattered at the sound and she clenched her teeth. "I'm so sorry, Fenn." *I'm sorry I left you; I'm sorry I might have to rob you.*

Fenn froze. "Sorry?" He sounded perplexed. When she did not answer, he took her face in his hands and forced her to look at him full on. Of all things, his handsome features were split into a blissful smile. "Oh, Verve. You think I'm angry with you?" His magic responded to his apparent relief, filling the air with the scent of limes and causing his skin to glow all the brighter. "May I join you?"

She trembled as he eyed the spot on the bed next to her covetously. "Yes, but I-I don't understand. I yelled at you and then I left and everything went horribly wrong and you probably should hate me if you don't already." Her breathing hitched as Fenn lay next to her and gathered her into his arms.

He sighed happily as her heart missed a beat. "You thought *I* would hate *you* after I drove you away?"

"You didn't," was all she managed to protest before his lips were on hers.

When Fenn came up for air, his eyes were terrifyingly dark, his magic barely leashed. "Verve, love, I saw the fear in your eyes every time I mentioned mastership magic. But, thinking I knew best, I told myself it had to be done. That you should simply yield to my so-called better judgement." He nuzzled into her neck. "*I* am so very sorry. Can you forgive me for my pride and cruelty?" Fenn pulled back now to look her in the eyes, his expression troubled and ashamed. "If you can't, I understand."

She laughed, and the weak sound broke the tension in his body; she could feel the weight lift off him as if it had been resting on her own shoulders. "I was angry, that is for certain. But I didn't run away from you, Fenn. I went to find answers about my curse and how to fix things."

He tucked her once more against his chest, his grasp tightening so there was no space between them. "And you found those answers." Fenn's heart leapt as she kissed his neck.

"I think so. Breaking with my mortality should have broken the curse, but there hasn't been another living soul to test that theory out on." Unbidden images entered Verve's mind, and she started to cry. "I killed them, Fenn. So many people." She tried to pull back to look into his eyes, to better gauge his reaction, but he seemed unwilling to release her and she was too weak at the moment to resist him. "I'm horrid. You shouldn't have anything to do with me."

Fenn stroked her hair as she sobbed. "Verve, there is nothing you could possibly do to make me agree with that sentiment."

"I killed Tilda," she blurted, wishing to get the worst of it over, though it wasn't entirely her fault the wretched fae was gone.

"And did you do so out of malice?" he asked patiently, his voice suggesting he knew the answer.

Verve struggled, and Fenn loosened his hold, but still refused to release her entirely. "Does it matter why? She's dead and at my hands. The last of your family, Fenn. I did that." Hating herself more and more, she tried pushing away from him, only to be seized gently by the chin.

"*You* are my family." He rolled her onto her back and pinned her beneath his weight. "And I know you." His breath was hot on her neck as he leaned down and spoke the words directly into her ear. "You are fiery, just, kind, loyal, and good. I could not ask for a better mate for my soul to be bound to." Fenn wiped away a few stray tears as he studied her face.

Her body relaxed as he began probing, looking her over for wounds. His touch was clinical and careful, but even so Verve struggled to breathe. She could have been lost to him forever, and he to her, but now….

Fenn gave her a concerned look. "Are you all right? You're rather flushed. And your heart—" He stilled as she reached for him, took his hand and placed it on her breast. A contented sigh slipped from his lips, and he leaned in to kiss her once more. His tongue pressed against the line of her lips, and she let him in with a sigh of her own. Too soon, though, he pulled away, though it was clear to Verve he wanted more; he was glowing so brightly, she began seeing spots. "You need to rest."

Now she was cold, the weight of what she had promised Igraine threatening to crush her. She gasped as Fenn continued examining her, his touch still feather-light. "Distract me?"

The look he gave her warmed her through. "I will. Good and thoroughly when you are rested and I'm certain no damage has been done to you." He leaned in and whispered once more. "Don't be mistaken: I have plans for you, wife." His teeth tugged at her lower lip as the fingers of his right hand stroked the space over her heart.

Verve whimpered, and he chuckled softly. She tried to remain still and calm as he turned her this way and that, pulling her out of her clothes and giving her body a more thorough examination.

At length he ceased his prodding and covered them both with a blanket, then lay down next to her. "The curse is gone." He pecked her on the lips. "I sense no trace of it." Again Fenn took her into his arms, and it became apparent he was afraid she would run off. "How do you feel?"

"Sad," she replied. "Relieved."

He squeezed her. "Go on."

"What happened at the estate? When I found it in ruins, I thought the worst."

Fenn's breath rippled through her hair and his hold tightened further still. When he spoke, there was anger in his voice, and though she knew it wasn't directed at her, it made Verve shiver. "Tilda left a little present for us when she departed. The gateway she took you through sealed in front of me before the estate exploded. Had you not left and had I not pursued you, we would have been both seriously injured." Fenn took to rubbing gentle, soothing circles on her back. "But you're all right. I'm all right."

"And she can't hurt you now," Verve murmured, earning herself another kiss atop her head.

"The deed is done, my love. It would not do to dwell on it."

They lay in silence for a few moments, his hand still tracing soothing patterns, her thoughts scudding here and there, unable to land on any one thing until it alighted on Helena, on Father and the promise. *Should I tell him?*

"Is Dacre going to be a problem for us still?"

Verve jumped at the sound of Fenn's voice, and he froze. "What?" she asked.

"I'm sorry," Fenn said, "that was perhaps too blunt of me."

"No, you just startled me from my thoughts, that's all." She waited a moment before committing her worries to the air. "Well, he's not dead. I left him weak and sealed in Ithalamore, but I don't think that will stop him." Verve swallowed. "He's grown strong, Fenn. Too strong. He's been bathing in the pools of the other realms, taking on the power of their dead."

Fenn stilled. "And he's still there?" There was a note of dread in Fenn's voice, and Verve's heart began to race. If he was worried, that doubled her own concerns.

"Yes. I don't know how many he managed to bathe in before…he found me." She did not plan on telling him about her struggle with her other selves or her near death. He did not need another thing to pity her for. "You don't think he could open Death's Maw…do you?"

"*But two shall hold the key*," Fenn said, quoting part of the poem he had recited for her weeks prior. He didn't need to say anything more than that to confirm Verve's fear.

They lay for a while next to one another, Fenn's grip tightening from time to time as though the ghost of some thought or other were plaguing him. Finally, the guilt and fear became unbearable and Verve could stand keeping her burning question in no longer. "Fenn?" she asked.

He stilled, his heart picking up its pace. "What's wrong?"

"Did you ever steal anyone's power?"

That made him pull back and he looked down at her face, his expression confused. "No. It's not something I'm even capable of. You have to be a siphon in order to take someone's magic."

Verve could have died of relief. "It's a coincidence, then."

Fenn's frown deepened, and she could feel his muscles tensing. "What's a coincidence?"

The thought of sharing the particulars of her hastily made deal with Igraine was not appealing. Instead, she simply said, "There was talk in Ithalamore of a man named Larknott who took someone's magic."

Hurt flashed across his features before he drew in a deep breath. "And you suspected me of being this thief?"

"No – I mean, I wasn't sure because…well, there aren't many of your family left." At once she wished the words back. Now not only did he have a suspicious wife but a thoughtless one. She felt the blood rush to her face. "I'm sorry, Fenn. I shouldn't have doubted you."

He sighed, his features softening. "I forget we haven't known each other for overly long – or been around each other for much time."

Verve cringed. That had been her fault as well, the lack of time spent together, as she had refused to leave Etterhea.

"And you don't even know my – and your – own last name, which is a further testament of how little I've shared with you." Fenn leaned down and kissed her slowly, softly. Then he whispered, "It's not Larknott, love. That was my father's name. Though few know it, I took my mother's. If you choose to take the name, it's Letorheas."

Verve blinked. "But that's…that's the place. Your name is really Letorheas?"

Fenn shrugged and settled back down next to her, his hurt apparently forgotten, at least for now. "It's thought to be the name of the founder of this realm. The first human with magic."

She rolled over to face him and rested her hands against his chest. "No wonder you wanted to keep that name, then."

He pushed away a strand of hair that had fallen into her face. "There were those in my father's family who were siphons, though I'm not certain they employed their gift by force." His eyes searched hers. "Who mentioned siphoning and the Larknotts to you?"

"Someone I met in Ithalamore."

"So you said." He waited a moment and whispered, "If you don't care to tell me, that's all right."

That was a relief. Verve knew someday soon, however, she would have to return to Ithalamore and then seek out this thief who shared Fenn's father's name. But that was weeks away. She had time to figure out how to tell Fenn what she must do.

And so they lay there, basking in each other's company until sleep found them and carried their worries away. Hours later, the couple would wake. Fenn would check that his magical wards were still in place while Verve began to plot her course. But that came later. This moment was peaceful, if not perfect. *Perfection is such a fragile thing anyway*, Verve mused in her dreams. *As fragile as glass*.